MAN OVERBOARD

MAN OVERBOARD

Susan F. Edwards

Cover design by OriginalSyn

This book is a work of fiction. All characters are invented and used fictitiously. The story is, however, based on the real-life 1926 disappearance of an actual person under suspicious circumstances. The mystery of his vanishing has never been solved.

Some of the characters in this book were inspired by photographs from the fabulous Burgert Brothers collection, an extraordinary historic archive preserved by the Tampa-Hillsborough Public Library. It contains almost 15,000 images of the Tampa Bay region from the late 1800s to the early 1960s. The library website aptly describes the collection as, "a unique pictorial record of the commercial, residential and social growth of Tampa Bay … area as it faced wars, natural disasters, economic booms and busts." The images capture people working in cigar factories, sponge docks and real estate offices, and playing at country clubs, tin-can tourist camps and beaches.

The photos of 1920s land boom Florida are especially wonderful. They evoke the excitement, glamour, exuberance and hype of that very special time and place.

The photos that inspired certain fictional characters in this book. The characters are in no way whatsoever based on or related to the actual people depicted in those photos. They are simply photos that piqued the author's imagination in creating fictional characters. They are shared merely to give the reader a feel for the time, place, and photographic collection.

The Burgert Brothers photos appear in this book courtesy of Tampa-Hillsborough County Public Library System.

You can order prints from the library for an incredibly modest fee here:
http://www.hcplc.org/hcplc/liblocales/jfg/H&G/burgert/ordering_burgert.html

Acknowledgements

Many thanks to Linda Bassett, who introduced me to the joys of historical research and the incredibly rich history of Florida. Thanks also to all the historians, journalists, raconteurs and librarians who have treasured and preserved Florida's amazing past in all its checkered glory, especially Gary Mormino, Robert Ingalls, Leland Hawes and Tony Pizzo.

Thanks to Porter Anderson for reading early drafts and giving me excellent feedback, to the late Lee Sokol Lippe for making me a better storyteller, and to Kellie VanWyck for teaching me the finer points of life insurance policies.

A big thank-you to Noel Smith for unearthing old photos from the Burgert Brothers archive that inspired some of the characters in this book, and for reading early drafts with and insightful and keen eye. Thanks to Michael Ross for teaching me discipline by example and to Ian Ross for retyping the entire manuscript after the digital copy was lost.

And thank you to Syneca Featherstone and Fawn Germer for their constant support and to Michael English for encouraging me to take this thing out of mothballs and publish it, and for giving me the time to do it.

Prologue

In 2015, city workers in Tampa, Florida, uncovered a series of underground passageways and rooms while installing a new storm drainage system in the old Latin town known as Ybor City. One chamber held an oak bar with empty liquor bottles, suggesting that the place might have been a speakeasy during Prohibition.

Also found in this room were boxes of premium handmade cigars, a straw fedora, a gold key-shaped pin with a missing stone and a file, dated 1928, containing the case notes of a private detective named William Heart, a.k.a. Billy Corazon. This is his story.

Chapter One
Tears and Red High Heels

There is something lonely about a city after a parade. The people are gone, but their smell, the echoes of their laughter remain, blowing around the empty streets along with torn paper streamers, a child's shoe and discarded bits of lunch.

The Gasparilla Parade began as usual this year when Tampa's most powerful men, dressed as pirates and already high on voodoo brew, stormed City Hall. As usual, the mayor gave up the keys to the city without a fight to this year's pirate king, who led his mates down the main street of town shooting pistols and tossing candy, cheap beads and fake coins to the cheering crowd.

My father always hated Gasparilla Day. He took us to the parade every year for a civics lesson. To him, Tampa's city fathers didn't have to dress up as pirates to pillage this town. He believed these bankers, lawyers and factory owners did their plundering every day of the year in board meetings and backroom deals. To my father, the charade was when they wore business suits and sipped brandy from snifters behind closed doors. He never doubted that they were dangerous men. Ten years ago, he found out how dangerous.

Dad devoted his short life to workers' rights. Words were his stock in trade. He used them the way a pirate uses a sword, with swashbuckling fury. He never let me catch the booty tossed from the pirates' floats. No son of Ramon Corazon would scramble in the streets for cheap baubles, he said. In those days I couldn't wait to grow up and go to the parade without him.

Now it only makes me miss him more.

Uniformed cops keep the peace on the parade route, breaking up fights and dragging kids and drunks out from under the horses' hooves. Plainclothes detectives and private dicks like me work the back of the crowds, watching mostly for pickpockets and bootleg

1

liquor. People seem to get drunker now than they ever did before Prohibition. Especially on Gasparilla Day when all of Tampa toasts the pirate Jose Gaspar, sacker of towns and ravisher of captive women.

This year's Gasparilla had an Egyptian motif, so King Quattlebaum brought in camels to draw the queen's float. He discovered too late that camels are foul-tempered beasts, and unlike horses, will not work in teams. They bit and spat and squalled like demons straight from hell. The queen plastered a smile over gritted teeth as the camels pulled in all directions and nearly tore her float apart. By the end of the parade, her Cleopatra wig was lopsided, and the tears had turned the kohl around her eyes to mud.

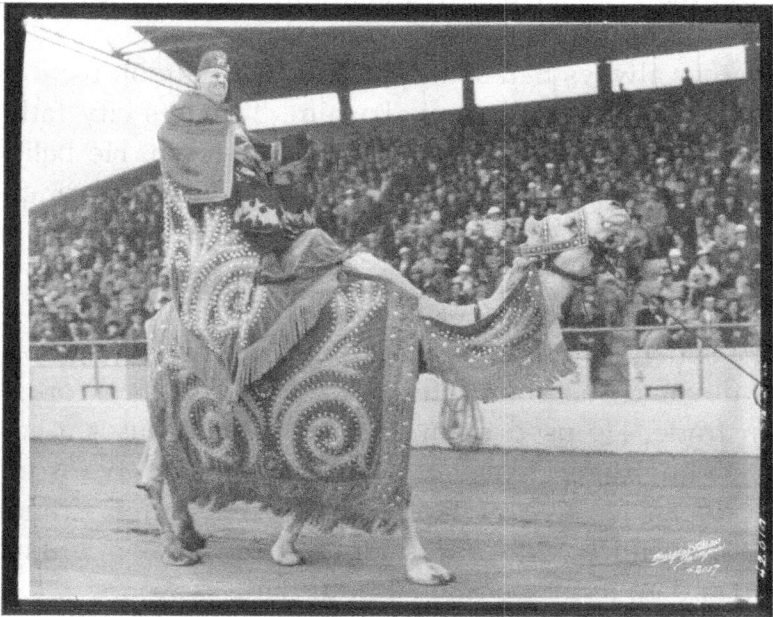

Photo courtesy of Tampa-Hillsborough County Public Library System

After the queen's float, came the mounted Rough Riders, prancing in their dress blues. Some of them had actually fought alongside Teddy Roosevelt in in Cuba during what the Anglos call the Spanish-

American War. The rest just like to dress up and play soldier on this one day each year.

I felt impatient as I watched them put their horses through precision military drills. But it would all be over soon. Then I could write up my report and be done with Gasparilla for another year.

I didn't know then that my troubles with pirates were just beginning.

The February evening was turning cool as I walked the nine blocks to my office. I passed the monstrous Tampa Bay Hotel with its silver minarets, where Negro men drew rickshaws bearing white guests on a sunset tour of the grounds. I drew up my collar against the wind coming off the Hillsborough River as I crossed the bridge into downtown. It was dark by the time I rounded the corner onto Zack Street.

The light in my office window told me I had a visitor. It wasn't a good sign. Decent men were already home hugging porcelain pots and renewing their pledges to obey Prohibition laws come tomorrow.

I took the back stairs in the dark and slipped up to the open door of my office. What I saw made me want to sneak back down the stairs and out into the night. But whatever else I am, I'm no coward. I stiffened my spine and went in.

She had made herself at home in my chair with her feet up on my desk. She was smoking one of my handmade Cuban Belvedere cigars and had even poured herself two fingers of the rum I keep in a drawer for medicinal purposes. She didn't introduce herself—she didn't have to. Everyone knew Nesta Edmunds was the daughter of one of the most prominent Tampa families, that she had been the Gasparilla Pirate Queen four years ago in 1924 and later that year had married the infamous EQ Edmunds.

The happy couple had divorced and remarried, and generally kept society matrons fueled with enough gossip to light up their luncheons until about a year ago. That's when Edmunds disappeared

3

from an ocean liner bound for England. The official story was accidental death. The insurance company made a great show of promptly paying off the million-dollar policy on his life.

"Drink?" asked Nesta Edmunds, like she owned the place.

I never agreed with my father's politics, but I did inherit his mistrust of a whole class of people. This dame was definitely a member of that class.

"Parade's over, lady. Your float left without you."

"You always treat your clients so politely?"

I pointed to the chair on the other side of the desk. "My clients usually sit there."

She took her time, but eventually she moved.

I settled in behind my desk and surveyed the drawers to see what else she might have filched. Everything was there, but the mess told me she had gone through it without the slightest finesse.

"Now. Am I to understand you're looking for a private investigator?"

"Yes." She crossed her legs and took out a compact. She inspected her face in the mirror and started to powder her nose. She wasn't what you'd call a doll. Her unpainted features were large and horsey, but she was handsome and well-groomed in an expensive-looking navy blue suit, her hair pulled back into a neat bun at the nape of her neck. Her buffed, unpolished fingernails had never touched dishwater. Her one vanity was a pair of red high heels. "I want you to find my husband," she said.

"You're remarried?"

She stopped powdering and shot me a look that could have withered a water oak. "No. I want you to find Mr. Edmunds."

I wondered why she would want to bring him back from the dead. By all accounts he had been a hard-drinking, womanizing little braggart and bully. But I didn't say that. All I asked was, "What makes you think he's alive?"

4

Her mouth drew into a hard, straight line. "My husband is a con and a liar, Mr. Heart. This wouldn't be the first time he tried to trick me."

"Leaving you with a million dollars in life insurance money hardly seems like a dirty trick."

The taut line of her mouth curved into a bitter smile. "Everyone assumes I was the beneficiary of that policy, but the truth is, I didn't get a dime."

"Who did?"

"My husband."

"Kinda tough for a corpse to spend a million bucks."

"Oh, he spent it long before he disappeared."

She dangled it out there like bait on a hook. I wasn't about to bite. I waited, stone-faced, for her to go on.

"It was a neat little sting, actually. Edward so loved the art of the sting."

"That's what land speculation is all about, isn't it?" I ignored the look she shot me, cold and sharp as a shark's tooth. "Please continue," I said.

"When the bottom started falling out of the real estate market here, Edward sold Edmunds Island for one million dollars to a real estate syndicate called Liberty Limited. For a tiny fraction of its value. He held the contract and title, and they made monthly payments to him. Liberty took out a one-million-dollar insurance policy on his life. The deal was if Edward died, I would inherit the contract and title. Liberty Limited would sign the insurance check over to me in exchange for the papers. They'd own Edmunds Island, and I'd be a rich widow."

I took my time digesting that. I had to hand it to the Anglos. They knew how to work a buck. One thing I didn't understand though. "So how did your husband end up with the money?"

"You can use a life insurance policy as collateral for bank loans up to the limit of the benefit. After Edward disappeared, we discovered that he had borrowed a million dollars against the policy. The benefit paid off his loan."

"I'm not sure I follow."

"The bank placed a lien on the policy. The loan balance had to be paid before anyone else. In effect, by taking out that loan, Edward placed the bank as beneficiary in line ahead of me."

"So Edmunds got his million, the bank got its million and you and Liberty were left out in the cold."

"Mostly me. It turned out Edward had also run up over five million dollars in debt claims against Edmunds Island. The property can't be sold until the debtors are paid. When Liberty Limited found that out, they pointed to some fine print in their contract and bailed out of the purchase. I now own a development that's over five million dollars in debt. I'm broke, Mr. Heart. Worse than broke. I'm personally liable for all those debts."

I poured myself a stiff dose of island tonic and downed it. I didn't have to ask who owned stock in Liberty Limited. The same handful of men owned everything in this town. This case would have me nosing around some pretty powerful closets, and I didn't like the smell of it.

"Why don't you talk to Meade and Barkin up on Franklin Street? This is more up their alley than mine."

"I can't. They won't—" She stopped, and the look on her face told me I hadn't been her first choice. Probably not her third or fourth either. It made sense that the uptown dicks would sit this one out. They wouldn't want to uncover dirty laundry on their own people.

"I have no one else to turn to, Mr. Heart," she sobbed.

Something about a woman's tears brings out the Corazon in me. No Corazon man could stand by while a woman cried. My father couldn't, and neither could his. It's one of the reasons women love us. Even though I didn't much like her, Nesta Edmunds' tears worked on me.

"Why don't you tell me what you think happened to your husband."

"I was in London at the time." She dabbed at her nose with a crisply ironed monogrammed hankie. "Edward was supposed to meet me there, and we were going to go on to Italy. He wanted to look into doing some developments on the Riviera."

"What was the date of Mr. Edmunds' disappearance?"

"September 27, 1927. It was my twenty-seventh birthday. I think he picked that day on purpose."

That made her six months younger than me. She looked older than twenty-eight. I guess bitterness will do that to a person. I probably look at least fifty.

"How did you hear of his disappearance?"

"I got a wire from Saul Stone the next morning. It said Edward had fallen overboard and that the ship had circled for five hours before giving up the search."

"Saul Stone?"

"Saul was the business manager for Edmunds Enterprises. He was Edward's right hand."

"Was Stone on the ship with Edmunds?"

"No. The steamship company notified him at the Edmunds Island office."

"I seem to remember reading that there was a witness who said he fell out a porthole."

Dark petals of red bloomed on her face. "Lola Flores."

"And you don't believe her?"

"Lola Flores is a prostitute, Mr. Heart. She could easily have been bribed to say what she did."

"Your husband was traveling with other people, was he not?"

"Yes. Dominic Boudreaux, that's his lawyer, and Dom's wife Hedda."

"And what do they have to say about the disappearance?"

"They seem to believe he fell."

7

"Why don't you think he fell?"

"My husband was broke and deeply in debt. He was being investigated by the Internal Revenue Service for tax evasion."

"Maybe he committed suicide."

"That's not his style. This is just the kind of stunt Edward would pull to get out of a spot like that. The only one who saw him go overboard was a gold-digging harlot. And I happen to know he had at least fifty thousand dollars in cash on his person when he disappeared."

"Where was the ship when it happened?"

"Just about midway between the States and Europe."

"How does someone disappear off a ship in the middle of the Atlantic Ocean?"

"That's what I want you to find out."

This case was about as inviting as a swamp full of alligators. But I, like everyone else in this town, was curious about what really happened to EQ Edmunds. The papers and radio stations had been full of contradictory stories at first. Then the official report from the insurance investigator and the steamship line had come out in the *Tampa Chronicle*, the favorite paper of Anglo Tampa.

Edward Quincy Edmunds had accidentally fallen from a porthole and been lost at sea. Case closed.

The only problem was that the porthole was four feet off the floor and only three and a half feet in diameter. At just over five feet tall, Edmunds would have been hard pressed to simply fall out of it. The *Chronicle* article suggested Edmunds had been showing off when the incident occurred.

Coverage had stopped abruptly after that although people continued to gossip for some time, especially about the mysterious female witness. Some had suggested a hoax or publicity stunt to boost sagging sales. Edmunds had often staged grandiose events to call attention to himself and his developments.

Eventually, life had gone on for most of us, and the disappearance of EQ Edmunds had faded from our minds.

But for Edmunds' wife, the question still gnawed. "Please, Mr. Heart. You're my only hope of finding the truth." Her tears were beginning again.

I knew I should walk away from this one. The last time a Corazon had taken on the Anglos, he'd left a bereaved widow and an angry young son behind. I felt the cycle beginning again.

"Twenty-five dollars a day plus expenses." I usually get ten, but I figured she could afford the Meade and Barkin rate.

"All I can afford is fifteen, including expenses."

"Is that what you offered Meade and Barkin? Or is fifteen just the Dago price?"

Her eyes grew wide under arched eyebrows. "I wasn't lying when I told you I was broke. I'm selling my jewelry to pay you. It's all I have left." She began to sob.

We settled on twenty, including expenses. Twice my usual, but not much for the trouble I was about to stir up.

SUSAN F. EDWARDS

Chapter Two
Blind Otto and the Ripe Mango

In a case like this, it's always best to follow the money. I planned to start with the insurance company that had paid off the claim, Victory Life. But first I wanted to find out what my friend Otto knew about EQ Edmunds and Lola Flores, the dame rumored to be the only witness to his death.

You don't need to read the paper if you stop by Otto's newsstand in City Hall. He can tell you everything that's going on, most of which never gets into the papers. But you give him your nickel, and he gives you the lowdown, and you take the paper for form's sake. And, of course, to read the official party line, as my father would say. I buy the *Tampa Herald*, never the *Chronicle*, for reasons of my own.

"Lola Flores," he said when I asked. A sly smile snaked up the left side of his face. He had a way of pointing his dark glasses at you as if he could look right through you even though he'd been blind since birth. "A ripe mango with a steel pit. I believe you'll find she has a lifetime rent-free lease on a penthouse in Edmunds Towers."

Sounded like a convenient way to keep a mistress. "What do you know about her?"

"Word has it she was a taxi dancer in Cuba. Edmunds added her to his entourage when he was down there before his first marriage."

"He was married before?"

Otto nodded. "The first Mrs. Edmunds died. Some sort of swamp fever, I think." He paused and seemed to study me for a moment. "Tell me you're not investigating Edmunds' disappearance."

"Maybe."

"Dangerous waters, Corazon. You go fishing there, you're liable to lose a lot more than your pole."

Otto's warning didn't do much to stir up my gusto for the case, but it was too late now. I had given my word to a lady in tears. Damn that Corazon blood.

I took a *Herald* and flipped him a nickel, which he caught in mid-air and felt with his thumb. "Brand new Indian head," he said with a smile. "You've been to the bank this morning."

Not much gets by Otto.

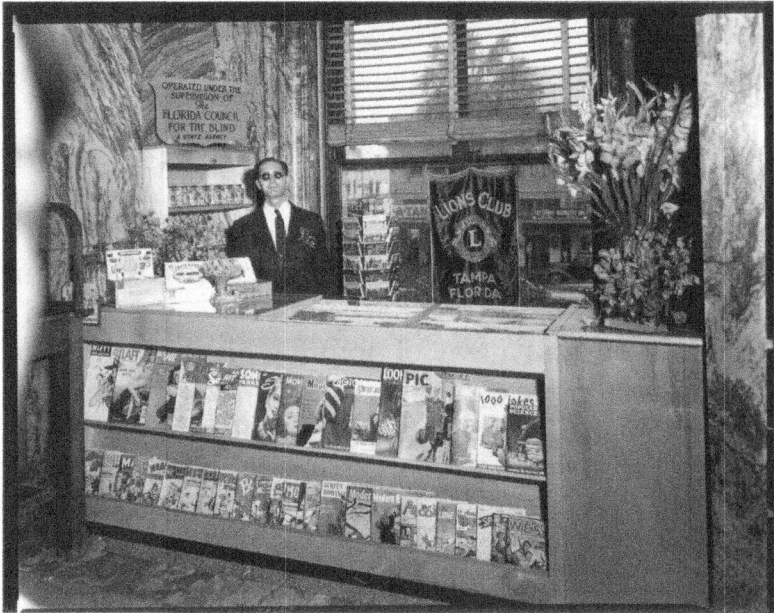

Photo courtesy of Tampa-Hillsborough County Public Library System

Victory Life was closer, but Lola sounded more interesting, so I hopped the Bayshore streetcar headed south out of town. Tampa sits on a fat finger of land surrounded by Hillsborough Bay to the east and Tampa Bay to the west and south. Bayshore Boulevard runs south along Hillsborough Bay from downtown to the tip of the peninsula. Tampa's wealthiest citizens live in columned mansions along this stretch of road with views of blue water meeting bluer sky, interrupted only by a couple of grassy keys where snowy egrets and great blue herons nest.

It was on those keys that Edmunds originally planned to place his development. But Tampa's elite didn't want their view obstructed, so they pressured city council members not to grant the needed permits. They had underestimated Edmunds, though.

He managed to bribe, charm and probably blackmail a four-to-three decision in his favor. The mayor, who lives on Bayshore, was none too happy, so Edmunds made him an offer he couldn't refuse.

Edmunds had quietly bought up another key off the southern tip of the peninsula a couple miles south of the end of Bayshore Boulevard. He told the mayor he would put his development on this island on two conditions. One was that the city would extend Bayshore Boulevard and the streetcar line all the way to his island and build a bridge to it. The second condition was that the city would purchase the other two keys at three times the price he had paid and pledge in writing never to develop them. The mayor haggled on the price a little but otherwise pretty much gave in.

I had the streetcar almost to myself this morning. The only people headed south on a weekday morning were a few Cuban and Negro women on their way to cook, clean and tend children in the sparkling bayside homes. They eyed me curiously. A Latin man, especially one in a suit, is a rarity on the Bayshore streetcar.

It was ten a.m. by the time the streetcar stopped at Edmunds Towers. The whole island was done in a new style called Mediterranean Revival with textured stucco facades, deep colonnaded porches, arched windows, hand-painted tile courtyards and lots of fancy turrets that made the houses look like what they were: fake castles. The place was supposed to look like the Italian Riviera, and I suppose it did, minus of course the Italians. We stayed in Ybor City where there were none of the signs common in Tampa that said, "No Dagos Allowed."

13

Edmunds Towers was the first building on the island, and Edmunds had spared no expense on its opulence. It was, after all, the model he used for selling plots. It looked like a twelve-story-high wedding cake with frosting the rosy tint of a tropical sunrise. Brilliant scarlet bougainvillea draped over the central arch that led to the inner courtyard replete with fountains spilling into a deep blue pool.

I entered the lobby and found Lola's apartment listed as penthouse two. The white-gloved Negro elevator operator eyed me with suspicion when I told him my destination but said nothing. On the ride up, I noticed a small gnarled bit of tree root with a piece of fabric tied around it fixed over the door. A Haitian root doll, put there no doubt by the operator to keep evil from crossing the threshold of his elevator. I wondered if it had done its work.

I knocked on the door of penthouse two and waited a long time for an answer. Lola Flores opened the door wearing a purple satin robe and matching high-heeled slippers. Even fresh out of bed, her glossy black hair not yet combed, she was a delectable dish with copper skin as smooth and flawless as the satin of her robe, and fine high bones. But it was her eyes that made her beauty most arresting. They were the most startling shade of gold, a color seen more in cats than in people. They held not a trace of warmth as she looked me up and down.

"Salesman are not allowed in this building," she said, and started to close the door.

"I'm a private investigator. My name is William Heart." I handed her my card, which she inspected briefly. "I wonder if I might ask you a few questions."

"You don't look like a Heart, *guajiro*." The word means something like Cuban hillbilly. It was no compliment, but I needed answers. I had to let it slide.

"May I ask you some questions?"

She made no move to let me in. "What's your real name?"

14

"Corazon."

"Spanish?"

I nodded. "My mother's Italian." She looked me over some more, taking her time, probably thinking I looked more like my Sicilian mother's side of the family, with my dark features and sizable beak.

"Why'd you change it?"

"It's a long sad story, Miss Flores. I'll tell you mine if you tell me yours."

"About what?"

"The disappearance of EQ Edmunds."

Her eyes narrowed. "Who are you working for?"

"Mr. Edmunds' wife."

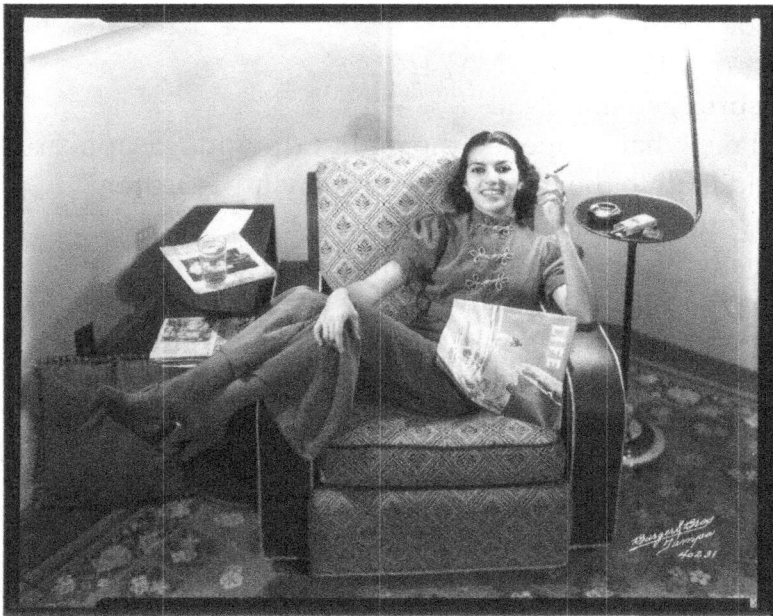

Photo courtesy of Tampa-Hillsborough County Public Library System

She rolled her eyes and let out an exaggerated sigh as she gestured me in. I followed her through the luxuriously appointed apartment, stuffed full of brocade furniture and huge potted palms. Shimmery bits of clothing were draped about amid overflowing ashtrays and half-empty glasses with lipstick smudges on their rims. The place had the musky smell of an overripe papaya. Her fluid movements, like her eyes, reminded me of a cat. Otto had been right about her.

Lola draped herself across a chair on the terrace and lit a cigarette. I took in the magnificent view of the bay, the bridge and the tail end of Bayshore. From here its houses looked dwarfed and inconsequential. It was a view that could give a person a false sense of power.

Her voice cut through my musings. "So what is it this week, did I push him, or did he jump overboard and swim to Europe?"

I turned to face her as she poured herself a demitasse of black café solo. She threw it back like a shot of whisky, the way men in Ybor do. She made no offer to me.

I gestured to a chair. "May I?"

She shrugged and I sat.

"Tell me what happened the night Edmunds disappeared."

"I told it all to the insurance company investigator."

"Do you remember his name?"

"Usually I forget names, but his was so stupid."

"What was it?"

"Les Moore. Do you believe it? Who would name a kid Les Moore?"

"So what did you tell him?"

"Can't you just get it from his report? He wrote it all down, and then he made me sign it."

"I'd rather hear it from you."

She sighed and fingered her cup. "Eddie liked to show off. He was dancing on the table. I told him he would fall and hurt himself. He said nothing could hurt him, he could fly like an angel." She laughed. "A devil is more like it."

She rolled her eyes and sighed. A light flush mottled the smooth curves of her breasts and traveled up her neck. Some people blush when they're embarrassed, some in anger, and some when they lie. I didn't know Lola Flores well enough yet to guess which one applied to her.

"You were alone with him?"

"No, this was earlier. Everyone was there. He flapped his arms like wings and ran around the room pretending to fly. He climbed into the window. He said he would fly around the ship. We had to pull him out. He was kicking and waving his arms. He kicked Dom right in the mouth."

"Who else was there?"

"Dom's wife Hedda and Mrs. Conti." The flush reached her face now.

"The papers said your mother was there."

"The papers never get anything right. Mrs. Conti is my *duenna*."

I couldn't help it; my eyebrows shot up at the thought of this former taxi dancer doing something so virtuous and old-fashioned as traveling with a chaperon.

She noticed my surprise and smiled. "A Spanish lady always travels with a duenna."

"You're Spanish?"

She lifted her chin, defying me to contradict her. "Of course. What did you think?"

I shrugged. I knew she was Cuban, but we all had our reasons to alter history.

"Was Edmunds drunk that night?"

She laughed. The sound came from deep in her throat like a growl. I could feel my blood and parts farther south surging in response. "Very drunk. He stayed up all the night before drinking and he drank all that day."

"Any particular reason?"

She shrugged. The flush was gone from that magnificent chest. "He liked to drink. He was not a large man, but he could drink until everyone else was crawling on the floor."

17

"Then what happened?"

"Everyone left to go to bed. But he wanted me to stay."

"You stayed without your chaperon?"

Her nostrils flared. "Listen, Linguini Boy, I don't have to talk to you at all, you know." The flush again. It was definitely anger that brought it out.

Our eyes locked. Linguini Boy? This was one tough cookie, and she wasn't about to crumble under a little pressure. "Look, Miss Flores. I'm afraid we got off on the wrong foot. I'm just a poor *paesan* with no manners. I'm not used to questioning a Spanish princess. Forgive me if I was rude." I dropped my head in surrender.

"Don't overdo it," she muttered.

"What happened next?"

"He kept saying he could fly. He got in the window again. I couldn't pull him out by myself. And then..." She stared at the bottom of her empty cup. I waited. "He just...slipped out."

"What did you do?"

"At first I was stunned. I couldn't believe he was gone. And then I guess I started screaming. The steward came. I couldn't stop screaming. Then a doctor was there. He gave me a shot. That's all I remember until..."

"Until what?"

"Many days later in London. They said he was dead. *She* was there. She called me a liar and a whore."

"Mrs. Edmunds?"

"Yes."

The flush rose to her face again, and I stood. She looked at me as if just remembering my presence.

"Thank you, Miss Flores."

"That's all?"

"For now."

She made no move to rise. "She must not be paying you very much. Les Moore asked a lot more questions."

"I'll see myself out."

The day was beginning to heat up as the streetcar passed over the bridge from the island. The sluggish breeze stirred up by our movement was too warm and damp to be cooling, too heavy to remove the musky smell that clung to my nostrils. On the ride back to town I thought about Lola. Women who make their living pleasing men could lie without the usual telltale signs, but a woman of passion cannot hide other emotions. She hated Nesta Edmunds. That much was clear and not surprising. But she'd had the same red-faced response when she described the others in the room. Which one did she hate, her chaperon, Edmunds' lawyer or Hedda Boudreaux?

Chapter Three
Victory Life

L es Moore had a face to match his name, soft and undecided with no discernable bone structure under flaccid, colorless skin. His hair, eyes, and even his suit resembled the indistinct color of dirt. His expression betrayed no emotion, nor did his toneless voice.

"As far as Victory Life is concerned, the case is closed. It was an accidental death, and we have no further interest in the subject."

"I'd like to get a look at the files, if you don't mind."

"Look. We have cooperated with Mrs. Edmunds in every conceivable way. She has seen the files many times. We have gone over everything with her dozens of times. In fact she made such a nuisance of herself that we had to have her escorted from the premises. She was rude, abusive and threatening to the receptionist, to me, and even to Mr. Quattlebaum."

Terrance Quattlebaum, king of Gasparilla, owned Victory Life. He also sat on Tampa City Council, the Tampa Port Authority and most of the other commissions that made the decisions in this town. I had to smile at the thought of the former Gasparilla queen going toe-to-toe with old Q-Head.

"She actually punched him in the stomach. After that, he instructed us to have nothing further to do with her. I shouldn't even be talking to you."

"Didn't it seem strange to you that Edmunds named a real estate syndicate as the beneficiary of his policy instead of his wife?"

"It isn't uncommon for syndicates to require such a policy from a developer in whom they have invested heavily. It's just sound business practice."

"How long did it take you to complete your investigation?"

"I met the ship in Miami when it returned. My report was on Mr. Q's desk two weeks later."

"And the company paid off right away?"

"Within the month."

"You know, when my father died, it took us two years to collect his four-thousand-dollar policy."

"He obviously chose the wrong company."

"Actually it was Victory Life."

If Moore had been the sympathetic type, this might have stopped him for a moment. But his answer was slick and brusque. "This was a very high-profile case. Mr. Quattlebaum was anxious to settle it as quickly as possible."

"I see."

Moore stood in a gesture of dismissal. "I really must ask you to leave now. I have work to do."

"Of course. Thank you for your time, Mr. Moore." I picked up my hat and headed for the door. When I got there I turned back to him. "One thing I'm curious about, though."

He sighed and glanced up from his papers. "What is it?"

"You probably know more about this case than anyone, right?"

"That's right."

"Reports aside, off the record. Do you personally think Edmunds fell out of that porthole?"

Most people either blink excessively or not at all when they're lying. Moore's eyelids did a quick tap dance as he answered my question. "No doubt about it."

In the hallway, I spied a door to a corner office and figured it must be Quattlebaum's. I was halfway there when his secretary stepped in front of me. A fragile-looking porcelain woman of about fifty-five, she had a guileless smile. Her prim pink dress gave her pale skin the only hint of color about her except for her light blue eyes. Even her hair had a shining translucence about it, the hueless brilliance of a ray of sun.

"May I help you?"

"I'd like to have a word with Mr. Quattlebaum."

"He's in a meeting and can't be disturbed."

"Maybe I can make an appointment."

She steered me to the reception lobby. "You can leave a card, and we'll call you."

I handed her a card. As she looked it over, her lips drew down in a slight frown. "Will he know what this is about, Mr. Heart?"

"Just tell him it's in reference to an investigation I'm conducting."

She placed the card carefully onto her immaculate desk next to a name plate that said Dottie Adams. "I'll see to it that he gets the message."

I was sure Les Moore would see to it that Quattlebaum heard all about my visit before Dottie had a chance to give him my card.

Chapter Four
In Liberty We Trust

I figured I'd better try a different tack with Liberty Limited in case Nesta had used her charm on them as well. The receptionist there was extremely friendly when I told her I was interested in investing in real estate. In less than five minutes I was sitting in the office of a young and enthusiastic sales representative. He looked lean and hungry, and his trouser cuffs fell a shade short of his worn but polished shoes.

"You've picked an excellent time to invest in real estate, Mr. Heart. Costs are lower than they have been in ten years."

That was an understatement. The bottom had fallen out of the real estate market two years before—the slide had begun just before Edmunds disappeared. Everyone had said it was just a lull, that in a few months things would return to their frenetic pace of the early 1920s when a piece of property might be bought and sold fifteen times in one day, increasing in price with each sale. Property sold so fast, they didn't even bother with deeds. Instead they dealt in binders that entitled the holder to get the deed. In those days people all over Florida became millionaires almost literally overnight buying and selling lots they never even saw.

Those who flooded into Florida later to get in on the action weren't so lucky. When the bust hit, most of them found they had spent their life savings on undeveloped lots in the middle of mosquito- and snake-infested swamps. I wasn't surprised that this young man was eager to make a sale.

"Yes, I guess people are hesitant to invest in real estate these days."

"That's the beauty of a syndicate. By pooling resources with other investors, you increase your buying power. And our experienced analysts purchase only the choicest properties. There's almost no risk."

"Yes, well, I've spoken to a couple other syndicates. I have only a couple hundred thousand dollars to play with, and I'd like to invest it all with one company so I can keep an eye on it, you understand."

His eyes bulged slightly at this and he licked his lips. I was sure he was counting up his commission in his head. "Liberty Limited pays excellent dividends. Let me show you—"

"I've already compared your annual reports with the others. They're all pretty much in line. What I'd like to have is a list of your board of directors and major stockholders. I've found that the success of a company depends on the people who make the decisions."

He leaped up from his desk. "Yes, sir. Excellent reasoning. I'll put together a portfolio for you right away. I'm sure you'll be quite impressed with our other investors. Liberty Limited is the most prestigious company in this part of the state."

He was right. Back in my office, I looked over the list of corporate officers and major stockholders. It appeared that the entire power structure of Tampa stood to gain from the accidental death of Edward Edmunds. The list held the names of almost all the Gasparilla pirates as well as the mayor and chief of police. Saul Stone, chief executive officer of Edmunds Estates, was treasurer of the board. No surprise there. He'd built Edmunds' empire with skill and precision. Dominic and Hedda Boudreaux were major shareholders, and so was Terrance Quattlebaum.

Two other names among the major stockholders caught my interest. One was Santo Ciega, *padrone* of Ybor City. Ciega ran most of the gambling, bootlegging and prostitution operations in Ybor under the direction of Charlie Dorr, a favorite son of Anglo Tampa. Rumor had it that Dorr and the Tampa Board of Trade had hired Ciega almost forty years ago—right after Jose Vincente Ybor opened his first cigar factory in Tampa.

Until then, Tampa had some seasonal industry, shipping, cattle and citrus. But the cigar industry promised a more stable, year-round economy. This made Tampa's city fathers attentive to Ybor's needs. After opening his first factory, he complained that his workers missed Cuba, where they were accustomed to betting on a numbers game called bolita. They were also lonely, Ybor said. And Tampa's prostitutes charged more money than cigar workers could afford on their wages.

Eager to please Ybor, the Tampa Board of Trade had put Charlie Dorr on the job. He hired Ciega, then a part-time bootlegger, to oversee bolita operations and houses of female companionship. As a bonus, Ciega had brought in boxing, cockfighting and pit bulls. Now we had a town worth moving to. As the cigar industry grew, so did gambling. Although it was technically illegal, everyone played bolita, even the south Tampa matrons, who bought their tickets from their housekeepers.

The other name that caught my eye on Liberty Limited's list of major stockholders was Randall Stroven, owner, publisher and editor of the *Tampa Chronicle*. The man responsible for my father's death.

SUSAN F. EDWARDS

Chapter Five
The Godfather of Ybor City

The clanging of the streetcar roused me from black thoughts as it stopped at Twenty-Second Street and Seventh Avenue. I had missed my stop at Fourteenth Street and traveled the length of Seventh Avenue — the main street of Ybor, the Latin city within the city of Tampa. Cigar capital of the world.

Ybor is not just a separate city — it is a different nation where the rhythms of Spanish replace the drone of English. The quiet, staid streets of Tampa give way in Ybor to shouting, laughter, singing and music. Tampa does not exist in the nose, but Ybor is filled with the smells of fresh tobacco, roasting coffee, baking bread and sizzling garlic.

Every evening, families promenade down Seventh Avenue, buying mondongo, sweet guava pies, piruli candy, and shots of hot, black Cuban coffee from street vendors. On weekends we watch open air movies projected on sheets hung from balconies. Old men smoke cigars and play dominoes in the cantinas and squares of the social clubs.

As I walked through the crowd, I had no intention of stopping at El Dorado. My feet seemed to have other ideas. They took me across the street and to the door. Suddenly I was inside the dragon's lair. Blue ribbons of cigar smoke curled in the air under paddle fans. El Dorado was Ybor City's most lavish gambling emporium. Roulette wheels spun and dice clicked among red brocade and gilt. A huge crystal bowl holding one hundred ivory bolita balls sat next to a red velvet drawstring bag draped upon an altar on the stage.

Through the haze I saw Santo Ciega sitting in his huge hand-painted wooden throne at his table next to the stage. He was holding court with his thugs, everything about him larger than life: The huge Santo Cigarro made especially for him at the Cuesta Ray factory was

27

always stuck into his face under a bushy black mustache. His trademark perfectly tailored white linen suit draped on his bulky six-foot-four frame. He looked as though he could pluck a palm tree out of the earth and use it for a toothpick.

Suddenly the lights dimmed and a drum roll sounded. A rustle ran through the crowd as people took out their bolita tickets. A man in a black tie and tails appeared in a pool of light onstage and took up the red bag with a flourish. He dropped each bolita ball into the bag and mixed them together dramatically. Then he tied the drawstring tightly and handed the bag to Ciega, who shook it and rolled it around to mix the balls further. Then he handed the bag to a painted blond he had been eyeing at a nearby table. She fondled the balls through the bag flirtatiously and finally selected one.

The man in the penguin suit leapt off the stage and tied a black ribbon around the ball. Then he brandished a knife, cut the velvet fabric around the ball and held it aloft triumphantly. Fourteen, the wildcat. The band played a fanfare. Curses and cheers went up around the room from losers and winners.

Ciega's laughter rumbled like thunder through the surrounding din and raised the hairs on the back of my neck. Suddenly I felt hot and dizzy. I backed out the door, never taking my eyes off Santo Ciega, and went home to bed.

I awoke late the next morning, sweating and tangled in the sheets. The last smoky vapors of a nightmare dissipated in the blazing morning light. In the dream I had been on Seventh Avenue, which was eerily quiet and empty. Thunder rumbled under roiling storm clouds, shaking the glass in windows. A flash of lightning illuminated the sky, revealing the leering face of Santo Ciega, laughing as he sent a giant tidal wave, three stories high, racing up Seventh Avenue toward me. I was running for my life when I woke up.

I shook off the dream and stumbled out of bed toward my watch. Nine-fifteen.

Chapter Six
Spanish Heart

I downed a café solo on my way to the streetcar. It was still early enough that the breeze was not yet hot. By the time I got to my office, I felt somewhat revived. When I opened the door and saw Nesta there, I wished I'd drunk two coffees. At least she'd had the decency not to take up residence in my chair today.

"You always start your day at ten o'clock? No wonder you can't afford a secretary."

It hadn't taken her long to go from damsel in distress to matron of the manor. I took my seat behind the desk before replying. "Don't worry, you'll get your money's worth out of me."

"And what has my money bought so far?"

"I went to Victory Life yesterday."

"What did you find out there?"

"For starters, they're not crazy about you."

"I don't need a private eye to tell me that."

I told her Les Moore hadn't been much help, to which she replied that she had gotten more out of him than I had. Then I ran down my visit with Lola, dwelling on Lola's intimate knowledge of Edmunds' character and habits longer than was really necessary or kind. But Nesta Edmunds wasn't the sort who brought out the best in a man. Then I showed her the list of Liberty Limited's stockholders and board members and asked if anyone on the list might have helped her husband disappear.

She wetted a finger and ran it down the first column. She paused at the names of Hedda and Dominic Boudreaux and gave me a significant look.

"They're already on my list to question," I told her.

When she got to Quattlebaum's name, she let out a small gasp and her lips tightened in a satisfied smile. She stabbed at the name with a

29

neatly buffed fingernail. "That figures. He probably thought he was just shifting the money from one pocket into the other. Ha! Did he get a surprise."

"He couldn't have expected to gain much. He only owns thirteen percent of the stock."

"He probably paid less than five percent of the policy, if that."

I didn't follow her, and my face must have shown it because she explained. "With a big policy like that, the company reinsures parts of it with other insurance companies. It spreads out the income, but it also diffuses the liability. Old Mullethead made money on this deal."

"Mullethead?"

"Quattlebaum's nickname. I thought everyone knew it."

"Why Mullethead?"

"I take it you haven't seen him up close yet."

As I explained that I hadn't been able to get past the receptionist, Nesta took out a cigarette and held it up for me to light, a princess accustomed to servants. I wanted to ignore the gesture, but my mother raised a gentleman, so I obliged. Nesta sat back and blew a thick stream of smoke in my direction.

She finished the list without another hitch. "The rest of these names mean nothing to me. I know most of them, but so what?"

"Do you know Randall Stroven?"

"Vaguely," she replied, wrinkling her nose in distaste. "Nasty little man."

"Did your husband ever have business dealings with him?"

"Edward had business dealings with everyone, Mr. Heart. Everyone."

"Were they friends?"

"God, no. No one actually likes Randall Stroven. But everyone has to be nice to him. He's tremendously powerful. He gave us wonderful coverage when the Island opened. Of course it was the least he could do. Edward spent thousands for advertisements in his paper."

"Is it possible that Stroven might have helped your husband disappear, Mrs. Edmunds?"

"I doubt it. He would have been the last person Edward would trust. Randall Stroven is not a man you tell your secrets to."

I pointed out Ciega's name. "What about him?"

She shrugged.

"Did your husband know him?"

"I have no idea. Edward knew a lot of people I never met or heard about."

"You've never heard the name Santo Ciega?"

"Never. Why? Who is he?"

I gave her the particulars, and she shook her head. "My husband prefers to keep company with the rich and powerful, not criminals."

"Santo Ciega is one of the richest men in Florida. And one of the most powerful."

She eyed me with a haughty smirk. "Not in our world, Mr. Heart."

"You might be surprised. Santo Ciega is Charlie Dorr's right-hand man." Everyone knows the name Charlie Dorr, the Anglo Big Boss of all gambling operations in Ybor. All the Latin boliteras operated under his direction and protection, and they paid dearly for the privilege. Dorr took care of all the payoffs to local and state officials and would orchestrate occasional police shakedowns to weed out those who weren't paying him enough, and to appease reformers. Because Dorr controlled such large sums of money, he carried a lot of weight in state and local politics and commerce.

She studied me through the smoke of her cigarette. "You're Latin, aren't you?"

When Anglos say Latin, they mean anyone brown. "I'm Spanish and Italian."

"But Heart isn't an Italian name."

"My father was Spanish. Heart's the English translation of his last name."

"Which is?"

"Corazon."

She stubbed out her cigarette with an amused smile. The name obviously meant nothing to her. She probably thought I had changed it to be more like an Anglo.

"Look. Mr. — Heart." That smile again. "Edward may be a liar and a cheat. But he likes to mingle with the elite. I don't think he would have turned to your Santo Ciega for help."

My Santo Ciega. I felt my jaw tighten. If she had been a man, I would have wiped that smile off her face with the back of my hand, client or not. But she was a woman, if not a lady.

"I was thinking more of murder."

"Murder?" Her smile vanished. I was getting a rise out of her now. "You mean you think that this…this mobster might have killed him?"

"Possibly."

Her laughter was sharp and metallic. "That's ridiculous. I'm telling you Edward is alive. He's somewhere sipping rum at this very moment and laughing at me. I want him found."

"What do you know about Saul Stone?"

Her nostrils flared for an instant, but otherwise her expression didn't change. "Forget him. He was loyal to my husband, but he wouldn't be a party to fraud."

"How do you know?"

"Edward complained constantly about Saul's rigid morals. He said Saul lacked imagination. He was always refusing to play a part in Edward's more creative ventures."

"Such as?"

"You remember the grand opening of sales for Edmunds Island?"

I nodded. Who could forget the wild weeklong hoopla? Tampa had never seen such a show. Fireworks, speedboat races, society balls, radio broadcasts, stunt planes, parades, bathing beauties, and countless celebrities. People had waited in line for three days to make sure they could buy plots of land. There was practically a riot when the offices finally opened.

"Edward sold half the plots on the island in four days, and then he shut down the office with hundreds still in line. For a week people bought and sold those properties, driving the price up to hundreds of times its original price."

I remembered the frenzy. It had been like a carnival for weeks.

"Then Edward reopened the office and sold the rest at wildly inflated prices. He made millions and millions."

"What does this have to do with Saul Stone?"

"Saul thought the plan was unconscionable. He refused to take part, even after Edward threatened to fire him."

"So why didn't he fire him?"

"Because he knew Saul was the best numbers man in the business. And the only one Edward trusted not to pilfer the till."

Her smile told me she enjoyed the irony of this.

"There's no need to bother Mr. Stone. He's pure as Ivory Soap."

"Even Ivory's not one hundred percent pure."

"Close enough," she said, rising to leave. When she got to the door, she turned back to look at me. "Perhaps I made a mistake in hiring you. Maybe you don't know enough about our world to succeed in this investigation."

"Don't kid yourself. Greed and jealousy are pretty much the same in every world."

"I'm talking about high finance."

"It's been one day, Mrs. Edmunds. Surely you didn't expect me to find him overnight."

"A woman wants many things from a man, Mr. Heart. But she actually expects very few."

SUSAN F. EDWARDS

Chapter Seven
Man Overboard

I hadn't taken time for my usual morning Cuban toast, but that wasn't the only reason for the cold, hard lump that throbbed in the pit of my stomach. Nesta Edmunds had gotten to me. No longer the tearful supplicant, she was a razor seeking a jugular with cool precision, and she had found mine. *Our world,* she said, as if the Anglos inhabited a separate planet.

I bought a crab cake as big as my fist from a street vendor and slathered it with tart hot red pepper sauce. It was like swallowing a ray of sun. Fiery fingers melted the icy spot in my gut and radiated warmth and energy up from my stomach. I washed it down with a yeasty malta and felt my body perk up. I was ready for my next move.

I walked three blocks to the offices of the Whitestar Cruise Line on the corner of Franklin and Cass. The receptionist was a ravishing brunette with a fringe of dark eyelashes so long they brushed her cheeks when she looked down. A man could spend a lifetime deciphering the language of those brown eyes. I hoped the man who had given her the diamond chip engagement ring on her finger would try.

A woman can smell a man's attraction even if she's not aware of it. She responded to mine with a smothered smile, a pretty blush and a downward sweet of those fan-like lashes. "Can I help you?" she asked with her eyes still fixed on the desktop. I placed a card on it to give her something to look at. She studied it intently, still young enough to be impressed by the title.

"I wonder if it's possible to get a list of everyone who bought a ticket in Tampa for the Royal Cruise to London on September 25, 1927?"

The lashes flew upward, and she looked me in the eye for the first time. "That would take some digging."

"I know it's a lot to ask. You've probably got too much work to do as it is."

"I didn't say it was impossible." Her smile was as dazzling as her eyes. I couldn't help but smile back. "It will just take some time. You know, to go through all those old records."

"I could pay you for your time."

"Oh no. I'm happy to help. Is this for a case?"

I nodded. "Can you keep a secret?"

"Oh, yes."

"You remember the disappearance of EQ Edmunds?"

Her eyes grew wide and she nodded.

"Some people don't believe it was an accident," I whispered.

"But what—"

I put a finger to my lips in a shushing gesture. "When can I check back?"

"Give me a couple of days."

"Thank you. You are as kind as you are beautiful."

She blushed again, more deeply this time, and my blood answered by rushing to some very pleasant places.

I stopped at Victory Life on my way back to the office. Yes, the receptionist told me apologetically, Mr. Quattlebaum had received my card and message. He would call me when he could, but he was a very busy man.

City Hall was the next stop. I hadn't had time to get my paper this morning either. Otto smiled and thumped his heart with a fist when he heard my steps or smelled me or did whatever he did to identify me as I approached.

"Corazon," he said and slapped a *Herald* on the counter. He caught the nickel I tossed him and palmed it. I looked at the paper and hesitated. "Give me a *Chronicle* today instead."

His eyebrows shot up to twin peaks above his glasses. He knew I never bought a *Chronicle* and why. "What's up?"

I told him that Randall Stroven was a stockholder in Liberty Limited, the company that had taken out a million-dollar insurance policy on Edmunds' life.

"So what? I'll bet half the Krewe of Gasparilla had a piece of that pie. It doesn't prove anything."

"Call me curious. I just want to have a look at what Stroven's up to these days."

"Dios mio, Billy. Why don't you just strip naked and lie down in a pit of hungry alligators? You'd have a better chance of surviving." He slapped a *Chronicle* down on the counter and flipped my nickel back at me. "I wouldn't want you putting a nickel in Randall Stoven's pocket. I dreamed of the running of the bulls last night. Put that on fifteen tonight."

"You know I don't play bolita."

"The only man in Tampa who doesn't play bolita, and he's Italian. You're a discredit to your people. And you hold too many grudges."

I took the newspaper up to my office and stared at it a while. The usual murders, bootleg busts and real estate stories marched down the columns in a dreary procession. There was an editorial by Stroven prominently displayed criticizing a city council decision to fund a Spanish language library in Ybor City. Stroven wrote that if "those people in Ybor want to read, let them read in English like decent Americans." He chose to ignore the fact that most of the books in question were historical documents originally written in Spanish. Things like transcripts of letters from Don Pedro Menendez from Florida to the Spanish crown in the sixteenth century, long before English was spoken here.

In particular, Stroven attacked one city council member who had spearheaded the drive, Rudy Garcia. It was an ill-kept secret that Stroven planned to run against Garcia in the next city council election.

SUSAN F. EDWARDS

The fan overhead strained to cut through the heavy, damp heat, creaking rhythmically, hypnotizing me into sleep.

Chapter Eight
The Dandy and the Aviatrix

I awoke to the whistle from the three o'clock train two blocks away. A good time to visit Dominic Boudreaux. Liberty Limited had listed him as an attorney with the Stern and Ernest law firm on Zack Street. The receptionist only fit half the description. A stern fireplug of a woman with nothing particularly earnest about her. She took my card and rose from her desk.

"Mr. Boudreaux is just on his way out, but I'll see if he has a moment."

She disappeared down a hallway and returned moments later followed by a tan, fit man who looked to be in his early thirties. Women would probably find him handsome, with his crown of dark, silky curls and a face almost too pretty for a man. His perfectly tailored taupe silk suit draped his frame elegantly and attested to his wealth and his vanity. His boyish smile revealed a fine expanse of even, white teeth, as highly polished as the manicured nails on the hand he extended to me.

"I'm Dominic Boudreaux," he drawled in a warm, honeyed voice as he took my hand and squeezed it in both of his. It was less a handshake than an embrace.

He chuckled when I explained that I was working for Mrs. Edmunds and looking into her husband's disappearance.

"She still thinks old Eddie took a powder, huh?" He drew each vowel out until it drooped like a piece of stretched taffy. It took forever for him to complete a sentence.

"You don't think so?"

"Tell you what. I'm headed to the club to meet my wife. Why don't ya'll come with me and we can talk about it?

"Sounds good to me."

He draped an arm around my shoulders in a fraternal pose. "Hedda loves private eyes." He blew a kiss at the receptionist. "Bye, Elsie. If Stern asks where I've gone —"

"You're at City Hall filing those affidavits," she finished for him.

He grasped his breast theatrically. "You're the sun in my sky, dearest Elsie. I swear, if I weren't already married —"

She slapped a thick file down on the desk. "Just make sure you file them on your way in tomorrow."

He gave me a mock-wounded pout. "She never takes me seriously though it's clear that I love her."

Elsie rolled her eyes and tapped the file. "Before noon tomorrow or your goose is cooked."

He seized the file and saluted. "This mission will be accomplished, or I will die trying." He clicked his heels and marched out the door.

By "the club," I figured Boudreaux meant Edmunds Island Yacht Club because he drove his shiny gold Stoddard-Dayton straight for Bayshore. Although autos are much more common than they were five years ago, people still have a tendency to stare, especially at such a fine machine as this. Boudreaux honked and waved, a one-man parade in a shiny new car.

On Bayshore, Boudreaux caught up with the outbound streetcar and kept pace with it for a while, waving and winking at its occupants while I inspected the creamy leather interior of his car. At length, he tired of his game and stomped the gas pedal with an alligator shoe.

I grabbed the handhold as the car leapt forward and sped south. I watched the speedometer climb from thirty to forty and beyond. When we hit fifty miles per hour, Boudreaux slapped the steering wheel and howled like a wolf, as if the speed and freedom of that ride had somehow released a wild animal inside of him. I have to admit, I felt like howling too. By the time we reached the yacht club, my blood was singing and every pore in my body felt cleansed and alive.

The Edmunds Island Yacht Club had a respectable crowd for four o'clock on a Wednesday afternoon. White-clad figures bounded around the tennis courts, and children splashed in the pool under the watchful eyes of colored nannas. Slavery was abolished more than sixty years ago, but you would never know it to look at this place with its old plantation feel. Gleaming sailboats with silver-haired men at the helms sliced the water soundlessly. In the main hall, men in business suits lingered in groups over cigars and coffee. I followed Boudreaux to the lounge tucked away in a back corner of the building overlooking the bay.

As we entered the plush hunter green lounge, a handsome, well-tended woman in safari khakis eyed us lazily from an overstuffed divan and lifted a cool drink to her lips. She had a robust physique and the high rosy color that comes from good health and exercise. Her blonde hair fell almost to her shoulders in rows of shiny marcelled waves. "There you are, naughty boy," she said.

Boudreaux leaned over and kissed her on the forehead.

"You missed my moment of glory," she said with a pout identical to the one her husband had given Elsie. I wondered who had picked up the expression from whom.

"I'm sorry, darlin'. Old Stern had me on a short leash all day. I even suffered through lunch with him."

"You could make it up to me by spicing my drink a bit."

"I'll do better than that. I brought you a surprise," he said, gesturing to me.

She appraised me coolly while her husband produced a silver flask from a pocket, uncorked it, and poured a generous slug of fragrant amber liquid into her glass. Scotch, I guessed from the smell.

"This is Mr. William Heart. He's a private eye."

She sat up and clapped her hands in delight. "Well now the afternoon is getting interesting!" She took a long pull from her drink, and Boudreaux motioned to the bartender.

Even though the building had been built during Prohibition, the lounge had a massive polished oak bar. Where liquor might have stood in less puritanical times, an impressive array of seltzers, sodas, and other mixers were arranged. The bartender poured some sort of clear bubbly liquid into three glasses and brought them to our table, ignoring the glass of amber liquid and its smell of alcohol.

When the waiter had departed, Boudreaux topped off my glass with his flask. "None of that sticky Caribbean swill. This is pure Scottish brew from the emerald highlands." It had clean, metallic taste going down, followed by a hot bite, sort of like swallowing a sword.

A rowdy group entered and cheered in our direction. "Nice flying, Ace," one of them called to Hedda. She smiled and raised her glass to them.

"Hedda's a pilot," Dominic explained. "She flew an exhibition today. Showed 'em her new double corkscrew maneuver, and I missed it. Can you ever forgive me, love?"

She rolled her eyes.

"Dangerous hobby," I said.

"I'm a dangerous woman," she replied, licking the edge of her glass.

Dominic looked at her with exaggerated dog-like devotion. "Can you imagine, the daring, the skill? And she's mine. All mine."

Hedda handed him a cigarette holder and turned to me with a slow, seductive smile. "It's just something to break up monotony." Dominic loaded a cigarette into the holder, lit it and handed it back to her. "Ah, but you wouldn't know about boredom, would you? Out spying on people, solving mysteries. Tell us about a case, Detective Billy."

She seemed disappointed at first when I told her I was looking into Edmunds' disappearance, but then giggled when I told her who I was working for. "You've got to give the old girl credit for tenacity," she said.

42

Finally I was in the driver's seat. "Did he act at all unusual on the day of his disappearance?"

"It's hard to say what would be unusual for Eddie. He was an uncommon man." The twinkle in her eyes betrayed an affection for Edmunds, I thought, though her husband didn't seem to notice. "I'd say he was himself that day, only more so."

Dominic leaned in with an earnest look. "He *was* acting a bit strange that day, though. He was giving Lola a devil of a time all day."

Hedda clucked her tongue impatiently. "After the scene she made the night before, who could blame him?"

"What was that about?"

Hedda stubbed out her cigarette. "She found out Eddie was going to meet Nesta in London, and she pitched one hell of a fit. Screaming, crying, throwing things."

"She didn't know before?"

Hedda gave me a disdainful look. "Apparently not."

Dominic was agitated. "He was always doing things like that to the poor girl. Cruel things."

"Nonsense. He simply liked to tease, and she was so easy to get a rise out of. That's why he kept her around. He thrived on dramatic scenes, and he could always count on that hot Cuban blood of hers to give him one."

I wanted to ask her what she knew about hot Cuban blood, but Dominic cut in.

"He sure got one that night. She threatened to kill him, but even that he turned against her. He said he would kill himself before she got the chance." Dominic turned to Hedda. "Remember the song he kept singing to her all day?"

"Oh, yes. How did it go?"

They sang it together to the tune of a popular song. "I can make money or spend it, live my life or end it. It all depends on you."

"Do you think he was suicidal?" I asked.

Hedda snorted. "Not at all. He may have been threatening suicide when he fell, but I'm positive he had no intention of actually killing himself."

Dominic nodded in agreement. "He wasn't the type to commit suicide. The sea was rough that night. A wave probably hit the boat, and he lost his balance."

Hedda smiled slyly. "Or maybe she'd had enough and pushed him."

I had a feeling she was toying with me. "You think she's capable of murder?"

She shrugged. "In a moment of anger perhaps, aren't we all?"

Hedda grilled me about my investigation so far. I chose to tell them only about my visit to Victory Life and my unsuccessful attempts to see Quattlebaum.

"Forget his office," Dominic advised. "He's hardly ever there anyway."

"I don't think he'd appreciate my calling him at his home."

"Oh, he's never there either. If you ever meet his wife, you'll understand why," Dominic drawled.

"So where does he spend his time?"

"Mostly private gentlemen's clubs." He didn't say the obvious, that these clubs wouldn't let me in the door.

Hedda brightened. "Wait. Dom, didn't you tell me he goes to the YMCA almost every night for a steambath?"

Dominic nodded. "That's right. He goes after dinner around seven. I've met him there a few times to get his signature on papers for Eddie."

I stood. "Thank you. You've both been very helpful."

"You aren't leaving so soon? Won't you join us for dinner?" Hedda gave me the Boudreaux pout. On her it looked a little more contrived than on him. I decided she had picked it up from him.

"I'm afraid not, Mrs. Boudreaux. I've got lots of work to do."

"Call me Hedda. And I shall call you Detective Billy."

They insisted on driving me back to town although the streetcar would have been safer, given Dominic's state of inebriation. After a hair-raising ride up Bayshore, we screeched to a stop in front of my office. As I was getting out of the car, Dominic clapped me on the shoulder and Hedda planted a kiss on my cheek. Then they were off, blowing kisses and waving scarves in the wind. It was hard to tell if they were hiding anything. Life was one big stage show to them, and they were the stars. People like that don't so much lie as act a part.

SUSAN F. EDWARDS

Chapter Nine
The Mullethead Trail

I had an hour to kill before going to the YMCA. Compared to Ybor, downtown Tampa is pretty quiet at night. I thought about getting a bite to eat, but Tampa food is so bland it killed my appetite just to think about it. I figured I'd go to my office and get some paperwork done.

When I got there, I discovered a slip from Western Union. A telegram is always more interesting than paperwork. I snatched the slip and headed over to see what was up.

The telegram was from the Continental Detective Agency in San Francisco. Continental gave me my start in the detective business nine years ago when I was eighteen.

I had gotten into some trouble here after my father died, and my mother sent me to stay with her sister in San Francisco to keep me from following in his footsteps. I knocked around there, drinking and getting into fights. One night I got in way over my head and was facing the points of about six stilettos.

An overweight, nondescript man broke up the party with surprising ferocity. He told me I owed him a favor and sent me over to a waterfront bar. He told me to sit at the bar and keep my mouth shut and watch for a man he described to me. I was to listen to everything he said to anyone and report back. He paid me for the job and sent me on a few more. It turned out he worked for the Continental Detective Agency, and they took me on and trained me. I learned almost everything I know about the private eye business from that man. In some ways, I owe him and the Continental Agency my life.

A few years later, I moved back here and set up shop. This county never would have granted a P.I. License to a man with a Latin name, but I had another reason for changing my name to Heart. Continental contacted me from time to time for information on runaways, cons, fugitives, and the other loose marbles that roll to this end of the continent. All they wanted this time was a make on a Florida automobile license plate. I would run it down tomorrow and telegraph back.

Usually I'm not big on steam baths. The air in Florida is hot and humid enough most days, but in March the Tampa nights could get pretty cold. An icy damp wind chilled me to the bone on this night and made me pull my thin jacket closed against it. I found myself looking forward to the hot hiss of steam.

It was seven on the dot when I wrapped a towel around my waist and entered the searing fog of the steam room. Only two occupants sat talking on the bench. One was a slender man in his twenties. The other was Quattlebaum, a rotund but solid barrel of a man in his late forties with dark thinning hair.

I sat down next to him. He and the younger man were arguing boxing. The young fellow felt Sugarcane Alejandro would take Kid Muldoon in the upcoming match on Friday. He was willing to wager ten dollars on a knockout before the fifth round. The big man took the bet and turned to me. "What about you? You want to get in on this action?"

"Tell you what," I said. " You're Terrance Quattlebaum, right?"

He nodded.

"I'll spot you ten on a split decision, Sugarcane over The Kid. But you've got to answer a question for me first." I paused to make sure I had his full attention.

He leaned in, eager for the challenge. "What's that?"

"Why did your company pay off so fast on EQ Edmunds' life insurance policy?"

He straightened up and narrowed his tiny, round fish eyes, so far apart they were closer to his ears than to his nose. "Who are you?"

"William Heart. I've been trying to get in to see you for days."

I could see him scanning his memory for the name. "Ah, yes. Nesta's new dick."

I didn't like the way he put it, but his witticism seemed to please him. He smiled, baring pointy teeth too small for his large mouth. He made me think of a 'possum. Then I remembered his nickname. Mullethead. The small teeth, the wide-set wall-eyed stare, the round, bullish head set on a neck so thick it looked like an extension of his head. It kept me from feeling too bad about being referred to as Nesta's dick. I smiled.

Mullethead emitted a series of snorts that I took for laughter. He clapped me on the back. "I gotta give you credit for finding me, though. Who told you where to look?"

"Let's just say a little fishie told me."

His smile vanished for a moment and then returned to his mouth but not his eyes. It was the practiced, insincere expression that businessmen and prostitutes cultivate. "You know, son, there's a lot of insurance companies out there trying to get your confidence, and not all of 'em earn that trust. A fella feels like he pays and pays in good faith and then when the chips are down, that company does not come through for him. Am I right?"

His false folksy manner annoyed me. I knew this age-old sales trick. Get the mark to agree with you and keep agreeing with you until he agrees to sign on the dotted line. As much as I hated to do it, I had to give ol' Mullethead a little more line. "That certainly was my experience when my father died."

"Exactly!" he crowed, triumphant at getting an affirmative out of me. "You probably don't trust insurance companies any more, do you?"

"That's right."

"And that's why I paid off Edmunds' policy as soon as I could. The whole city was watching. Hell, the whole state was watching. I wanted people to know that no matter how hard-nosed and, yes, even unscrupulous some insurance companies are when it comes to paying off, they could count on Victory Life to do the right thing." He gestured to an imaginary sign in the air. "Victory Life—we'll come through for you." I thought he might weep at the largesse of his generosity and empathy. Then he recovered and eyed me with compassion. "I'll bet you don't even have insurance. Am I right?"

"Right again."

"You're young, healthy, strong. You probably think nothing's ever going to happen to you. But we all get sick. We all die. Now's the time to plan for the problems we all face down the road. I can set you up now with a policy that will cost you pennies and pay you dollars. What could be a better investment than that?"

"If you really want to do me a favor, how about letting me get a look at your investigator's report on the Edmunds case?"

He shook his head, setting his jowls aquiver. "We closed the book on that one. A clear-cut case of accidental death. We did the right thing, and no one has anything to gain by reopening it, least of all your client." He mopped his dripping brow and stood up. "You come see me when you're ready to invest in your future. Then we'll talk."

I felt a little dizzy and sleepy from the heat while I dressed. The cold air on the Ybor streetcar revived me some and reminded me how hungry I was. I stopped at the Gold Ring on Seventh Avenue and Fourteenth Street and wolfed down a Cuban sandwich and a bowl of caldo gallego soup, a dish of navy beans and turnip greens.

I wondered if Mullethead's refusal meant he had something to hide beyond the fact that he was a major shareholder in the company that stood to receive the million-dollar payoff. There was a good chance he had not discovered until later that Edmunds had mortgaged the policy to the hilt. I had a hunch Les Moore's report would reveal little more than a hasty and halfhearted investigation designed to arrive at a conclusion of accidental death. Nonetheless, it would also have the London police reports, and I wanted to see those.

MAN OVERBOARD

Maybe I should have leaned on old Fish Face a little harder. No, let him sit tight for a while thinking I might go away. I still had a few leads to run down before push came to shove. The more I knew when I saw Victory's file, the more it might tell me. The long steam bath and late dinner combined to make me sleepy. I went home and slept like an old dog under a porch.

SUSAN F. EDWARDS

Chapter Ten
My Left Boot

I awoke early the next morning and figured I would use the extra time to visit the police station and get the job done for Continental Detective Agency before visiting Saul Stone, Edmunds' accountant and former business partner.

For reasons of my own, I'm not keen on visiting the headquarters of the Tampa Police Department. I had made a few friends on the force since my return. No one recognized the grown man William Heart as the angry punk named Billy Corazon. Most of the Tampa cops I had worked with knew me only as a private dick who always repaid a favor. I had even helped one of the detectives crack a case that had gotten him a promotion.

Boot Sims owed me a big one, and he always helped me out when he could. As long as I had to go in anyway, I figured might as well pay Boot a visit and see what I could pick up on Ciega's activities over the past couple of years. The police kept tabs on the top mobster even though he operated under their protection. I guess they needed to keep his file up to date in case he failed to make his payments to the brass on time.

Jimmy Reilly was in records, and he gave me the dope I needed for the Continental job without so much as a grumble. He must be about a hundred and four, but he says he'd rot if he retired. Word has it he never was much of a copper, but he's a crackerjack records man. He loves to know everybody's business and pass it around with a few additions of his own for drama's sake. For spreading the word through the ranks, Jimmy's faster than a memo, but you've got to divide whatever he says by at least four. I listened to his tale of the latest bootleg bust and then asked if Boot Sims was around. He nodded and waved me upstairs.

Sims was on the phone at his desk, so I sat down across from him and read his papers upside-down. Boot was the only cop on the force who knew my real name and my reasons for changing it. He was good about keeping my secret, but I liked to keep him in my debt just to make sure. I hated to call in a chit for Nesta Edmunds, but a job was a job.

He dropped the phone into its cradle and gave me a broad grin. "Billy Boy. How's tricks?"

I told him I was fine and asked about his family. He bragged about his oldest boy and told me he and the wife had another on the way, their third. When he asked, I made up some stuff about my love life, and then finally got down to business. I told him about the case I was working on and we kicked around theories for a while, just like the old days.

Since Edmunds had disappeared in international waters, the Tampa Police had not been informed on the investigations. Sims didn't know even as much as I did about it, but he had a copper's sense of skepticism about the accidental death ruling.

"What about Ciega?" I asked.

His smile disappeared and his face reddened. "What about him?"

"You boys ever turn up any connection between him and Edmunds?"

"Why should we?"

I told him Ciega was a major stockholder in Liberty Limited, the real estate syndicate that made a half million dollars off Edmunds' accidental death.

"So what? You think he'd knock off Edmunds for a little blip in his portfolio? That's feeble, Heart. And you know it."

"Maybe there was something else between them."

"Like what?"

"That's what I'm asking you. Maybe Edmunds bought whiskey or women from Ciega. Maybe he used Ciega's muscle to collect on delinquent accounts. Could be anything."

"I got nothing like that, Billy."

"How about Randall Stroven?"

"What about him?"

"He have any dealings with Ciega?"

"You never learn, do you?"

"Look, I didn't come here for advice. I came for information."

"No, you came for a bullet in your head. I won't be a part of it."

"Does that mean you know something you're not telling me?"

"Grow up. Even if there was some connection, you couldn't pin this on Stroven and you know it. He's too big. Jeez, Billy, even the chief of police is scared stiff of Randall Stroven."

"Look, if you don't know anything, just say so. I know you boys have your instructions to look the other way when it comes to certain people."

"What are you, stupid? You so much as whisper Stroven's name again and I don't know you."

I guess I should have expected him to react that way. Boot had always been one to play it safe, and he wanted me to do the same. I had tried to goad him into telling me what he knew, and it backfired. I couldn't blame him for striking back. Still, my fists itched as I walked the five blocks to my office. I wanted to punch somebody, but no likely targets crossed my path.

Until I opened the door and found her waiting again.

Nesta Edmunds looked at her watch. "Late again. Or don't you usually start your day until eleven?"

"If I wanted to punch a time clock, I'd work in a cigar factory."

"Testy this morning, aren't we?" She took a cigarette out of her purse and posed, ready for a light. I snatched the pallid little tube of stale tobacco out of her hand and threw it in the wastebasket.

"Let's get something straight. You hired me to do a job, and I'm doing it. But that doesn't mean you can treat me like your servant. I'll report to you once a week, on Fridays. If at that time, I haven't worn out enough shoe leather to suit you, you can fire me." I didn't wait for her reply. I left the office and slammed the door, fists still itching.

* * * * *

I sent the telegram off to San Francisco. They'd have the information they requested less than a day after they asked for it. It made me feel better to get something accomplished with no arguments, no condescension and no advice. Maybe I should have stayed in San Francisco.

I bought a café solo, threw it down my gullet, and hopped the Bayshore street car. It dropped me off right in front of the offices of Edmunds Estates, a division of Liberty Limited, the sign said.

The receptionist was apparently away from her desk, so I nosed around until I found Saul Stone. It wasn't hard. His was the first office I came to, and his name and title were posted on the open door. He was a thin, tidy man of about forty with a generous nose and mouth, deep-set dark eyes, and thick, wavy salt-and-pepper hair, smoothed back and tamed with a hot comb I suspected.

He looked up without curiosity when I entered. "Can I help you?"

"I'm here on behalf of Nesta Edmunds."

His eyes narrowed as I handed him my card. He caught his breath and shook his head as he read it.

"Is something wrong?" I asked with as much innocence as I could muster.

He realized then that I was watching him and struggled to compose his face. "Not at all." He gave me a wan smile and gestured me to a chair. "Please. Sit down."

I settled into the rich leather chair across from him and explained what Nesta had hired me for.

"Did Mrs. Edmunds send you here?"

"No, but I thought it necessary to ask you some questions, if you have no objections."

"Look. I've been through this dozens of times. Mr. Edmunds' death was ruled accidental in an official investigation. I don't see why his wife is dredging it all up again."

"She doesn't think he's dead."

"I've heard all her theories. Frankly, they're bunk. She just won't accept it."

"Did Edmunds have financial problems, Mr. Stone?"

"No. The man was a millionaire several times over."

"Then why did he sell Edmunds Estates?"

"He was bored."

"Bored?"

"Edward liked the excitement of new beginnings, the challenge of building something from nothing. Once Edmunds Estates was up and running, he lost interest."

"How much did Liberty pay for Edmunds Estates?"

"I don't know the exact figure." A series of quick blinks told me he was probably lying.

"Give me an estimate."

"Maybe three million."

"Actually it was one million. I'm surprised you wouldn't know that, being business manager for Edmunds Enterprises and treasurer for Liberty Limited."

He flushed at that. He apparently hadn't expected me to know that much about him.

"Why would he sell a multi-million-dollar investment for so little, Mr. Stone? He may have been bored but he was still a businessman."

Stone picked up a pencil and drummed it on his blotter. "It's no secret the bottom was falling out of the real estate market here. He wanted some cash to start a development in Europe, where things where ripe for the sort of thing he'd done here."

"But you said he had plenty of money."

He drummed the pencil faster. "Not liquid, for heaven's sake. You don't keep those kinds of assets under a mattress, you know."

"Wouldn't his assets have gone to his wife?"

"Yes of course. What was left after his liabilities were paid off."

"Liabilities like the loan he took out using his life insurance policy as collateral?"

Stone dropped the pencil and lit a cigarette.

"Did Edmunds wire that million dollars to Europe?" I asked.

"I have no idea." *Blink blink blink.*

"Oh, come now, Mr. Stone, you were his accountant and business manager. If he'd wanted the money sent to Europe, wouldn't he have had you do that?"

"Yes I suppose so."

"Well, did you?"

"No."

"Then he must have taken cash."

"I don't know."

"You expect me to believe that a meticulous man like yourself didn't know exactly where and in what form a million dollars of his client's money was?"

"All right. He did have cash. That doesn't prove anything." Stone's shoulders sagged, and he stubbed out his cigarette in a crystal ashtray.

"Why did you lie about Edmunds' financial status?"

Stone straightened up. "The money game is all about confidence, Mr. Heart." His voice took on the patronizing tone of a schoolteacher to a slow student. "If people have confidence in you, if they think you can protect their money and make it grow, they give it all to you. If people had known their investments in Edmunds Enterprises were in trouble, they would have rushed to pull out their money. Then we would have big problems. As it is, I've been able to hold things together somewhat and start to pay off the debts Edward left for his wife. She's not helping matters by stirring the pot like this."

"Have you explained that to her?"

"Many times. But you know Nesta. She always thinks she knows better than anyone else how things should be done."

"How would you characterize her relationship with her husband?"

His eyes widened at this question. "That is none of my affair, Mr. Heart." He rose. "And now, if you'll excuse me, I have work to do." *None of his affair.* Interesting choice of words.

I thanked him and went to the door where I stopped and fired one more question. "Did Edmunds Estates have any dealings with Randall Stroven?"

I watched him closely for any change in expression, but there was none. He was a lousy liar, but maybe he was just too tired to react. "We bought quite a bit of ad space from him. Why?"

"Just curious. He's a stockholder in Liberty Limited, you know."

"So are a lot of people."

"Yeah, like Santo Ciega."

Stone's face remained blank. "Good day, Mr. Heart."

The day had turned hot, and I was hungry. I stopped at a downtown lunch counter and gobbled down a plate of tasteless roast beef and mashed potatoes before heading to my office for some think time.

I approached my door warily in case Nesta was still there. To my relief, she was gone. I hung up my jacket and hat and lay on the sofa under the fan.

I hadn't made much headway on the Ciega angle, even less on Stroven. It was like wrestling two full-grown alligators at once. You had to approach them carefully or they would eat you alive. Maybe I was letting my personal feelings lead me off the scent.

Edmunds had been broke and deeply in debt when he disappeared. That fact could point to suicide or an engineered disappearance. Dominic Boudreaux had said Edmunds threatened suicide on the day he disappeared but neither he nor Hedda had taken it seriously. If anything, it sounded like Edmunds had been in high spirits that day, quite the opposite of a man planning to take his own life, especially in such a horrible way. But also quite the opposite of a man who had just lost his entire fortune. Of course, he had a million dollars. But that was nothing to a man like Edmunds. And why carry cash? Why not wire the money to Europe if he intended to spend it there?

Was EQ Edmunds drinking rum somewhere and laughing at his wife? Or was he dead at the bottom of the sea with a million dollars in his pockets? And if he was dead, had he jumped? Or had someone pushed him? I seemed no nearer the answer now than five days ago when I found that cursed woman drinking my stash, smoking my cigars and warming my chair.

Sometimes when you hit a dead end, it's best to sleep on it. I've found new leads and even an occasional solution during a siesta. On this afternoon, I awoke with neither in the stuffy air of my office.

The girl in the steamship office had said to give her a couple of days, but in the absence of anything else to do, I decided to pay her another visit and see how she was coming with the list of ticketholders. And maybe to get another gander at those gorgeous peepers.

I needed a smile to pick up my day, so I stopped on the way and bought a single pink rose. It didn't hold a candle to the blush on her cheeks when I gave it to her. If that flower had an ounce of self-respect, it would have wilted in shame on the spot.

"I've only got about half the names," she said in a hoarse whisper, not looking at me. I hoped I hadn't embarrassed her too much. She handed me the list, written in a loopy, childish script. I scanned it, finding the names of Edmunds and his entourage among many others that meant nothing to me.

Then I saw three names I knew, and an icy finger tickled the back of my neck. There they were in black and white. Frankie, Aldo and Rocky Vincetti. In my elation, I kissed her on the cheek before I knew what I was doing. "You're an angel," I shouted. Then I saw her turn crimson. "I'm sorry, I just, uh… It's good news…"

I mumbled my thanks and told her I'd be back for the rest of the list later, and then made tracks before she could recover and deliver the slap I deserved. I felt like a heel, but the trail was heating up, and the chase was on. I would square it with her later somehow.

Rocky Vincetti had a place in Ybor City called the Punch House where people gathered to gamble, drink liquor and watch boxing. Vincetti was Ciega's right hand man, and his brothers, Aldo and Frankie were bagmen and arm breakers and anything else Ciega wanted them to be. This was the break I was looking for. Three of Ciega's boys had been on the same ship as Edmunds when he disappeared.

I could feel my grip tightening around Ciega's throat. I couldn't wait to tell Mama.

SUSAN F. EDWARDS

Chapter Eleven
Mama's Pesto

Mama was in her garden when I arrived, watering her tomato and romaine plants with an old coffee can. I caught her up in my arms and danced her around the yard. In the old days she loved to dance. Every Saturday night, she and my father used to take me to Fraterno Italiano. I would sneak Cuban coffee with lots of sugar and watch my parents whirl around the dance floor, laughing and kissing. She had been beautiful and gay in those days with an easy smile and eyes only for the dashing figure of her husband.

Like almost everyone else in Ybor, my mother had worked in a cigar factory, stripping tobacco leaves for the Cuban artisans to mold into fine cigars while the lector sat high above the room reading in a loud, booming voice to chase the boredom away. In those days every cigar factory had a lector, elected by popular vote of the workers, and chosen for his dramatic flair, his literary taste and his politics.

The lectors were entertainers, but they were also political labor leaders. They read Cervantes and Lorca, but they also read revolutionary manifestos of the greatest political theorists of all time as well as socialist and anarchist newspapers from all over the world.

The lector's job was not just to entertain, but to inform and sometimes to inflame workers to stand up for their rights and to unite in the cause of fair labor practices. Partly due to the lectors, Ybor had one of the most cohesive and sophisticated labor movements in the world. The voices of Ybor cigar workers were heard and heeded, not just in Ybor, where the cigars were made, but in Cuba where the tobacco was grown, and on the sugar and banana plantations of the Caribbean and South America.

My father had been lector in the Cuesta Rey factory where my mother worked. It was there, listening to his voice that she fell in love with him. It was there that he courted her, reading love poems before three hundred other workers, but for her alone, a blushing and beautiful seventeen-year-old. She was always that girl around him, smiling, laughing, blushing.

It was that girl I saw as I danced my mother around her yard.

She let me dance her around a little and then had me pick some basil and follow her to the kitchen.

Inside, Mama peeled cloves of garlic and mashed them with the flat edge of a knife while I poured glasses of Mrs. Mazzarelli's homemade red wine and told her about the Edmunds case. She enjoys hearing about my cases and speculating with me. She is a keen observer of human nature, and her insights have often proven valuable. But this case was closer to home in a lot of ways.

Mama's lips tightened when I told her that Rocky Vincetti and his brothers had been on the ship with Edmunds.

"You remember your promise to me?" She fixed the stern glare on me that had always turned my knees to water as a child. That look meant I was courting a date with the switch. Although I was too old now for a whipping, the look still had the same effect on me. My neck grew hot under my collar.

"I'm just going to have a talk with Vincetti."

"Don't play semantics with me, nino. You step on Rocky Vincetti's tail, and the Yellow Rat bites you. We both know that."

Yellow Rat had been Mama's name for Ciega since my father's disappearance. She said Ciega could have stopped it, but that he was too much a yellow rat. And that's what she called him forever after when she spoke of him at all, which was seldom.

She chopped the garlic and some pecans with a vengeance, her knife pounding on the cutting board with the rhythmic blast of machine gun fire. I decided to keep my mouth shut about the Stroven angle.

She slapped a chunk of parmesan down on the table in front of me with a grater. I dutifully grated cheese while she poured the nuts and

64

garlic into a large porcelain mortar bowl and went after the fragrant bouquet of basil I had picked with her knife.

She put the chopped basil into the bowl with the garlic and nuts and poured in some olive oil. Then she picked up a large pestle and mashed the mixture with strong sure strokes, adding in a little of the cheese I had grated. The aroma that arose was heady and sharp. It always made me slightly drunk.

My thoughts drifted to Stroven as Mama beat the pesto into submission with her porcelain club. It turned smooth and creamy under the drubbing she was giving it. If he was involved in Edmunds' disappearance, and if I could prove it... Vengeance would truly be mine.

Mama dipped a wooden spoon into the mixture and tasted it. She extended the spoon to me, and froze in mid-gesture. Her eyes narrowed and fixed upon me. "What is it?" she demanded.

"Nothing," I mumbled, feeling like a guilty six-year-old and turning my eyes away from her. She grabbed a fist full of my hair and yanked my head up to face her. I don't know if all mothers can read their children's minds, but I had no doubt that mine could.

"There's something else, isn't there?"

"No," I whined, trying to untangle her hand from my hair. But she had a good grip, and she shook my head.

"Tell me!"

It was no use resisting. "It's Randall Stroven," I said. "I think he might have been in on it somehow."

She gasped and released my hair. She backed away from me, a look of horror on her face. "No." She was still holding the wooden spoon. Pesto dripped from it onto the floor.

"He was one of the major stockholders in Liberty Limited, Mama. They bought Edmunds Island for a million dollars. Then they took out a million-dollar insurance policy on his life."

She sank into a chair. "You must drop this case, son."

"I can't do that. I gave my word."

"Don't be a fool!"

"A fool? What am I now, Mama? What is a man who lets the murder of his father go unavenged?"

She smacked me on the jaw with the spoon, splattering my face with pesto. "Are you blind? You can't win a blood-and-guts battle with Randall Stroven. He will pulverize you like that pesto. Did you forget everything he did to us before?"

"No, Mama. That's why —"

She raised the spoon to stop my words. "Your father is dead. We are lucky you did not follow him to his grave. Do you think we will be so blessed next time?"

"Maybe it would be better to die than to let that pig get away with murder again."

My mother slapped me hard, a look of horror on her face. The sting, the deep ache of her blow felt good somehow, as if the pain inside me finally had a small outlet. I felt it seeping slowly out. I wanted someone to hit me again and again, until it all bled out.

Mama began to weep. The sound of her sobs made the need worse. I pounded my head on the table over and over until she whacked me again.

We ate our vermicelli buttered with pesto in uncomfortable silence. I tried once or twice to get her to talk about her favorite subject, which was our club, Fraterno Italiano. Everyone in Ybor belongs to a mutual aid society like Fraterno. They're the center of our social lives. The Spaniards have Centro Espanol and Centro Asturiano. The Cubans have Circulo Cubano, and the Negro Cubans have Marti Maceo. All the clubs have grand buildings with ballrooms, auditoriums, cantinas, libraries, and medical clinics.

My mother was Fraterno Italiano's librarian. In that capacity she served as secretary and voting member of the board of directors. It was a position of authority that she wielded with a strong sense of responsibility and solid judgment. When she spoke, people listened because what she said always made sense. Usually she loved to tell me about new programs or political maneuvers at the club, but tonight, she had no warmth for the subject.

When I was getting ready to leave, my mother came to me and held my face in her hands. She studied me as if she felt she might never see me again. I felt the hard shell on my heart crack.

"My heart," she said to me, "You're all I have left in this world. Everyone I ever loved except for you is dead."

"Please, Mama. I'm not going to die—"

"If you let your hatred for Stroven control you, then he doesn't just beat you. He beats me too. He took my husband, and you would let him take my son. Your vengeance is his knife in my heart."

I wanted to say something, to tell her everything was going to be all right. But the words stuck in my throat. She wouldn't have believed them anyway. I didn't myself. I kissed her on the forehead and went out into the night with a heavy heart.

My thoughts buzzed in crazy circles like bugs around a candle as my feet carried me toward the man who knew the answers to some of my questions. I doubted he would give it to me straight, but I had to rattle his cage a little, see what he might do.

Chapter Twelve
Punch House

Punch House, as Vincetti's boxing establishment was known to locals, sat on the inside of a city block ringed by two-story buildings set end to end. On the first floor of these buildings were bodegas, fabric shops, magic stores, and other small businesses. On the second floor, cafes spilled out of the buildings onto balconies overlooking the streets in front and the courtyard surrounding Punch House in the back. You could reach Punch House through the four alleys that lead in from the streets, but I chose to enter through one of the arcades that run through the buildings from street to courtyard.

The arcade was lined with shoeshine boys, barbers, and vendors of a thousand spicy morsels and cold drinks. I flipped a prune-faced old man a nickel in exchange for a fresh mango helado, what Anglos might call a sherbet. It soothed away the knot in my throat, but not the one in my gut.

You can smell the blue cloud of cigar smoke that shrouds the Punch House before you see it. A mournful violin wept bitterly somewhere above when I stepped into the courtyard and headed for the thick of things.

I dropped a dollar on the counter, collected my ticket, and walked in. Rocky Vincetti wasn't hard to find. He was at his table on the mezzanine overlooking the floor and the boxing ring. This was where the elite sat, with snowy linen tablecloths, silver services and fresh flowers in cut crystal vases. Admittance to the Mez was strictly prohibited to all except those who owned a Gold Key pin, and only the richest and most powerful men belonged to the Gold Key Club. Curtained, raised booths at the back of the mezzanine shielded occupants from observation while affording them ample view of the action.

It was common knowledge that hidden stairways provided private access to The Mez for those who did not wish to be seen entering a known hotbed of bootleg gambling. It was also common knowledge that separate curtained booths were always reserved for the mayor, the chief of police, the state prosecutor, and of course, Charlie Dorr. Each could enter without ever seeing the other. It was a tidy setup.

I knew where both secret stairways were and also that they were heavily guarded by cousins with machine guns. I also knew I could get up to the mezzanine easily through the kitchen. I had done it before. But in deference to my mother, I decided not to piss off Vincetti any more than I had to.

I took out one of my business cards and wrote on the back of it, "*Pido cinco minutos de su tiempo.*" I knew he wasn't crazy about me, but a polite request in the mother tongue was rarely refused by anyone from the island. I gave it to the guard at the stairway and asked him to pass it on to Vincetti. I knew Vincetti would take his time getting to me to let me know who was top dog, so I settled back against a post to watch the bout.

It was a warm-up for the main event, and it wasn't much of a fight. A pale, freckled redhead, all joints and teeth lurched around the ring throwing wild punches at the compact Cuban lightning bolt who flashed under Red's flailing gloves and hammered his upper body like a heavy bag, and then backed off for a shot at that shiny glass jaw. It wasn't long in coming. One swift upper cut sent Red reeling back against the ropes and bounced him onto the floor face down and out cold.

The crowd cheered as if the Cuban Lightning Bolt had just brought down the entire Anglo nation. He strutted around the ring like a rooster while Red's trainer and the ring doctor worked to revive him. God, I love boxing.

I finished my mango helado and lit a cigar. I passed the time before the upcoming main event by watching the busy cigar and cigarette girls circulate in their tiny tight costumes, teasing and dodging amorous hands with the grace of young deer. Finally the lights went down and the drums and congas commenced playing a meringue beat that made the crowd go wild. Sugar Cane was a favorite, and this was his song. Everyone rose when he entered, punching the air and dancing to the beat.

The fight went the full fifteen rounds and both pugs came away bloody, dizzy and lead-footed. But it was clear before the decision that Sugar Cane had bested The Kid from Atlanta. With one eye swollen shut and a nose full of gauze, Sugar Cane raised his gloves and staggered around the ring for his accolades. I wondered if Quattlebaum was good for his nut.

I felt a tap on my shoulder and turned to see a man mountain with a squashed nose crook a meaty finger at me. I followed him to The Mez where Vincetti kicked a chair out and gestured me into it. He inspected me through narrowed eyes before speaking. "I hear you're a big businessman now. Got a new name and everything."

"I'm investigating the disappearance of EQ Edmunds." I watched for a response, but wasn't surprised not to see one. Rocky Vincetti could garrote his own grandmother without so much as a guilty twitch.

"So what?"

"I understand you and your brothers were there when he went over."

"You should watch how you say things, Corazon." He smiled and bit down on his Bering Magnifico cigar. It was large, neatly wrapped, and shaped like a dirigible. "You aren't careful, you could get run out of town again, this time by your own people."

I might be half Italian, but this man was not my people. I bit back the thought and forced out a smile of my own. "I just wondered if you saw anything. If you had any ideas about what might have happened that night, but if you don't know anything…"

"Why would I tell you if I did?"

71

I shrugged. "Maybe you're feeling generous."

This got a sneer from him. "You want to talk about generous? Every night I got half of Tampa's biggest players up here, sometimes even Stroven himself. What do you think they'd pay to know the son of Ramon Corazon is back in town pretending to be some Anglo private eye, huh? But I keep your secret. That's generous."

I wasn't about to acknowledge a debt to Vincetti. We both knew he would never turn me in. An Italian man would rather die than violate the code of omerta, silence.

"Any particular reason you and your brothers took a cruise to Europe?"

"Not that it's any of your business."

"Of course not."

"Mama was sick. We went to Santo Stefano to be with her."

"I hope she's feeling better."

"She'll live."

"I didn't see Frankie or Aldo tonight."

"They stayed with her until she's better. The Vincetti boys take care of their own."

"Your mother must be very proud."

Vincetti gestured to a waiter who set down two snifters filled with fragrant cognac. He lifted his glass to me. "*Salute. Y force in el canute.*" It was a Catalan toast, and too ribald to translate. He laughed and grabbed his canute for emphasis.

We drained our glasses. The fiery liquid suffused my limbs and put a warm glow on things. It softened Rocky's sharp, ferret-like features and made his smile look less like a snarl. It must have made him feel expansive as well, for he said, "You know, it's too bad you got into so much trouble with the Anglos. I coulda used a smart boy like you in the business."

"I don't slither that fast."

His face reddened, and he slammed his glass down on the table. "You're a fool, just like your father. You think you're better than everybody else. That's the Corazon downfall."

Rage filled my eyes and drenched the scene before me in red. I lunged toward Vincetti, but I felt a paw clamp onto my shoulder and jerk me back in mid-flight. Suddenly I was surrounded by hard, thick bodies that dragged me down the stairs and out to the alley. They threw me onto the bricks and started to leave me there.

But I hadn't had enough yet. I needed a fight. I threw myself at the back of the pack, kicking and punching for all I was worth. The blows felt good, like scratching an itch until it bled. We slugged it out until their fists and shoes sang me a syncopated lullaby and finally put me to sleep.

I awoke just before sunrise in a steady rain. Small rivers of water ran down the cracks between the bricks. I lay there for a long while, letting the rain penetrate my clothes and hair and wash me clean down to the skin.

SUSAN F. EDWARDS

Chapter Thirteen
Tio Diego and La Voz

At my apartment the next morning, I showered and shaved and put on fresh clothes. My body ached from last night's fight, but my heart felt lighter. I stopped at Julio's Bakery and bought two sweet cafe con leches and a large Cuban toast. I balanced them on my lap for the ride downtown.

Nesta was surprised and I think a little touched when I shared my breakfast with her. But that didn't keep her from ripping into me as she washed down the buttery bread with a swig of rich, creamy coffee.

"I thought I made it quite clear to you that I wanted Saul Stone left out of this investigation."

"If I'm going to find your husband I have to know as much about him and his associates as possible."

"All Saul knows is numbers. If you want to know Edward's financial business, come to me. I know as much as Saul does."

"If your husband planned his own disappearance, he must have had some help. Mr. Stone is a likely accomplice."

"Are you crazy? I told you before, Saul would never have anything to do with Edward's scams. The very mention of anything untoward sends him into seizures. The poor man called me absolutely hysterical after you grilled him. I insist—"

"Why would he be hysterical if he's innocent?"

She replied with the kind of icy patience adults reserve for very stupid children. "I'm sure you noticed that Saul is a man of—delicate sensibilities. He was very upset by your strong-arm tactics. And your nasty insinuations."

"I didn't insinuate anything."

"You asked him about my relations with my husband. That has nothing to do with this investigation. Nor is it any of your business."

She turned red as a boiled lobster, and I expected to see steam coming out of her ears at any moment. She simply lit another of her anemic-looking cigarettes instead and fixed me with a glare. "Do you have any real leads, or are you just nosing around for dirt?"

I told her about Ciega's muscle being on the same cruise as Edmunds and asked her again if she knew of any connection.

"I'm not paying you to look for murder, Mr. Heart. I wish you would remember that."

"Maybe it wasn't murder. Maybe they were his accomplices."

"You're grasping at straws. You have nothing at all after a whole week's work. Admit it."

It wasn't worth explaining to her that gumshoe work was the slow accumulation of odd bits of information, rooted out painstakingly and put together in a thousand different ways until you came up with a picture that made sense and fit the facts. Something about this dame got under my skin. I knew she wouldn't listen even if I gave it to her straight.

"You want to fire me?" I almost hoped she's say yes. I didn't like this case or the places it was taking me. I was dismayed to see her face crumple into tears.

"I'm sorry. I just..." She looked at me with pleading eyes. "Please. Don't quit. I know I can be...brittle. That's what Edward always said. Brittle and prickly. He said it was because I never had to work for a living, never had to learn to get along with people. He resented my privileged background. He punished me for it."

She was sobbing now into her lacy handkerchief. I wondered who washed it, hung it out to dry and ironed it. "He said I needed to see what it felt like to want things I couldn't have." She blew her nose with a loud honk. "That's why he did this. He wanted to break me. To leave me broke and alone."

I pasted the most sympathetic look on my face I could muster, and let her cry for a while. I didn't much feel like comforting her even if I had known how to. Then I hustled her out with assurances that I would stay on the case, that I would do everything I could to make certain she would have what she wanted.

But what did Nesta Edmunds want? Did she think even if I did find her husband alive that she could put a leash on him, bring him home, and turn him into the faithful husband he never was? Or did she simply want vengeance, to see him brought back, humiliated and stripped of the money he had left? I wasn't so sure she'd be happy, even if I did find her husband.

It had begun to rain again by the time I left my office. Fat, warm drops that hammered my hat while I waited for the streetcar. By the time I got to Ybor, the streets were flooded. I stepped off the car into ankle-deep rushing water and knew I would have to change clothes to survive this weather and to be taken seriously in Ybor.

I squished up the stairs to my apartment and peeled off my soggy suit, socks and shoes. I replaced them with a guayabera, summer-weight chinos, sandals, and a panama hat. Latins know how to dress for the tropics, in light fabrics that dry fast and don't hold moisture next to the body.

I walked the length of Seventh Avenue, keeping fairly dry under the overhangs of balconies, stepping out into the rain only to cross streets. By the time I got to Circulo Cubano, I was ready for a café solo with plenty of sugar and a bowl of black beans and yellow rice. I shook my hat out and looked around the cantina.

Tio Diego was at his usual table, playing dominoes and chewing on the end of a great dark Aromatico cigar with the rest of the old Cuban gentlemen. I placed my order at the counter and wandered over to watch the game.

"Billy Boy," said Tio when I sat down. Tio Diego is not really my uncle, just an old friend of my father. After his death, Diego made it a point to drop in and check on my mother and me at least once a week. He usually brought an armload of groceries when he came. He was old now, maybe seventy-five, but he still kept a sharp eye out and knew everything that happened in Ybor.

When the game ended, Tio Diego asked after my health, my mother and her garden, nodding at my responses that I was fine, she was fine, and her garden still yielded the best rosemary, basil and tomatoes in Ybor. The others simply listened and nodded politely.

"Tio," I said, using the term of affection and respect, "if I wanted a passport with a different name, who is the best person to ask?"

Bushy gray eyebrows shot up all around the table. Diego fixed his watery brown eyes on me and blew a long plume of thick smoke over my head. "Who do you want to be this time," he asked. "Billy Ace of Spades?"

Grunts and chuckles percolated around the table. It was no secret in Ybor that I went by the name Heart instead of Corazon in Tampa, and most people disapproved.

I explained that I was looking for a greedy Anglo who had disappeared and left his wife broke and alone.

The old gents seemed to like the idea of helping me track down such a dishonorable son of a dog, as they called him. They gave me several names of printers, engravers, and forgers who specialized in the making of false papers for crossing national boundaries. My lunch came, and I played a game of dominoes with the group. I came in dead last, which made them even more willing to help. By the time I left, I had enough leads to keep me busy all weekend.

Everyone had agreed that Miguel Casals was the best printer and engraver in town and had probably taught most of the rest everything they knew. Edmunds was a man who went straight for the best, so I decided to try Casals first. He was master printer for *La Voz*, Ybor's major Spanish language newspaper.

Most Ybor people read at least three newspapers a day. And if they worked in a cigar factory, the lector read to them from many more. The socialists, the anarchists, the communists, the Italians, Cubans, Spaniards, each had their own newspapers, full of party creeds, nationalist rhetoric and news from abroad. The names were a litany of ideologies and loyalties: *L'Aurora, La Poliglota, Liverdad, El Machete, Sociale, Igualdad, Proletaria, La Comune.*

In addition to these, everyone read an Anglo paper, not out of interest, but in self-defense. And everyone in Ybor read *La Voz*, the voice of Ybor City with its local, national and international news. It had an international circulation almost as large as its local readership and chronicled for the world our strikes, our victories and defeats, our social programs, and our own peculiar Utopia.

Miguel Casals was lord and master of *La Voz's* printing presses. He was a small wiry man of about fifty-five with a head as smooth and hairless as a nutmeg shell. His eyes were a startling blue, and his stubby hands were black with ink. He gave me a suspicious once-over when I showed him Edmunds' picture and asked if he had ever seen him. He pushed the picture back toward me and replied, "Is there anyone in Florida who has not seen EQ Edmunds?"

"I have reason to believe he might have purchased traveling papers somewhere in Ybor."

Casals fixed me with a steady gaze. "So?"

I thought a little flattery might help grease the wheels. "Everyone knows you're the best printer in this country. Anyone who could make a decent passport must have been learned his skill from you. I—"

He interrupted me with an impatient wave of his hand. "I have trained hundreds of men. I have no control or knowledge of what they do when they leave me."

"I'm not a cop. I'm just trying to find this name for his wife because he—"

Again Casals did not give me a chance to finish before he cut in with, "Don't you read the Anglo papers? This man is dead."

"You and I both know better than to believe everything we read in Anglo papers, my friend."

His stern mouth curved upward at this, and his eyes softened for a moment. "Forget this Edmunds," he said. "If he is alive and doesn't want to be found, you will only make trouble for yourself."

Casals would tell me no more, so I thanked him and left.

I spent most of the weekend wearing out shoe leather in the pouring rain, visiting the printers Diego and his friends had named and getting stonewalled every step of the way. No one admitted to making a passport for, nor to ever meeting EQ Edmunds.

The rain finally let up on Sunday night, but the dampness by then had permeated every stick of furniture, every fabric in my home, and every pore in my body. Mildew formed on the wallpaper, spreading its mossy smell throughout my apartment. I sat watching the wallpaper curl up from the baseboards and wondering what to do next.

I reviewed what I knew so far. Edmunds had left Tampa with over a million dollars in cash and set sail for Europe on the same boat with three of Ciega's thugs. His financial empire was in ruin, and yet by all accounts he was cheerful even though he had threatened suicide repeatedly. His girlfriend, who had threatened to kill him, had been the only witness to his disappearance. And the man I hated most in the world had somehow been in on the deal.

It wasn't much. I needed more information. I had to see the original reports from the ship and the London police, and those were in the possession of the insurance company. It was time to play hardball with Terrance Quattlebaum.

Before heading for Victory Life the next day, I made a couple of phone calls and found out that the Majestic, the ship from which Edmunds had disappeared, was in port in Miami and was scheduled to leave for Europe in two days. The man who had been captain on the fateful voyage had since left the company and was now in

Australia. I made one more phone call and reserved a ticket for Miami on the evening train.

SUSAN F. EDWARDS

Chapter Fourteen
The Mullet Flops

Monday morning is a good time to find executives in their offices. I presented myself at Victory Life early and asked to see Mr. Quattlebaum. Dottie, the receptionist, said he was in a meeting and couldn't be disturbed. I took a piece of stationary from her desk and wrote on it, "I have an appointment at noon with a *Tampa Herald* reporter about your Liberty Limited investments." I folded the note and clipped it to one of my cards. I gave it to her and said, "I think he'll want to be disturbed for this."

She took the card and disappeared down the hallway.

Moments later, Mullethead appeared, jowls red and quivering in irritation. He motioned me to follow him. Once we were both in his office, he closed the door carefully and scowled at me. "What is this all about?" he demanded.

"I just thought the *Herald* might be interested in knowing why you really paid off Edmunds' life insurance claim so fast and what it really cost you. And you know what? I was right. They're very interested."

His tiny fish eyes rolled in his head. "What are you talking about?"

"I'm talking about the fact that you're a major stockholder in Liberty Limited, the beneficiary of Edmunds' policy. I'm talking about the fact that you reinsured almost the whole policy so that you didn't lose a penny in the deal. In fact you probably made money. Shouldn't take a reporter long to dig out the figures. Of course I didn't go to *Chronicle* because of Randall Stroven's involvement in Liberty Limited."

Quattlebaum's jowls were almost purple now, and beads of sweat formed on his forehead.

I continued. "I don't know if it's illegal to pull a scam like that, but I do know it won't look good in the papers. What will the companies that reinsured the policy do when they find out how you bilked them? Think they'll be eager to do business with you again?"

"What do you want from me?" He growled.

"All I want is a look at your files from the investigation."

His colorless lips squirmed and twitched like two fat worms trapped on his face. "How do I know you'll keep quiet if I show you the files?"

I grinned. "You'll just have to trust me."

He looked at me with contempt. "You don't know who you're dealing with, young man. If you make trouble for me, I'll have your license pulled so fast, it'll make you cross-eyed."

"Look. I know you're a big, powerful man. All that means to me is that you've got a lot to lose. Once you're tainted with scandal, your so-called friends will desert you like rats off a sinking garbage scow, and you know it. They'll throw you off their boards and pull their money out of your company, and leave you flopping around high and dry like a mullet on the beach."

He slapped his fleshy palms on the desk and rose, his jowls flapping and mottled with rage. I guessed he was sensitive about any references to mullet. His eyes bored into mine, and I stared back without flinching. Finally he punched a button on his desk and summoned Les Moore. Moore appeared almost instantly, and Mullethead muttered without taking his eyes off me, "Get the Edmunds files."

Moore gave me a hostile look. "That will take some time, sir. They've been boxed up already. "

"Now," roared Mullet, and Moore ducked out, giving me another poisonous look.

"Oh by the way," I said casually, "You owe me ten bucks."

He looked at me blankly.

"Sugarcane beat The Kid Friday night. Don't you read the *Chronicle*?"

A guttural sound rumbled in his throat as he pulled a money clip out of his pocket and peeled off a ten spot. He tossed it on the desk. I pocketed it and thanked him politely.

Mullethead drew the line at letting me leave with the files, but he did set me up rather nicely in the conference room. I sat in a fine leather chair and spread the files on the polished mahogany table and went to work. Dottie even brought me a cup of coffee, sweet and black the way I like it.

I started with the report from the ship's captain. In it he stated that at 1:10 a.m. a steward who had been outside the door to Edmunds' stateroom had heard screaming. He had entered and found Lola Flores alone and distraught. She told him that Edmunds had jumped from the porthole. The ship had circled for five hours, searching in the darkness without finding Edmunds.

The captain questioned the steward, who stated that he was outside the door to the stateroom at eleven p.m. when Edmunds, Lola Flores and Dominic and Hedda Boudreaux entered. He had remained outside the door and had seen the Boudreauxs leave at approximately twelve-thirty a.m. No one else entered or exited. Upon further questioning, the steward stated that he had heard loud voices arguing, and possibly the sounds of a struggle shortly after the Boudreauxs had left.

The captain had interviewed Miss Flores, but stated that she was incoherent and hysterical and babbled in Spanish. He asked her if Edmunds had jumped, and she replied in the affirmative, saying she had tried to stop him. He sent for the ship's doctor and had her sedated because her screams were beginning to disturb other passengers. The captain had also briefly questioned Mr. and Mrs. Dominic Boudreaux and Mrs. Conti, and determined that the three knew nothing about the mishap.

The report from the London Police said that Miss Flores appeared confused and disoriented. She said she and Edmunds had argued and that he had climbed into the porthole and threatened to jump. She had struggled with him to try to pull him back inside, but there had been a jolt and he had fallen.

An official inventory of the stateroom turned up a button on the floor near the porthole, identified by Miss Flores as belonging to Edmunds' jacket, scratches on the porthole, a broken lamp, assorted bottles, glasses, and personal items belonging to Edmunds, Flores, and the Boudreauxs. The inventory further noted that the room was in an extreme state of disarray, and that a brass handrail next to the exit door was bent and one end was pulled out of the wall to which it had been secured.

Les Moore's report was a perfunctory review of his interviews with Lola, the Boudreauxs, the captain, and the steward. He concluded that Edmunds had fallen through the porthole, and he declared the incident an accident. He recommended full payment of premiums to the policy beneficiaries.

Dottie came in at a little after five o'clock to tell me it was time to close up shop. Everyone else had already gone. She eyed the files and my person with some discomfort, and I realized she had probably been instructed to make sure that I didn't steal any papers. I smiled and opened my coat and palms to her. She blushed and gathered up the files.

When she had put them away and locked up, I walked her to the streetcar stop, talking mostly about the weather and the price of real estate.

Dottie told me her husband had caught the real estate fever at the height of the land boom and had made enough money buying and selling land for them both to retire in luxury. She had wanted to put their earnings in the bank, but he insisted on continuing to reinvest in new land deals to increase the money. When the bust hit, they were left with several acres of worthless swampland in Pasco County that they couldn't give away, but they still had to pay taxes on.

It was a familiar and sad story in a time when businesses were going belly up daily. Dottie's husband had lost his job at the paper company when it went broke, and she was left working to support them both and pay taxes on the land. She liked her job and was good at it, but her husband was ashamed to be supported by a woman. He spent his days at a speakie with legions of unemployed paper executives, stockbrokers, and real estate men. He came home only to eat and fall asleep. She carried on and hoped things would get better eventually.

Dottie boarded the streetcar and waved to me from the platform as if she were going on a cruise and I were her uncle, come to see her off. Her prim skirts swayed in the breeze.

I hopped the Ybor streetcar, my thoughts still on the unfortunate Dottie with her unflagging hopes and shy smile. Some men might say she had been a beauty in her day and was still good-looking despite her fifty-odd years. But to me she was more beautiful now than she probably had been at a dewy-skinned twenty. The lines in her face showed character, and her full figure a ripeness I doubted her husband appreciated. She had a grace and elegance that no twenty-year-old could match.

SUSAN F. EDWARDS

Chapter Fifteen
The Majestic

I slept well on the all-night train ride to Miami. There was something mesmerizing about the steady rocking and chugging of the train. It was like sleeping in the lap of a strong fat mother with a loud, contented snore.

At the docks, I introduced myself as a prospective traveler and asked to see suite 200, the stateroom from which Edmunds had disappeared. A Negro steward was assigned the task of ushering me. He led me silently to the upper deck and along an interior hallway. He stopped at a door marked 200 and unlocked it.

He followed me into the spacious stateroom. The infamous porthole was set into the wall directly across from the door. It was less than four feet in diameter, and its bottom edge was a good four and a half feet above the floor. At a trim five feet, three inches, Edmunds could easily have fit into the window, but he would have to climb onto something to do it. Two sofas, a couple of chairs and a low coffee table were arranged around the porthole. The polished brass frame of the porthole still bore faint scratches, but the table was unmarred.

A small mirrored bar covered the back wall of the stateroom. Doors on the opposite side led to a suite of rooms that included a sleeping compartment, a bathroom, a mirrored vanity lounge and closet. There was an exit from the sleeping compartment that led directly into the hall through a door marked 202. I went back to the stateroom and examined the brass handrail next to the exit door. It was bolted solidly to the wall, but the neat patch of wall paper around it was a shade less faded than the rest, indicating the repair that had been made. I gripped the rail. It seemed solid enough.

SUSAN F. EDWARDS

The steward watched me out of the corner of his eye. "Were you on the ship the year before last in September when the man went overboard out that porthole?" I asked him.

"Yes sir," he replied, lowering his head.

"I heard there was a steward right outside the door when it happened."

He nodded, still not looking at me.

"You know where I can find him?"

Again he nodded. "Wait here," he said and disappeared. About ten minutes later he returned, followed by a stout Cuban man. "This is Ignacio," he said and bobbed his head in thanks when I handed him a tip for his trouble. Ignacio licked his lips and tried to see the denominations of the folded bills.

I gestured for Ignacio to sit and offered him a fine handmade Sobrano cigar. He took it and sniffed it, but declined my offer of a light. He put it into his pocket instead and patted the fabric over it.

"You remember EQ Edmunds, Ignacio?"

He nodded, his solemn brown eyes fixed on mine. "The man who went overboard. I remember him well."

"You saw him come in here that night?"

"Yes. Eleven o'clock, as I told the captain and the police. I know because I just came on duty. My shift was eleven to seven in the morning."

"Who was with him?"

"The Señorita Flores and the other two. A man and his wife. I forgot their names, but they traveled with him."

"What did you do after they entered?"

"I brought them ice and some scotch, a few things like that. Mr. Edmunds gave me ten dollars. He told me to stay outside the door because maybe they will need something else. So I brought a chair and sat outside the door."

"Did you see him get into the porthole?"

"No, but I did see him push the table under it."

90

"This table?"

"No, a different table. We had to change it because it was so scratched from his shoes."

"Was the rail by the door damaged when you came in?"

Ignacio looked at the rail. "I don't remember. Maybe."

"Did you hear anything while you were sitting outside the door?"

"I could hear their voices, but not the words. They were very loud, sometimes laughing, sometimes shouting."

"And you were outside the door the whole time?"

"Yes."

"And no one else came."

"No. The other two left about twelve-thirty. They went to their cabin."

"Then what happened?"

"Mr. Edmunds went out for about fifteen minutes."

"Where did he go?"

Ignacio shrugged. "Down the hall and out. Maybe he went up on the deck. I don't know."

"Did he bring anything back with him? Or anyone?"

"No."

"Then what?"

"He went back in and it was quiet for a while. Then they started to argue."

"You heard both voices?"

"Yes."

"Are you sure?"

He thought about it for a moment. "Yes. They were arguing, but I didn't think about it. They always argued, threw things. Very noisy, like always. But when she screamed, it was different. I went to the door, but it was locked."

"Did they usually lock the door?"

"Not until they went to bed."

"What did you do?"

"She was screaming and screaming. I knocked on the door and told her to unlock it. The two others came from their room and talked to her through the door. Finally, she unlocked it, and we went in. Mr. Edmunds was gone. We looked everywhere for him. The señorita was crying and talking in Spanish. She said he jumped out the window."

"Are you sure she said jumped and not fell?"

"She said 'saltar,'" he told me, not bothering to translate. There's no mistaking it in Spanish. We both knew *saltar* means to jump.

"There was no way Mr. Edmunds could have gone out the bedroom door?"

"No. My chair was between the two doors. I would see him if he came out."

"Then what happened?"

"They told me to get the captain, and that's what I did."

I asked Ignacio to show me the Boudreauxs' cabin next door to Edmunds' and the one farther down the hall that Lola supposedly shared with Mrs. Conti. He said Miss Flores spent most nights in Edmunds' cabin. I thanked him and gave him five dollars. With tips and travel, this job was starting to cost me money.

Outside I stood on the dock and studied the ship. With its huge bulk, smooth curves and three neat rows of portholes, it looked more like one of those big art deco hotels going up all over Miami Beach than something that could float on water and move across the Atlantic Ocean.

The porthole Edmunds had come out of was in the middle row toward the front. His drop to the water below would have been a good twenty-five feet. The fall alone could have killed him or knocked him unconscious. I shuddered at the thought of a watery death, of the strong smothering embrace of the sea. I was ready to get back on the train and head inland over solid ground.

MAN OVERBOARD

Chapter Sixteen
The Pineapple Toss

Wednesday is wash day in Ybor. As I walked the seven blocks from my apartment to my mother's house, women were taking laundry off the lines, and the smell of garlic filled the air. Mama was still ironing when I entered her house through the back door. My folded shirts were stacked in neat, starched piles on the kitchen table. Chorizo sausage sizzled in a pan on the stove next to a simmering pot of garbanzo soup.

She surveyed the cuts and bruises on my face. "So you beat your face against Rocky Vincetti's fist." It was an old family joke.

I gave her a sheepish grin. "I asked for it."

"You always do." She cupped my face tenderly in her hand. "Just like your father."

It was the second time this week someone had accused me of being like my father. This time I didn't want to hit anyone. "I can't change what I am."

"I know," she said, tragedy and love in her eyes. "I don't want you to be a different person. But you could try to learn from his mistakes." She patted my face and returned to her ironing. Her reluctance to accept my involvement in this case did not stop her from wringing information from me. She always said she would rather see a train coming at her than be caught unaware.

I took her at her word and told her all about my meeting with Mullethead, omitting only his threats.

"It doesn't work to push people around. When will you learn that? Especially Anglos."

"Mullethead poses no danger to me, Mama. He's too afraid of being exposed for the fraud he is."

"Don't ever underestimate an Anglo. Even if he looks soft and white and fat like a marshmallow, he can be like a razor inside."

93

"Anglos don't scare me."

"That's what your father said before the 1915 strike. He said the Anglos need the cigar industry. They will roll over like dogs and show their bellies when we strike. Do you remember that strike?"

I remembered it well.

* * * * *

All the workers in Ybor had sat down and refused to work because of unreasonable demands made by factory owners. It started when owners instituted a seven-day work week. The lectors had led resistance to the move. The owners accused the lectors of anti-American tactics, and fired them.

The lectors were replaced with inspectors who sat atop the high chairs shouting through megaphones at workers, telling them to work faster. Owners imposed quotas on the number of cigars workers had to make per shift or face disciplinary action and pay cuts.

When labor leaders called a strike, they were jailed.

Randall Stroven had used his newspaper to inflame the Anglo citizens of Tampa against the strikers. He denounced them as Bolshevik agitators, socialists, dangerous to the American way of life. He said these striking workers and their leaders threatened the very fabric of American democracy, and he challenged right-thinking men to take a stand and put an end to their treason.

In response, Tampa's most powerful men met at the Board of Trade. They arranged to bring cigar workers from Haiti to replace the strikers. Then they formed The Committee, a cadre of one hundred businessmen who patrolled the streets of Ybor on foot and horseback with pistols, bayonets, and shotguns to keep the peace and escort the strike breakers into the factories.

Three weeks into the strike, an Anglo bookkeeper for one of the factories was shot as he entered the building. Two Spanish drifters were arrested and charged with the crime.

The prisoners were to be transferred from the Tampa jail to the State facility in Jacksonville in a move heavily publicized by Randall Stroven in the *Tampa Chronicle*. Ten miles out of Tampa, the light guard was overpowered easily by a band of mounted men. They hanged the prisoners and shot their bodies full of holes.

Such lynchings had happened before in Tampa. Some men called them "necktie parties," and bragged about taking part in them.

No one expected that the men who hanged the two Spaniards would be found and prosecuted. The joke in some circles was that when the sheriff went to cut the bodies down, a local judge stopped him, saying he had paid good money for that rope and did not want it cut into pieces.

Stroven hailed the move as a victory for the forces of good old American law and order. The strike was broken, although The Committee continued to patrol the streets of Ybor for several weeks afterward.

But the war against organized labor was not over. Stroven named labor leaders in his paper who he said threatened the American way of life. Those he named were rounded up at night by a group of armed, masked or sheet-covered men, and put on boats for South America. They were told never to return to Tampa if they valued their lives. Others were arrested and beaten, or targeted for terrorism, their houses burned, rocks thrown through their windows with threats written on them.

When Stroven named my father the most dangerous anarchist agitator in Ybor City, *La Voz* printed a rebuttal editorial saying that Ramon Corazon was a hero of the labor movement. That afternoon, masked men smashed La Voz's printing presses and beat the printers nearly to death.

Though my father forbade it, my mother went to Santo Ciega and begged him to intervene. She knew he was the only Latin man who might have some power with the Anglos. After all, Ciega knew

Charlie Dorr personally, and Charlie Dorr could easily put a stop to the hunt.

Ciega told my mother he could do nothing. He said that my father had brought his troubles upon himself and now would have to face the consequences.

I was seventeen and had just finished high school. My father had been fired like the rest of the lectors, and I worked at a grocery cooperative to help support the family. For days we waited for something to happen, slept with pails of water at the ready, in case they set fire to our home.

On the evening of the third day, my father, against my mother's protests, left the house to attend a meeting of strikers. He never arrived and was never heard from again. Deprived of most of its leaders and without even a martyred victim to rally around, the strike was broken. The unions and the cigar factories were never the same again.

For the first week, we waited at the post office with the other families of men who had disappeared that night. At the end of the second week, a card came from Honduras. Seventeen men had been kidnapped and put on a boat with the usual warning. Ramon Corazon, they wrote, had been with them at the boat and was leading the group in singing workers' songs, but he was pulled off at the last moment. He had gone with his head unbowed, singing the American national anthem at the top of his voice.

I do not remember rushing into the *Chronicle* offices brandishing a machete and calling for the blood of Wallace Stroven. Nor do I recall the arrest, the beatings, or being dumped in the streets in front of Fraterno Italiano, half dead after two days in jail.

I do remember the polite-sounding voices of the men who came to visit my mother. They sounded so concerned for us when they said it would be best for me to leave town. Otherwise they could not guarantee my safety. I tried to forget the sound of my mother's weeping as she put me on the train bound for San Francisco two days before my eighteenth birthday, knowing it was the only way to keep me alive.

* * * * *

My mother and I ate in silence again that night, remembering the cold terror of those days and the ruthlessness of our Anglo neighbors in breaking the great strike of 1915.

After dinner we sat on the porch with our coffee and talked about happier things, her brother Vito's new grandchild, plans for painting the ballroom at Fraterno Italiano, calm, everyday things.

At midnight I rose to go and picked up my basket of clean pressed shirts. When I kissed my mother goodbye, she looked old to me for the first time. Instead of the proud erect woman, I saw a slightly stooped tired woman with a deeply furrowed brow. She gave me a forced smile, patted my face and sent me on my way. She stood on the porch, watching me walk down the dark street as if she thought she might never see me again.

As I rounded the corner onto Seventh Avenue, I heard sirens and saw a fire truck streak by. It didn't occur to me until I reached my block and saw the flames and smoke that it was my apartment on fire.

Smoke poured out of my front window over the neon Ritz Theatre sign, and flames licked the curtains that flapped out through the broken glass. A crowd had gathered around the building, and firemen streamed off the truck and up the stairs. I broke into a run. A young cop in charge of crowd control tried to stop me, but I shook him off and ran up the stairs, too late to stop the axes from splintering my door.

The front room was full of smoke, but only the sofa and curtains were burning. There was nothing for me to do but watch as the firemen covered every square inch of the room with water and foam.

By one a.m. everyone had left except for a fire inspector named Chapman. I stood next to him in the middle of the charred room, examining the gnarled and jagged chunk of pipe in his hand. "Pipe bomb," he said matter-of-factly. "Looks like they chucked it through this window." He looked from the broken window to me. "Know anybody who might want to bomb you out?"

"Does it look like a professional job?"

He shrugged. "Not really. Anybody can make a pipe bomb with the right stuff."

After Chapman left, I closed what was left of the door and nailed some boards across it to hold it together. I pulled the Murphy bed out of the wall and found its mattress soaked through. The room popped and sizzled. Water dripped from the ceiling. I opened all the windows to let out the sweet, smoky stench. I found a dry blanket in the bathroom cupboard and threw it into the tub. I poured myself two fingers of rye whiskey, lit a cigar and settled into the tub, arms, legs and head draped over the sides.

A thought came to me as I lay there amid the charred and smelly remnants of my home. Someone had intended to scare me off, but all he had done was tip his hand. It was true that anyone could make a pipe bomb, but what Chapman had left unsaid, what everyone in Ybor knew, was that pipe bombs were the signature weapons of Santo Ciega's gang. This was clearly a warning from Rocky Vincetti. I figured if Vincetti was threatened enough to warn me off, I must be on the right trail. Maybe my nosing around printers and forgers was making him nervous.

I dozed off and on for the next few hours until my complaining joints would have no more of it. I arose in the predawn darkness and proceeded to clean up the mess in my front room. The smell of roasting coffee from the mills added to the burnt smell in my apartment and almost overpowered me. I piled the remains of the curtains onto the blackened sofa and dragged it down the stairs and out to the curb.

An old man in a tattered jacket sat propped against the building across the street. He yawned and eyed me briefly from under his

Panama hat and then settled back to his sleep. But something wasn't right about him. He looked better fed than most of the bums, and the soles of his shoes looked almost new.

Back upstairs I put the soggy mattress and bedclothes on the tiny wrought iron balcony to dry and air out. Then I sopped up watery ash by the bucketful and dumped it out the back windows into the alley below.

SUSAN F. EDWARDS

Chapter Seventeen
To Squeeze a Mango

By the time the sun rose, I had showered, shaved and dressed. I knew Vincetti wouldn't be at Punch House until later in the afternoon, so I took my time over a plate of eggs and yellow rice before heading to my office.

Otto sniffed at me when I stopped to buy a *Chronicle* from him. "Been chasing fire trucks this morning, Corazon?"

"Yeah, right to my apartment."

His eyebrows rose above the dark, round disks that hid his sightless eyes.

"Vincetti tossed me a pineapple last night," I explained.

"How do you know it was Vincetti?"

"I've been rattling his chain pretty hard lately."

"You been pestering anyone else?"

"Nobody who throws pipe bombs."

I told Otto I had spent the weekend questioning forgers about fake papers for Edmunds, and I thought that was what had made Vincetti nervous enough to threaten me.

"What does Vincetti have to do with Edmunds getting a fake passport?"

"I'm not sure yet. Maybe he helped Edmunds get it."

"That sort of shoots your theory about Ciega having your boy murdered, then doesn't it?"

"Not necessarily."

"Why get him papers if they were planning to shove him over?"

"Maybe Ciega wanted him to think they were going to help him disappear. Maybe Ciega knew Edmunds would have a million dollars in cash, and he sent his boys to skim the cash and help Edmunds disappear—only not the way Edmunds expected."

"You giving up on the Stroven angle?"

I shrugged. "Maybe Ciega was working for him."

"That's reaching."

"Maybe. Maybe not."

"What about Lola?"

"Wouldn't have been too hard to shut her up. A few threats, a little traveling money. I'm going to lean on her hard this morning, see what I can squeeze out of her."

I decided to avoid Nesta, so I took my paper to a coffee shop up the street before heading out to Edmunds Island.

Lola Flores answered her door in emerald green silk Chinese pajamas. She looked like an exotic hand-painted doll. She tossed her head in a pretty gesture, sending her glossy hair waving about her shoulders. "It is very rude to show up at a lady's door so early. I have not even combed my hair yet."

"You look all right to me," I said, following her down the hallway. She entered her bedroom, and I stopped at the doorway.

"Of course I do. That's not the point." She picked up a red dress off the bed and held it against her body in front of a full-length mirror. "I have an appointment at eleven. If you want to talk, you must do it while I get ready." She looked at me still in the doorway. "Come in. Sit. Sit." She motioned to the huge, rumpled bed, lush with overstuffed pillows and goose down coverlet. She disappeared into the adjoining bathroom calling out to me, "I'll be out in two minutes."

I heard the shower come on and went to her dresser to take a look. The top drawer contained a hairbrush, makeup and earrings. The next drawer held silk and lace undergarments. I ran my hand through the piles and felt something hard at the back of the drawer. I drew out a small pearl handled .32 caliber revolver, fully loaded. I replaced it carefully and checked the rest of the drawers. Clothing, sachets, but no papers or other weapons.

The jewelry box on top of the dresser was open. There, lying among neatly arranged rings and necklaces was a small gold key pin with four tiny sapphires set into the top. The sound of the shower stopped, and moments later Lola appeared, wearing a terrycloth robe carelessly belted and barely closed. The smile on her face froze as she saw me holding the pin.

"So you do know Rocky Vincetti after all," I said.

She took the pin from me and replaced it carefully in the jewelry box. "It belongs to a friend. I meet him there sometimes."

"Nobody gets up there without Vincetti's approval. You can't tell me you've never met."

"Maybe I did meet him once. So what?"

"So you know what he looks like."

She shrugged. "I suppose."

"And you never saw him on the ship with Edmunds."

"No."

"You're lying."

She let her robe fall off one glistening shoulder as she bent to pick up the red dress. I couldn't see her face, but her movements had lost their fluidity and become jerky. "You know so much, you tell me."

"Okay, how's this." I continued talking as she took the dress and some underclothes behind a dressing screen. It was in front of a window, and the light coming in silhouetted her naked body against it. I scanned the room for something, anything to look at besides those breasts, those hips. I locked onto a hand-painted tin piece hanging on one wall. A scene of a Haitian village with children playing amid colorful shacks.

"You were angry with Edmunds when you found out he was meeting his wife in Europe. So angry that, according to Hedda and Dominic Boudreaux, you threatened to kill him. The Vincetti boys overheard and approached you with a proposition. They'll toss him over the side and give you a cut of the one million clams they took off him before his big swim. All you've got to do is say he fell or jumped."

She came out from behind the screen smiling. The dress flowed over her figure like blood. "How did I get them past the steward?" she asked with amusement.

"He wouldn't have been any harder to buy off than you were."

She presented her bare back to me. "Button me up, please."

I obliged and she turned to face me when I was finished, her body inches from mine. I could feel her breath on my face as she spoke softly. "I was angry with him. Maybe I even threatened him. But no one killed him. He fell."

"Why did you first say he jumped and then change your story?"

"I was frightened. Confused. I knew I would be in trouble, and maybe they would say I pushed him." She bit savagely into her bottom lip to stop its trembling. I had to give her credit. She was good. "Everyone heard him saying he would kill himself and singing that stupid song over and over. So I said he jumped."

"Why did you change your story later?"

"It was Hedda. She told me, 'No, don't say he jumped. I know he wouldn't kill himself. Tell the truth. He fell.' I was so afraid… I…" Her trembling lip escaped her teeth and tears fell from her eyes. She buried her face in my chest, clutching my shirt. "Don't you understand? Oh, Billy. I was alone with all of these people shouting and asking questions. I didn't know what to say." She sobbed convincingly, her breasts convulsing against my chest.

I grasped her shoulders and held her away from me so I could see her face. She looked at me with pleading eyes. "I didn't kill him. I swear I didn't." She grasped my arms. "Please, Corazon. I know she hates me. She's a rich Anglo from a powerful family. I am just a poor Cuban girl. Don't let them do this to me again. I thought it was over."

So now she was Cuban. How convenient. I wrenched out of her grasp and backed away. "What happened that night, Lola?"

"I told you. He was in the window. He said he could fly, but he fell."

"How did the handrail next to the door get damaged?"

She turned away. "What handrail?"

I grabbed her arm and swung her around to face me. "The brass one next to the door. One end of it was pulled out of the wall. How did that happen?"

She buried her face in her hands. "I don't know. I don't know what you're talking about. Go away, please. Don't do this to me."

"You can turn off the waterworks, doll. I don't believe a word you're saying."

Her eyes grew round and glistened with tears. "You think I'm bad because I was with a married man." She sniffed and gave me a pathetic look.

"No, I just think you're a liar."

Her face reddened, and her eyes flashed angrily. "You have the nerve to call me a liar, you, William Heart? What kind of a name is that for a Latin man? You are the liar. At least I don't call myself Lulu Flowers. You change your name to be like the Anglos. Your father must be so ashamed. You turn against a poor Latin girl for a few dollars!" She was shouting now, and she picked up a hand mirror off her dressing table. "Get out! Mentiroso! Linguini Boy!"

I ducked through the door as the mirror flew toward me and hit the wall. The sound of shattering glass accompanied my retreat. "Traitor!" she shouted, and a small jeweled box whizzed past my ear.

Outside I watched the cars pass by on Edmunds Boulevard while I waited for a streetcar. Big Six Broughams, sport roadsters, custom sedans. Maybe I should buy a car. It sure would make the leg work easier. I spied an ugly tan 1924 Chevrolet coupe parked up the street. Those models were in the paper all the time for less than a hundred and fifty clams. That was two months on Nesta's payroll.

I rode the streetcar past the wide lawns and expansive skies of Bayshore Boulevard, toward the banana docks and wharf-side watering holes of dock workers. The streetcar followed the railroad tracks away from the docks and into the backside of Ybor City, where workers unloaded bales of tobacco from train cars and carried them into the loading docks of cigar factories. The smell of frying plantains reminded me I was hungry.

I stopped on Seventh Avenue and filled up on an eggplant sandwich, heavy on the mozzarella and oozing fragrant oregano-tinged tomato sauce. Thus armed with plenty of garlic and olive oil, I was ready to tackle Vincetti again.

Punch House smells of stale beer and sweat during the day. The sparring pair in the ring were spreading plenty of the latter around when I walked in. The coach looked like an old grizzled tomcat with small, ragged ears and a face flattened and scarred from the beatings he'd taken. He spat tobacco juice and circled the fighters with a wet towel, hollering, "Come on, you yellow belly! Keep your guard up. He's open—take him, right there!"

The coach twisted the towel and snapped it hard at the fighter who had his guard down. It hit him square in the nose with a stinging slap. The fighter jerked his gloves up to cover his face, and the trainer got him a good one in the stomach with the towel. Then he nailed the other fighter in the ear and shouted at him, "You! Wake up! I'm taking all your shots for you. What are you, a statue?"

I walked around the side of the ring and toured the offices in the back, watching the two young pugs take far more of a beating from their trainer than from each other.

The door to Vincetti's office was flanked with two slabs of human meat wearing identical greased-back hair and black suits. Vincetti sat on the other side of the open door with a stack of papers and an adding machine. I opened my coat to the meat, and each ran a hand up under my jacket and down my trouser legs.

Vincetti looked up as I was being patted down. "You again." He motioned to the meat to let me enter. "Make it fast. You're already starting to bore me."

"That why you hit my place last night, boredom?"

His eyebrows rose, and for an instant, I could swear he looked surprised. "What are you talking about?"

"The pineapple somebody tossed through my front window."

He chuckled and looked me over. "Sounds like you got some enemies, Corazon."

"Am I getting too close for you, Vincetti? Making you nervous?"

"Like a mosquito makes me nervous." He chewed on his cigar and eyed me. "What you been up to that's supposed to have me bombing your apartment, anyway?"

"Looks to me like you're worried I'm going to find out who made Edmunds' phony passport. Now why would that bother you?"

A smile twisted his rat-like face, and he opened his arms in an expansive gesture. "You tell me."

"Maybe you helped him get it. Maybe you promised to help him jump ship, told him all he needed was a new name and all the cash he could get his hands on to start a new life."

He sat back and laced his fingers over his narrow chest. "I like it so far. Then what?"

"Then you took his cash and shoved him over. Mission accomplished."

Vincetti laughed loud and long and then stopped abruptly with a snarl. "You're a sap, Corazon. You don't have a clue. The hell of it is, I wish you were right. I'd be richer, and you still couldn't touch me."

"We'll see about that."

"Beat it. Before I let the boys tie you up and use you for a heavy bag."

The meat moved in, and I went for the door. At the threshold I stopped and looked back. Vincetti had already turned to his adding machine.

I had gotten the name and address of Lola's duenna from the insurance files. I didn't expect to get much out of her, but she had to be questioned. The streets around the factories were lined with tiny identical cigar workers' houses set side by side in symmetrical rows of miniscule front porches adorned with gingerbread trim. The only differences between the houses were the plants and people on the porches and postage-stamp yards marked off with waist-high wooden fences. The cigar workers' houses were built by the factories, which rented or sold them to their workers. Rent was two bucks a week; the purchase price was usually about seven-fifty.

Lola's *duenna*, Maria Conti, lived in one of these houses on Fourteenth Street. One half of the front yard was cultivated in tomatoes, peppers, beans, and zucchini with a bright border of zinnias and nasturtium. In other half, four elevated wire cages, sat in the shade of an avocado tree. Each cage held a red rock fighting cock.

Maria Conti turned out to be younger than I expected. The pillowy, matronly woman was in her late thirties with thick black hair neatly braided, and an embroidered cotton muslin dress. She spoke little English, so we talked in Italian. She told me that Edmunds paid her well to act as Senorita Flores' traveling companion and that she had done it many times. Mostly that meant taking care of the senorita's wardrobe and occasionally accompanying her to dinner or other public social events. But mostly Maria stayed in her room or walked on deck to take the air.

On the night Edmunds had disappeared, Maria had not been asked to join the entourage and so had stayed in her room and gone to bed early. Her room was three doors down from the state room, and she had heard nothing that night until a ship's steward woke her and told her that Mr. Edmunds had jumped off the ship.

"He told you Edmunds jumped?"

She nodded. "Later they said he fell, but that night they said he jumped."

I asked if she had ever seen Edmunds with anyone besides Lola or the Boudreauxs during the cruise. "Only once," she replied. She was taking a walk on the deck alone. She had spotted Edmunds surrounded by three men going into a cabin. She described the men as similar in appearance, slender and dark and in their thirties, clearly the Vincetti boys. I wondered why I hadn't visited Maria sooner. I thanked her and left.

I stopped at Las Novedades for a plate of boliche and yucca. Boliche is an Ybor specialty, and Novedades has the best. A thick, tender slab of roast beef, cut across the grain with a perfect circle of chorizo sausage in the center and a warm blanket of golden gravy. The white starchy yucca is boiled and smothered in roast garlic.

I ate at the counter and read *La Voz*. There were articles about Mussolini in Italy, Stalin in Moscow, Chang Kai-Shek in China, and a review of Adolf Hitler's book, *Mein Kampf*, in Germany. The last British forces were leaving India and civil war was beginning there. Meanwhile, twenty-three nations had signed the Kellogg-Briand Pact, outlawing the war.

After dinner, I took up the *Chronicle* with a large cup of café con leche and a golden flan—egg custard with a burnt sugar sauce. In Tampa, the mayor's eldest daughter would wed an heir to the Blythefield fortune next month, a small child and his puppy had been rescued from a collapsed drainage pipe after a grueling six-hour ordeal, and brand new White Frost refrigerators were on sale for $125 and could be bought on an easy payment plan with only five dollars down.

In other news, Terrance Quattlebaum had been elected chairman of the Board of Trade. He pledged to bring new business to Tampa and predicted an upswing in the real estate market very soon. He was quoted as saying that by the early 'thirties, we wouldn't even remember this temporary economic dip we were experiencing now.

The flan seemed almost too rich tonight, too sweet. I left it and the *Chronicle* unfinished.

I went out the back door of Las Novedades, turned left in the alley and climbed a set of stairs two buildings over. Laughter and music spilled from the doorway above when the door opened and emitted a giggling, staggering couple. Few speakeasies had official names. What would be the point since they could not advertise or hang out a sign? But most had unofficial names. We called this one La Dulceria, the candy store.

Inside I ordered a double scotch and stood at the crowded bar. The cold, bitter edge of the scotch took the sugary taste from my mouth. I lit a panatela and added some smoke to the cloud that hung over the room. I felt a jostling at my elbow and turned to see Miguel Casals, the printer from La Voz, next to me.

"Don't look at me," he hissed through unmoving lips. I looked away and scanned the room. He ordered rum, and after taking a sniff, said, "Max Paredo on Fourth Avenue. That's your man. "

"Why are you telling me this?"

"You shoulda told me you was Ramon Corazon's boy before. He was a good man." Miguel downed his drink and left as quickly and quietly as he had come.

I finished my drink and had another, table-hopping and catching up with old friends. Most of them had heard about the fire in my place already and were quick to offer me places to stay. I turned them all down with thanks.

Until I ran into Alicia Garcia.

I had been in love with Alicia since the first time I saw her when I was ten and she fourteen. I followed her to and from school each day, begging to carry her books. She had laughed and said my arms were too spindly to take the weight of her books. She had married at nineteen, and her husband was killed a few years later in the war.

Although she had mourned him admirably, widowhood suited her. She had opened a fabric store with the money she got from the Army and became a hard-nosed businesswoman. She wore pants and smoked cigars and came and went as she pleased. Her short dark curls and Cleopatra-painted eyes devastated me utterly.

I told her the sad story of the pipe bombing and how my bed had been destroyed. "You can sleep on my sofa tonight if you want," she said. My face must have lit up like an electric bulb because she frowned and added, "But no funny business." I shook my head vigorously and bought her a double rum and then two more.

By the time we left, Alicia was leaning heavily on me and weaving. I put an arm around her waist and half carried her down the steps. At the bottom she turned to me, still encircled by my arm and cupped my face in her hands. She studied my eyes and said, "When did you grow into such a virile man from that skinny noodle I used to know?"

She slipped her arms around my neck and pulled me to her. Her lips were soft and aggressively yielding. Her whole body from her mouth down to her toes moved against me in electrifying circles. I wrapped myself around her and answered. When we came up for air, our eyes locked and every hair I had stood at attention. My blood throbbed in my veins. Alicia took my arm and we ambled up the alley. I was drunk on the smell of her hair, her neck, the way her dark curls framed her face. I wanted to start at her dewy eyelids and kiss every inch of her, touch the places I had only imagined as a boy.

At Alicia's place above the fabric store, we sat on the sofa, very close together. She closed her eyes as I traced a tendril of hair against her cheek with my finger and followed it with my lips. Suddenly she sat up straight and looked wildly around. Then she clapped a hand over her mouth and ran for the bathroom.

I could hear her retching and heaving, panting and then retching some more.

Vomiting is a private, primal act. When your whole body starts to buck and pitch and try to turn itself inside out, you don't want any witnesses. I sat on the sofa and tried not to hear the awful sounds. For over a half an hour she went on like that, sometimes with such violence I feared she might choke on her own esophagus, but I never went in to check. I knew she'd rather die than have anyone see her like that.

After she had been quiet for another half an hour, I went in. She lay sprawled on the floor with her head resting on the toilet seat. I gathered her up and carried her to her bed. She roused and smiled weakly at me through damp, red eyes. "Just let me die," she croaked as I laid her down and removed her shoes. I went to the icebox and chipped off a cupful of ice. I topped it off with water and took it back to her.

She was propped up on the pillows when I returned. I sat next to her and fed her ice chips. She sucked one lazily and held another to her head, glancing at me through half-closed eyes. "You didn't have to get me drunk to kiss me," she murmured.

"You kissed me."

"I had to. If I waited for you to do it, it would be another twenty years."

The top two buttons of my shirt were open and she ran her finger down my chest to the third button. She leaned over and kissed my chest, moving her hand to my trousers.

My blood began to throb and thrum again. She hooked a finger in the waistband and pulled it away from my body. She dipped her other hand inside.

Cold, wet ice chunks hit me like a jolt of lightning, sending me straight up off the bed.

She laughed as I barked and danced around to shake the ice out of my pants. "Next time, try the direct approach." She threw me a blanket and pillow. "The sofa, you heel."

Chapter Eighteen
Partners

I beat Nesta to my office by a full thirty minutes the next day. I was beginning to hope she might leave me alone until Friday. At ten, she showed up wearing a sad puppy dog face and dashed my hopes. "I missed you yesterday," she said, reproach dripping from every syllable.

"I wish I could say the same."

"You could say it just to be polite." She sat on the edge of my desk and lit up an Old Gold cigarette. It didn't even smell like real tobacco, more like newspaper burning.

"I don't think of lying as polite."

She met my steely gaze with equal steel, and no flinching on either side. "Where were you yesterday morning?"

"Victory Life Insurance Company."

"And?"

"I got a look at the files."

"Good work. You must have had to use two crowbars to pry them loose. What did you think?"

"I have to admit. It was a pretty sloppy investigation."

She slapped the desk and smiled. "What'd I tell you?" Are you starting to doubt just a little bit that the old boy just fell overboard?"

"There are questionable aspects to that version of events."

"So what's next?"

"I've got a line on a forger who may have made a false passport for your husband using a different name."

She snapped her fingers and leapt from the desk. "Great thinking!" She looked at me for a moment as if reappraising me. Her face glowed with excitement, and her eyes softened. "Listen. I know I've been a pain in the neck. You have every right not to like me."

I shrugged it off and mumbled, "Forget it."

"No, I mean it. I've been a perfect ass. Forgive me?" She held a hand out to me. I looked at her earnest smile and remembered I had found her handsome the first time I met her, before I knew her very well.

I took the offered hand, and we had a warm, hearty shake.

"Now then," she said and picked up her purse. "Shall we go?"

"Where to?"

"Why, to visit your forger, of course. This is our first big break, and I intend to be in on it."

"Oh no. Your job is to write the checks and call me on Fridays for your progress report."

"Don't be ridiculous. I'm offering my help."

"I didn't know you wanted to help. In that case I need to revise my rate."

A delighted grin lit up her face. "How much is it if I help?"

"Five hundred dollars a day," I said, picking up my hat and moving for the door.

She followed me down the steps. "So far I've been paying you to discover what I already know. You can't cut me out just when it's starting to get good."

Her high heels clicked behind me as I hurried for the street car. I leapt on just as it was starting to move, leaving her standing in the street, stamping her foot like a spoiled ten-year-old and shouting, "It's not fair!"

I chuckled to myself and took a window seat to enjoy the crisp morning air. I settled back and closed my eyes.

The sound of a car horn next to me disturbed my repose. I ignored it for a while, but its insistent bleating finally got to me. I sat up and opened my eyes and there was Nesta, driving her car alongside me and punching her horn. I moved to an interior seat, put my hat over my face and lay back.

I got off at Seventh Avenue and Sixteenth Street, intending to give her the slip, but she drove her car over the sidewalk and leapt out. I turned in the opposite direction, and she started to scream, "Please, someone! Stop that man. William Heart. He's done something terrible to me!"

A young woman and man stopped to stare at me with disgusted eyes. The man flexed his muscles and cracked his knuckles, preparing to tackle me and impress his lady with his gallantry. Several other people had slowed or stopped as well.

I went to Nesta, teeth clenched but smiling an innocent smile. She slipped an arm through mine and held on tight. She smiled and said, "That's better." As I walked down the sidewalk with Nesta clamped to my arm, she smiled and waved at onlookers. "It's okay now," she called. "Lover's spat."

I snorted and rolled my eyes and pulled my hat down over my eyes in the hope that no one recognized me. When we reached Fourteenth Street, I stopped and faced her. "Mrs. Edmunds, I—"

"Call me Nesta. We're partners now. What do your friends call you? Bill?"

"You're not my friend, and you're not my partner. You're a client, and you don't belong here."

"I can take care of myself. I've been to Ybor before."

"That's not what I'm worried about. You don't know how to act here. You're an outsider."

"As I recall, you got quite huffy when I said something similar to you."

We had arrived at Max Paredo's shop. I took her shoulders and flattened her against the wall. "Just stay out here and keep quiet. I'll tell you everything he said the minute I come out. Fair enough?"

She stamped a foot and made a whiny noise in her throat, but she stayed put when I let go of her shoulders. I ducked inside.

The intoxicating fumes of printers' ink invaded my sinuses as I entered. A compact man of about sixty stood behind the counter inspecting a sheet of newsprint with a magnifying glass. His thick plume of salt-and-pepper hair and erect carriage gave him a roosterish appearance.

"Mr. Paredo?"

He nodded.

"A mutual friend said you might be able to tell me the traveling name of a man I am looking for."

His eyes narrowed. "What friend?"

"He does not wish me to use his name. But he was a friend of my father, Ramon Corazon."

His eyes widened at this and he shook his head. "I can't help you."

"Please. All I want is a name." I took the photo out of my pocket and showed it to him.

Nesta sidled in the door, and Paredo looked from her to me. He shook his head once more and turned away.

"Please. You must help us," Nesta cried, coming forward. "We'll pay you." She slapped a roll of bills on the counter. "Just tell us what the name was that you put on the false passport."

His eyes grew wild, and he flew out from behind the counter. "You are mistaken. I only make flyers here. Posters and handbills." He propelled us out the door and closed it. I heard the lock turn and saw him pull all the shades down, shouting, "Go away from here. You are mistaken."

Nesta began beating on the door. I grabbed her arm and dragged her down the street. "Now you've done it. You've blown the best lead I had. I told you to let me do my job, but no. Your husband was right. You are a spoiled brat!"

"How was I to know he'd be so touchy?"

I opened her car door and shoved her in. "Get off my back, Mrs. Edmunds. Or I will quit this case, tears or no tears." I slammed the door and stalked off.

By the time I reached the Boudreaux house on Bayshore, my temper had begun to cool. The house was as modern and sleek as its occupants, and it stuck out self-consciously among its white-columned, antebellum-style neighbors. It was a new style popular in Miami called deco. A three-story cylinder rose in the center of a pair of two-story wings that ran back at forty-five degree angles. A deep gallery was cut into the first story of the smooth stucco cylinder, its roof supported by keystone marble columns. The whole thing was painted the color of a Florida sunset and trimmed in crisp white.

I entered the cool shade of the gallery and rang the bell. Friezes on either side of the door featured mermaids and porpoises cavorting among the waves. Hedda herself answered the door, and I noticed a strong resemblance between her and the naked fish women I had been admiring. She was barefoot and wearing a white sundress, and her wispy blonde hair was pulled back in a carelessly attractive tail at the back of her head. Strands that had escaped the blue grosgrain ribbon trailed down her neck.

She clapped her hands in delight when she recognized me. "Oh goody," she cried and called over her shoulder, "Rosalie, we'll be having a detective for lunch." The way she said it made me wonder if they would poach or fry me. She opened the door wide and ushered me into a spacious round atrium flooded with sun from the skylight three stories up. Dazzling gold terrazzo floors surrounded a central garden filled with orchids, ferns and graceful palms that almost reached the skylight. "You will stay for lunch, won't you?" Without waiting for an answer, she took me back through the grand room and out onto a veranda overlooking the rear courtyard. A giant swimming pool sparkled like a chest of aquamarine jewels.

"Detective Billy." She said it solemnly as she stepped behind the veranda bar and took up a quart of pre-Prohibition twelve-year-old Kentucky bourbon and sloshed half the bottle into a glass pitcher. South Tampa seemed to have an endless cistern of the stuff somewhere. All the judges and pols got cases of it for Christmas.

117

"What fun to have you all to myself." She smiled as she spooned sugar into the pitcher and stirred.

A squat, round woman with a pumpkin head and bronze skin waddled in with two silver glasses set in a mound of fine-cracked ice. Fresh-frozen stalks of sugared mint were arranged artfully on a silver-rimmed bone china plate.

"Tell me," Hedda demanded, dosing the pictcher with a dash of bitters and a slug of whisky. "Have you ever shot anyone?"

"No, ma'am. Detective work is more wearing out paper and shoe leather than shooting and spying."

"Oh god, please don't call me ma'am. Makes me sound like some frowsy matron at the market. Call me Hedda. Everyone does, even Rosalie." She stirred the concoction with a vengeance. "And I shall call you Billy. I love that name. Billy Heart. Sort of romantic and chancy. You know, like a deck of cards. King of hearts… Or are you the knave?" She smiled wickedly and scooped ice into the pitcher and stirred some more.

I pulled the glasses out of the ice, scooping some of it into each one, and set them up. "Just Billy Heart, Mrs. Boudreaux."

She topped off the glasses with the brew and garnished them with mint sprigs. The perfect mint julep. Ambrosia of the genteel South. The house may have been modern, but inside, the old South was alive and well.

She touched her glass to mine and looked deeply into my eyes. "To you, then. Just Billy Heart." We drank and gazed off at the blooming gardens in companionable silence until Rosalie began to serve lunch.

The first course was bland and creamy. Crabmeat swimming in a cheese-flavored, tomato-tinged white sauce, spooned over thin, white, crustless toast points and sprinkled with finely sliced mushrooms sautéed in butter. The last time I'd had mushrooms, they were large enough to shelter a frog, coarsely hacked in hearty hunks, sautéed in olive oil from the old county with a fistful of crushed whole garlic cloves and perfumed with a splash of Uncle Vito's homemade red wine and served with great crusty loaves of Cuban bread.

Hedda ate heartily and watched me with amused interest, as if I were some specimen of exotic species of bug she had just discovered on a tree in her atrium. "Have you gotten any big breaks in the case, as they say?" she asked, amused at her use of private eye lingo.

"Nothing earth-shattering. There is one thing, though, that you might be able to help with…"

"I'd love to, darling. Would that make me an assistant investigator?"

What was it with these dames, wanting to be my partner? "If you'd like. You could think of yourself as my deputy investigator."

"Mmmmm, fabulous!" she mooed. "We'll be partners. You could deputize me. We'll have a ceremony in the atrium and a party to celebrate! I'll have to get a badge. Something elegant, maybe an Erte pin. I know! A bronze eye in a circle of gold…"

Rosalie removed our plates and replaced them with fresh ones, and then set a platter in the center of the table. "Ah, Rosalie's special," said Hedda, "congealed salad."

Ybor City and south Tampa speak an entirely different language when it comes to food. My mother would not recognize this sleek and shiny object as a salad, or even food. To her, a salad is composed of the leafy romaine and fat, red tomatoes from her garden. This looked more like a car part, say a fender of a Bentley cruiser.

Hedda served another round of juleps as Rosalie carved a jiggling lump of salad for me. I was grateful for the drink to steel me against my first bite. "There's an inconsistency in Miss Flores' statements to the ship's captain and the London Police," I said, draining my glass and glancing at the object on my plate. I turned my attention to Hedda.

She smiled a little too casually, I thought, and replied, "You mean the business about whether he jumped or fell."

I nodded. "First, she said he jumped. That's what she told the captain when he questioned her."

Hedda took on a look of amused condescension. "She was hysterical, screaming in Spanish and English. She didn't know what she was saying."

"That why you explained to her that she shouldn't say he jumped?"

Her lips tightened. "Is that what she said?"" When I didn't answer, she continued. "I simply questioned her story, that's all. Look, Eddie wouldn't kill himself. I knew him too well to buy that. He was too full of life, too..." She looked at me and sighed. "Too passionate."

She took a bite of gelatinous mass and rolled it around in her mouth before swallowing. Then she set her fork down and leaned toward me. "I'm going to level with you. When she said he jumped, I knew she was lying. I figured the only reason she'd lie is if she helped him along. Oh, I didn't want to make a federal case of it. He had been tough on the poor girl. He was drunk and doing something foolish and risky like he always did. I'm sure she didn't plan it, but..." She put a hand on my arm and looked into my eyes. "I just told her I knew he wouldn't jump."

"Did you tell her to say he fell?"

She took her hand away and put it in her lap. "I might have asked her if she didn't mean to say he fell."

"Why?"

"I guess I wanted to give her an out. She was terrified."

"That's very kind, considering you thought she had murdered a dear friend."

Hedda sat up straight and grasped her breast in mock surprise. "Dear Billy. You are a hard-nosed dick, aren't you?"

"Is that your answer?"

"He was dead. In a flash of passion, this poor creature might have helped him over. What was I supposed to do, have her thrown in the brig? And what about Nesta? I figured if Lola said he jumped, Nesta wouldn't get the insurance money. Wasn't it bad enough that her husband was dead? That he was last seen in her company of — of a common harlot? Was she to mourn as a pauper?"

"But she didn't get any insurance money."

"I didn't know that at the time, did I? No one found out until later about all the insurance business."

"You and your husband were major stockholders in the company. You must have known—"

She waved me away. "Dom handles all those sorts of things. I just sign the papers." She took a long pull at her julep. "Really, Billy dear. You make me sound like some sort of racketeer." She gave me the Boudreaux pout. "I thought I was your deputy."

"I'm just asking questions. How you interpret them is up to you."

She made that mooing sound again and murmured, "I love it when you go all cold and hard on me, Billy Heart. Have you got a heart of steel, huh, Detective Billy?" She tickled my chin and teased a smile out of me. She was a piece of work all right.

She laughed and leapt to her feet, unbuttoning her dress. "It's too beautiful a day for all this seriousness." She dropped her dress around her feet and stepped out of it, wearing a swimsuit. She bounded to the pool and dove in, slicing the water cleanly. She swam the length of a pool and back in smooth, fast strokes. She got out and came toward me laughing and dripping, not even short of breath. She perched on my knee and flicked water on me from her hair. "Doesn't that feel good?"

It did. So did the feel of her firm, damp bottom on my knee, but instead of admitting it, I said, "You're quite a swimmer."

She smiled proudly. "I won the race around Edmunds Island for the grand opening, you know. Seven miles."

"A pilot, a swimmer. What else do you do?"

She stood and took a towel out of a cupboard, striking a number of poses for me while she smoothed it over her body. "Just about anything I get the chance to," she replied, stroking her thigh with the towel.

"How did the handrail in the stateroom get damaged?" I asked.

She stopped rubbing, bent over and shook out her hair. Women have so many ways of avoiding your eyes when they have something to hide. "What handrail?"

"The one next to the door, a brass thing screwed into the wall. The report said it was bent at one end and pulled out of the wall."

She toweled her hair, still hiding her face, and shrugged. "God knows. We were drunk half the time. Someone probably took it down passing out." She flipped her hair back and looked at me. "There's that steely look again. I honestly don't know how the damn thing got damaged. Do you have an idea?"

"Just curious."

"You don't give much away, do you?"

I smiled and rose to take my leave. "Thank you for lunch, Mrs… uh… Hedda. It was most interesting."

"But you didn't even touch your congealed salad…"

"Thanks, but I'm really not hungry."

I stopped at Emilio's for a meatball sandwich on my way downtown.

Chapter Nineteen
Apocryphal Angel

The *Tampa Chronicle* librarian brought me stacks of papers from 1925, the year Edmunds Island had its grand opening. It was front-page news for weeks that fall. It seemed as if every article had a connection with the opening of Edmunds Island. A full-page ad in the business section read, "Profits! The very word is synonymous with Edmunds Island! One purchaser of lots took a profit of $3,000 in four days. Another sold his property at a gain of $1,800 one hour after he bought it."

In the metro section another ad of equal size featured a drawing of a handsome couple on a gondola in a canal lined with palm trees and exotic Mediterranean architecture. The copy read, "Here are ceaselessly moving waters, ever lapping the foundation of Edmunds Island domiciles. Here, too, are the picturesque gondolas and other sorts of craft moored to fantastically colored poles—right at one's doorstep—ready for a moonlight sail to the accompaniment of music which steals across the bay."

The society page featured news of corps of Tampa's elite matrons setting out on shopping expeditions to Miami and New York in quests for the perfect gown to wear to the grand opening ball. It was to be held at the newly constructed lavish Edmunds Island Country Club Ballroom, which featured a roof that slid back for dancing under the stars. Duke Ellington would play for the ball, and WDAE radio station was to broadcast live from the festivities.

The sports pages featured articles about Edmunds Island opening events. Vincetti Productions staged a boxing match featuring Jack Dempsey. A famous golf pro was going to drive a golf ball from the mainland across the water to Edmunds Island. National speedboat races were to take place on a course set around the circumference of the island. Edmunds had dubbed the course Edmunds Island

Speedway. There was also to be a seven-mile swimming race around the island, with an award of ten thousand dollars to the winner. I figured it probably had paid for Hedda's ball gown and jewelry for the opening.

There was also an article about an unusual triathlon in which daredevil participants had to first water ski around the island behind a speeding boat and then grasp a ten-foot rope ladder dangling from a flying airplane and climb into the aircraft. In the second leg of the triathalon, participants had to rappel with ropes down the side of the one-hundred-foot tower of the new Palace of Florence Hotel. For the final leg, they drove a road race around the twisting roads of Edmunds Island. Each event was timed, and the total times determined the winner.

Hedda hadn't won this one, but she was prominently featured in the article as the only woman in this pack of adventurers. She did come in second, however, to a famous fearless Frenchman named Jean Claude DuBois. There was a stunning picture of her sitting on her plane next to the handsome DuBois, a wicked glint of amusement in her smile.

I stared at the picture, entranced. What a dame she was, bold and bright and brave. It took an iron set of *cojones* to love a woman like that. Or one like her husband, I supposed, who was content to let her wear the pants. Still, I wondered about her side of it. Could such a woman be satisfied with a pretty lapdog of a husband? Or would her larger-than-life appetite for excitement require more challenge?

As long as I was in the building, I figured I might as well pay a visit to Randall Stroven. All the blood seemed to drain out of me at the thought. So I stopped thinking and took the stairs up to the top floor to get my blood pumping. Nonetheless, my hand trembled slightly when I gave the receptionist my card.

Stroven motioned me in as he shouted into the mouthpiece of his phone. "I don't give a ram's testicle what he says. You get down to

City Hall, and you don't leave until you get some answers. These people are our public servants."

Stroven was a compact man on the small side of average with a hawkish nose upon which sat a pair of wire-rimmed glasses with thick lenses that magnified his eyes, making them seem out of proportion with the rest of his head. He had a nice crop of dark hair for a man in his late fifties. A thick vein throbbed in his neck just below the jawline.

I watched it as a cat does a lizard, wondering how close my knife had gotten to that vein ten years ago. I considered pouncing on it now and ripping it out with my teeth, tasting his blood.

"You're a reporter, for Crissakes. You figure it out!" Stroven slammed the phone down. "Reporters," he muttered to no one in particular. "In my day we knew how to get a story." He perused my card and then me, taking his time like a man used to authority. "PI, huh?" he squinted at me through his glasses. "You look familiar. Have we met?"

Fortunately, he was blind as a mole even with his glasses on. And anyway, there was little in the grown man before him to suggest the scrawny boy who had tried to kill him ten years before. "Never had the pleasure," I replied half truthfully, for it had been no pleasure, and we hadn't actually met.

This seemed to satisfy him. "What's on your mind, young man?'

"I'm investigating the disappearance of EQ Edmunds."

He rolled his monstrously magnified eyes and snickered. "Let me guess. Nesta Edmunds."

I nodded. "I read your paper's coverage of the disappearance, and I'm puzzled by something."

"What's that?"

"The story made the front page every day for about a week, and then, nothing."

"We followed it for as long as there was a story. Once we found out what happened and printed it, there wasn't much more to say."

"That's odd. I found lots of interesting things that weren't in your paper."

"Such as?"

"The fact that Liberty Limited stood to gain a multi-million-dollar development upon Edmunds' death for the cost of a few dollars paid on an insurance policy. The fact that Nesta Edmunds never received a penny of the money because Edmunds had already mortgaged the policy to the hilt."

Stroven's eyes narrowed as he bent over the desk to study me. "I'll be honest with you, son. Even though I don't have to tell you one damn thing. Nesta's uncle came to see me about a week after Edmunds disappeared. He's a very powerful man in these parts, and one with a good name to keep up. He wasn't happy about seeing his niece's name dragged through the mud in the paper with the likes of EQ Edmunds. It was bad enough she married him in the first place. An embarrassment to the family, if you know what I mean."

Stroven paused to give me time to agree. When I said nothing, he went on. "When Edmunds died, the family just wanted to put the whole thing behind them. The girl was still young, and they felt she still might marry a decent fellow if people could just be allowed to forget her mistake."

He spread his hands magnanimously. "This is a good town with good folks. I like to help keep it that way. Even though the story was selling like water on the desert, I dropped it for the girl's sake. I can't understand why she wants to keep stirring it up like this." Stroven fixed his owlish eyes on me. "You ask me, she needs a good psychiatrist, not another dick."

"I understand you're a major stockholder in Liberty Limited. You were in fact chairman of the board when the company bought Edmunds Island and took out the policy on his life."

Stroven sat back, the picture of casual indifference. "So?"

"You thought you had something to gain by Edmunds' death. I call that motive for murder."

126

"This conversation is starting to be ridiculous."

"Why did you take out the insurance policy?"

"It's a common practice, especially with a risky investment. Everyone dies eventually. Buying a life insurance policy is a way to make certain that the company recoups its investment even if the venture fails."

"What about—"

"That's all the time I have, Mr.—" He retrieved my card and read it. "Heart. I do have a newspaper to run."

"Just one more question."

Stroven rose and showed me the door. "I think I've been more than generous with you. You wouldn't want to try my patience."

I opened my mouth to speak, but Stroven called to a man at a nearby desk. "Jones, show Mr. Heart out." Stroven turned to me. "Take my advice and find yourself a different case. Nesta's family will not be pleased when they find out that you're taking her money for this nonsense."

I knew my mother would have heard by now about the bombing, so I figured I had better show my face. I also knew she wouldn't say, "I told you so," and she didn't. Once she realizes that I'm set on a course, she does her best to help. I think she genuinely enjoys mulling over my cases with me.

She had made my favorite, veal piccata, and we ate while I brought her up to date. I told her about the *Chronicle*'s coverage of the Edmunds Island opening and about Vincetti's staging of a boxing match on Edmunds Island. We discussed his denial of having been on the boat, and Maria's siting of them together. I related Vincetti's strange statement that he wished I was right in my theory that he had taken Edmunds' cash and thrown him overboard.

"What do you suppose he meant by that?"

I shrugged. "Maybe he was supposed to knock Edmunds off but didn't succeed. Maybe Edmunds pulled his disappearing stunt before the brothers could make the hit." I popped a perfect morsel of tender veal and capers into my mouth.

"Maybe he was so scared when he found out they were after him, he jumped." She put another veal medallion on my plate.

"It's possible he did jump. That's what Lola said at first. Then she changed her story and said he fell."

"Why would she change her story?"

"Maybe she was scared."

"Of what?"

"That's the big question. Maybe Vincetti. Hedda thinks Lola gave Edmunds a nudge to help him overboard and was afraid of being arrested."

"You've met this Lola?"

I nodded.

"Would she do such a thing? Could she?"

"Yes, she was definitely capable physically and emotionally of shoving him over in a moment of anger if he was already perched in the porthole."

"So the question is, did she?"

I chewed thoughtfully, the sublime taste and texture carrying me away for a moment from the puzzle at hand. "He just seemed too prepared for setting up a new life. He might have fallen or been pushed, but I don't think he jumped." I told her about the million dollars in cash he had on his person, and my almost positive proof that he had gotten a false passport.

She laughed when I told her how Nesta had balled up the mission to get the name on the passport. "It sounds like he might have left Tampa planning to disappear."

I nodded.

"Let's suppose he did. How would he disappear off a ship in the middle of the ocean?"

"There was only one exit, and the steward swore he saw Edmunds go in and not come out. If he's telling the truth, then Edmunds had to have gone out the porthole."

"Maybe Lola was telling the truth the first time. Maybe he jumped and had a boat waiting for him."

"That would be risky. A boat would have had a hell of a time finding a man in the ocean even on a sunny day. It was night and storming."

"Maybe he had some kind of flare or light he could flash."

"I suppose, but they were two days out at sea. Where would a boat come from? It would have to be an awful big boat to go out that far to sea. Wouldn't the crew of the ocean liner have seen it?'

We kicked around various scenarios over coffee and cookies. I told her about Hedda's prowess as a swimmer, a pilot and a general daredevil. Mama liked the idea of the daring and lusty Hedda as an accomplice—I had to admit the idea had its merits. After all, she had the means, by air or water, and the daring. She had been careful to tell Lola not to say it was suicide. But what was the motive?

"Maybe love," my mother said with a mischievous smile. "You said yourself her husband was a noodle. Maybe she and this Edmunds had plans to rendezvous again somewhere."

"But how could she get off the ship and onto a boat or plane? She was in the stateroom until almost midnight."

"She swam seven miles around Edmunds Island. Surely she could swim from one boat to another."

When I was ready to leave, Mama handed me a basket with pillows and fresh bedclothes and a bag full of food. She never said one word about the bombing, never asked me to stay with her. She respected my pride too much for that. I gratefully accepted the basket and kissed her on the forehead before slipping off down the street.

At home, I dragged my flimsy mattress in from the terrace and flopped it onto the bed. I made it up with the fresh linens from the basket and turned in. The place still smelled smoky and wet.

In my dreams the green-brown smell became the scent of a stormy sea. A ship passed through it and a man leapt from a porthole into the churning water. A plane flew back and forth overhead until a thin beam of light from the man overboard flashed on and off. A rope ladder dropped from the plane and a voluptuous woman in a diaphanous evening gown fluttered down it like some apocryphal angel. She scooped the man from the waves.

The plane flew slowly, trailing the couple clinging to each other, locked in a passionate embrace amid the wind, rain, and roiling waves. A flash of lightning revealed her naked breasts under the thin, soaked fabric of her dress, and a clap of thunder awoke me.

The storm had come up fast, and rain was blowing through my open window and onto the bed. I sat up wet and shivering, unable to shake the dream. When I rose to close the windows, I looked out and noticed a tan 1924 Chevrolet coupe parked down the street. With the darkness and rain, I couldn't see inside.

After I had showered and shaved and eaten breakfast, I peered out my window. The car was still there. I still couldn't tell if it was empty, but decided to leave by the back door just in case I had picked up a shadow.

The alley was empty except for the garbage collectors heaving the contents of overflowing cans into the back of a large truck. I slipped through the back streets and alleys, making sure I wasn't followed.

Chapter Twenty
Flying Heart

I arrived at Max Paredo's office at ten a.m. The shades were still drawn and the door locked. The hours on the window said nine to five. I listened at the door and heard no sound. I banged on the windows but got no response. I went around to the back of the building. A metal door set in brick was locked up tight. A garbage bin filled with paper sat next to the door. I sifted through the papers, mostly scraps of runs of posters and handbills that hadn't come out just right. At the very bottom, I came across some envelopes with Max Paredo's name and address on Thirty-Fourth Street, at the far eastern end of Ybor.

The streets east of Twenty-Second are really just narrow dirt roads lined with tiny tin-roofed houses amid fenced-in plots with chickens, goats, pigs, large gardens, and fruit trees. It's a mostly Italian neighborhood, but a few rural Cubans and Chinese also live there.

The house that matched the address on the envelope had a rickety porch and peeling paint. A few chickens scratched around the bare yard, and a litter of kittens trailed out from under the house. A tamarind tree, three Valencia orange trees, and a lemon tree shaded the front yard. I opened the gate, which swung roughly on a broken hinge, and entered the yard. A scrawny gray kitten lurched unsteadily toward me, mewing pitifully. I picked him up and he nestled into the crook of my elbow, hiding his head in the folds of my shirt, nudging and kneading, seeking a nipple he would not find there.

I heard the sounds of voices in back of the house and moved in that direction. I surprised a group of four gray-haired men sitting in metal chairs under a giant mango tree. Max Paredo was not among them. Before I had time to take in much more of the scene, four pistols where drawn, cocked and pointed at me. I stopped, put the kitten down, and showed my hands.

"Que quieres?" demanded one of the men through a prodigious gray mustache.

"My name is Guillermo Corazon. I'm looking for Max."

"It's him," another said. "The kid who brought the dame."

"She's my client," I explained. "She followed me. I came to apologize to Max."

The geezer with the mustache looked me over and squinted. "You're Ramon's boy."

I nodded when he mentioned my father's name, and he put his gun away. The others examined me with skepticism and relaxed their aim a bit. Another put his weapon away. The other two put theirs in their laps.

"You got Max in big trouble, Corazon," said Mustache.

"What happened?"

"Ciega's boys. They worked him over pretty good."

"How is he?"

"He'll live. But he ain't gonna be chewing mondongo any time soon. Won't be doing any pushups neither."

"What'd they do to him?"

"Stomped his butt."

"Why?"

"Probably for talking to you."

"Where is he now?"

Another man spoke up, one who hadn't put his gun away. "None of your god-damned business, and I don't care who your papa was. It's enough you almost got Max killed."

Mustache ignored him. "He's at Centro Asturiano Hospital. Make sure no one sees you go in."

I thanked him and left amid the violent argument that erupted in Spanish. I had no doubt Mustache could take care of himself, and I wanted to get out of there before one of the old guys decided to stop me with a bullet.

There were still no signs of my shadow, but I took precautions anyway. I took a streetcar downtown, got off and examined the other passengers. Then I hopped another car heading back to Ybor and was accompanied by none of the people who had come downtown with me.

I got off before we hit Seventh Avenue and hiked the northeast border of Ybor, coming up behind Centro Asturiano. It was a great red brick structure with clean white trim. I entered through a side door and made my way to the lobby where a Catholic sister told me Max's room number.

Max looked like a mummy lying in the hospital bed, bandaged and plastered from head to toe. They had stomped him to a bloody pulp, breaking fingers, ribs and small bones in his feet, and bruising all the meat and organs in between.

Tears came to my eyes at the sight of him, at the thought of the beating he had taken, thanks to me. I sank down on my knees at his bedside, shaking my head. "Ciega, the bastard. God damn him to hell!"

Max whispered hoarsely, "Get up."

I stood, trembling with hatred for the rats who had done this to an old man, snorting back the rising tide of tears.

"Stop it," he croaked and motioned me closer. "They wanted the name on the passport."

"They didn't know it?"

He gave me a puzzled look. "No. That's why they beat me."

"They didn't set Edmunds up with you?"

"No. It was a girl." The half of his mouth that wasn't bandaged curved up in a toothless smile. They had knocked out half of his teeth. "I knew her mother in Havana years ago. A real dish..." He held his bandaged hands a foot from his chest. "Coconuts out to here." His unbandaged eye took on a dreamy look that I hated to interrupt.

"What was her name?"

"Carmen," he whispered as if he were blowing in her ear. "Carmen Flores."

An electric jolt went through me. "What was the daughter's name?"

"I don't remember."

"Lola?"

"Yeah, I think that was it."

Lola had gotten Edmunds' false passport for him. So she had been in on his disappearance after all. "What was the name on the passport?"

He winced in pain and maneuvered himself into a more comfortable position. "Wallace Smithers." He smiled, and spelled it for me.

"Did you give the name to Ciega's boys?"

"I didn't give them nothing but a few bruises of their own to nurse." He chuckled and then grimaced in pain.

"Does it hurt to laugh?" I asked.

He nodded. "Pain. What would we do without it?" he asked. "It tells us we are still alive." He laughed again, and then lapsed into coughing.

I thanked him and asked him if there was anything else I could do for him. "Guava and cream cheese turnover," he replied, "and a pint of rum."

I promised I would return with the goods and then took my leave. At the door I stopped and turned around. "Why are you helping me?"

He grinned. "I already took the licking; I might as well do the deed."

"That's all?"

He hesitated and blinked. His lips trembled. "Your father," he said. "I used to take a break and go down to the Cuesta Rey factory to hear him. No one read Cervantes like Ramon Corazon."

I couldn't have spoken even if I had known what to say. I tipped my hat to him and ducked out. A fragment of Shakespeare's *Julius Caesar* came to me out of the blue. My father loved to read Marc Antony's grand eulogy over the great ruler in his deep voice. He read it the way a great tenor might sing an aria. "Friends, Romans, countrymen. Lend me your ears. I come to bury Caesar not to praise him. The evil that men do is left after them; and the good is oft interred with their bones."

Such was not the case with my father. His goodness radiated from the ground he had trod and reached up from his memory to touch me. Tampa's most powerful may have killed Ramon Corazon, but they had not silenced him, had not banished his spirit. I felt him all around me as I walked the darkening streets of Ybor toward Punch House.

Instead of approaching through an arcade, I went up a back service alley. A bakery truck sat at the loading dock, filled with boxes of bread. I sidled up and jumped into the truck, hoisted a stack of boxes and carried them into the kitchen with a couple of other guys. I carried the boxes through the main kitchen, up the stairs to the waiters' station on the mezzanine. There I deposited the boxes and went straight to Vincetti's table.

His face was a mask when I appeared before him. "I don't recall giving you a key pin," he said in a flat voice.

"Next time you want some information, why don't you come see me instead of pounding on defenseless old men."

Vincetti sucked his teeth and pulled a cigar out of his vest pocket. "There's an easy way and a hard way to do everything," he told me. "Max is like you. He always takes the hard way."

"Then how come I always seem to get there before you?"

He gave me a murderous glare.

"You want to know the name on Edmunds' passport, Vincetti? Ask me nice. Maybe I'll tell you."

"You know, I used to feel sorry for you. I thought you got some bad breaks. Now I see you got what you deserved."

"You can call your shadow off now. He can't keep up anyway."

His pencil-thin eyebrows shot up at this. "You got a tail?"

"Had," I replied.

"I don't got nobody on you, Corazon. Everyone in town saw that dame drag you up the sidewalk to Max's." He sucked his teeth and smirked at me. "You shouldn't let a broad push you around like that. It'll make you soft. If you aren't already." He laughed again. "Bombs, tails. Looks like me and the Edmunds dame ain't the only ones waiting for a piece of you when the time is ripe. The question is, which one of us gets to eat the heart?"

He motioned to his twin meatheads with a circular gesture of one hand. Suddenly four hands grasped me and flipped me backwards over the wrought iron railing. My feet hit a table down below and broke my fall enough that my head wasn't busted wide open when it hit the floor.

The people at the table were more surprised than anything at first. They looked from me to the mezzanine above and then back at me. I scrambled for my hat and got out there before their mood turned. The sound of Vincetti's laughter followed me out.

I didn't allow myself to limp until I was out of the courtyard and onto the street. By then, my head was pounding, my knee was threatening to buckle if I didn't give it a break, and my ankle was screaming in pain. I sank down on a bench and rested my joints, feeling for breaks. The knee was banged up pretty good. The bone felt bruised but not broken. No jagged edges in my ankle either, but the sharp ache in the little bones leading down to the toes probably meant some fractures. I just needed to get home and elevate it.

That turned out to be easier said than done. Halfway down the block, I broke into a cold sweat, and my head began to swim. I sank into a doorway and dropped my head. A cool darkness rushed up to meet me and carried me down, drifting, sinking in thick water.

A series of sharp tugs on my sleeve brought me out of it. I swam up out of blackness to the backs of my eyelids and pried them open. A woman was standing there, a wet, diaphanous gown clinging to every mound and cleft in her body. "Billy?" she said. "Billy, are you okay?"

I shook my head to clear it as the face came closer to mine, emerging through the sheets of pouring rain. It was the face of Alicia Garcia. "You call this the direct approach?" she asked as she helped me up.

Back at her place she made me a hot toddy and put me into her luscious bed, bad leg propped up on a stack of pillows. I got about halfway through the toddy before I drifted into a deep, dreamless sleep.

I awoke at dawn, stiff and throbbing all over. Alicia was sleeping with her head on my shoulder, her hair in a halo around her head. I would have stayed that way for a year if every joint in my body weren't groaning and begging to move. I eased her onto a pillow and unclenched my muscles one by one, moved my joints and finally crept out of bed, fighting to unbend. By the time I got to the door, I was almost upright, and both my legs were holding up, though not without complaint.

A hot bath helped a lot. Afterward, I drew on an oversize kimono hanging on a hook and made coffee. I drank two cups and took the third into the bedroom. Alicia was just waking up. She yawned and peered at me through sleepy eyes. "You look as if you might live after all."

"Thanks for taking me in last night."

"You want to tell me what happened?"

I shook my head. "It's better if you don't know."

"I've got a pretty good idea, Billy. Most of Ybor knows what you're up to." She took my hand and looked into my eyes. "You know, one of the reasons I never took you seriously before was because you were too young. Too immature. The other night, when we kissed... that was when I realized you were all grown up... that I could really fall for you. But you're still doing stupid things, Billy. Acting like... like some little *pendejito*."

I stood and said stiffly, "Yeah, well, like I said, thanks for taking me in last night. The *pendejito* has to go to work now."

She called after me as I walked out, "Billy. Don't take it that way. Come back."

Pendejito. I supposed it was better this way. To be reminded what she really thought of me. Little sausage. She wasn't kind, but she was honest. The man she finally chose to love would never have to wonder what she thought.

I wished I didn't have to stop at home to change clothes, but the ones I had on were dirty and crusted with dried blood. I knew my shadow would be waiting for me, and that I would have to go to the extra trouble of shaking him before heading to the steamship company to pick up the rest of the passenger list.

He was lounging inside the coffee shop across the street, watching the front of my building, still waiting for me to come out. The bum with the new shoes, the man in the tan Chevy coupe. I went into my building the back way.

After a shower and shave and a change of clothes, I felt even better. I poured half a bottle of rum into a flask and deposited it in my hip pocket. I went back out the back door and circled around the block, coming up on the door to the coffee shop from the side. There sat my shadow, nursing a café con leche with a newspaper spread open on the table and staring at my front door.

Our eyes met briefly when I entered. He blinked and turned hurriedly to his paper. I bought a half-dozen guava and cream cheese turnovers and a café solo. I took a seat at the table next to my shadow and watched him openly as I ate two turnovers slowly, savoring the sweet, sticky flavor and licking my fingers.

He ignored me and pretended to be deeply engrossed in the paper. He was a large, doughy man who had once been muscular. His close-cropped faded red hair was flecked with a dull gray. An aging Irish pug.

"You're not much of a tail, you know," I said conversationally.

He made no reply, acting as if he had not heard me at all.

I slugged back my café solo and rose. "For one thing you're too big to blend in with a crowd." I picked up my bag with the remaining pastries and leaned over his paper. "For another, Anglos always stand out in Ybor." I dropped a card on his newspaper. "You want to know what I'm up to, make an appointment. We'll swap stories."

I knew he wouldn't follow me when I left, but I was careful anyway. There was always the possibility he wasn't working alone. I rode the streetcars in every direction before making my way to the hospital.

I dropped off three pastries and flask of rum to Max. He examined my bruised and cut-up face with satisfaction while he munched a turnover. I hadn't taken the beating he had, but I had somehow in his eyes proved my mettle by taking a dive off the mezzanine at Punch House.

When I entered the steamship company and set a bag with the remaining turnover on the receptionist's desk, she smiled and pulled two neatly typed pages out of her top drawer and handed them to me. I folded them and put them into my vest pocket. "I appreciate all the trouble you went to here."

She smiled and opened the bag. "I was happy to help. And you are too nice to always bring me presents."

Suddenly I felt awkward, like the little pendejito Alicia had called me. "Listen, I… I'm sorry about last time. I just… I guess I just got carried away."

She blushed and smiled but didn't look away this time. "Don't worry. It's okay."

I tipped my hat and backed out the door.

On my way to my office, I stopped at Otto's stand for a paper. He smiled at my approach. "I hear Punch House was raining Corazon last night."

"Yeah, what else did you hear?"

"Word is, you're barking up the wrong tree."

"That's the word they would put out, isn't it?"

"I didn't say this was the party line."

"I'm telling you, Ciega and his boys are involved in this."

"Maybe so. But not the way you think." He slapped a *Chronicle* down, and waved away the nickel I produced. "Tell me something," he said leaning close and lowering his voice. "How is Hedda Boudreaux these days?"

"She's a real piece of work, Otto. You know her?"

He gave me a mysterious smile. "I used to."

I knew better than to ask for details. Otto tells you only what he wants to and when he wants to. No amount of prodding will get more than he wants to say out of him.

Up in my office, I sat down and opened the papers I had gotten from Miss Angel Eyes. Looked to be about fifty names altogether. She had even alphabetized the list and put suite numbers next to the names. I ran my finger down the first page, pretty much finding the names I expected to along with several that meant nothing to me. The second page was pretty much the same until I hit Ss and there it was. Wallace Smithers, Suite 102. Suddenly, it all fell into place. I knew exactly what happened to EQ Edmunds.

Chapter Twenty-One
Grilled Mango

Lola took her time getting to the door. When she did, I shoved past her into the living room.

"You have the manners of a dog," she said and closed the door.

"Tell me again, Miss Flores, exactly how Mr. Edmunds went through the porthole."

"Ay! The same question over and over. Don't you have a different one this time?"

"Okay. Does the name Wallace Smithers mean anything to you?"

She looked me in the eye, a Mona Lisa smile on her face and said, "So you do have new questions, eh Linguini?"

I didn't blink. "You want to tell me about Wallace Smithers, or would you rather talk to the police?"

She shrugged and turned away. "It was the name on his passport, but I'm sure you already know that. What else do you want to hear?" She turned back to me. Her eyes took mine in an earnest embrace. "I helped him get it years ago. He said you never know when you might want to disappear."

"How long did the two of you plan it?"

"We didn't plan anything. I told you, it was just in case."

"I suppose you didn't know Wallace Smithers had reserved suite 102 on the Majestic."

Her expression did not change, but two points of red blossomed and grew on her cheeks. Moisture glistened on her upper lip. She saw my scrutiny and flung herself on the sofa. "I don't know what you're talking about."

"Did the three of you plan it out together, or did he play you off against each other?"

Her eyes widened in what looked to be genuine surprise. "The three of us?"

141

"You and Edmunds and Hedda Boudreaux."

She smiled. "Is that what she said?"

"No, I figured it out all by myself. That's what detectives do."

"And what did you figure out?"

"That Edmunds never left the ship, for one thing."

"Oh, but he did. I saw him. I swear to you I saw him go out that porthole."

"Sure you did, and that's the truth — as far as it goes."

"That's the truth as far as I know it."

"How did the brass rail get damaged?"

"I don't know."

"That's a lie."

"You know everything, suppose you tell me."

"He tied a rope to that rail, and then attached the rope to the harness he had on, and climbed out the porthole. Then he rappelled down the side of the ship, just like Hedda taught him to do. Edmunds' stateroom was 202. Wallace Smithers' cozy little suite was one floor below. He had gone down earlier to make sure the porthole was open. It was just a few feet. It looked so easy."

She lit a cigarette, but that only gave away her shaking hands.

"It must have given you both quite a jolt when the rail pulled away from the wall."

She shuddered.

"Where is he, Lola?"

She burst into tears. "I don't know. I swear to you, I don't know."

"You're good, chica. I'll give you that. You can just cry on cue, can't you? Well I'm not buying it. You've lied to me; you've lied to the police. Do you know what the penalty is for aiding a felon in the commission of a crime?"

She stood and came over to me. She looked through her tears up into my eyes. "You must believe me, Billy. I don't know where he is. I didn't even know about the room below. Please, please don't tell

142

the police." She buried her face in my chest and wept in great heaving sobs. The tears that wet my shirt felt real. "I'm so afraid."

I let her go on like that for a while just to see how long she could keep it up. I told myself my heart had gotten harder on this case. Maybe Nesta had cured my allergic reaction to tears. Lola got more hysterical instead of less, and I began to tire of her game.

I stepped back away from her. "You come clean with me, and then we'll see what I can do for you."

Her face was red and tear-streaked, and she sobbed and sniffed as she spoke. "I didn't know he was going to do that. All day he was just picking, picking away at me. He could be very cruel." She started to cry again, and I handed her a handkerchief. She wiped her face and blew her nose. "That night when the others left, we had a fight. He was putting this thing on his chest with leather straps and buckles and a rope tied to it. He put rope around the rail. He told me our troubles were over. He said he will send for me. Then he got into the window. I didn't know what he was doing; I tried to stop him. He told me count to one hundred and then unhook the rope. He said, 'Tell them I fell.' I was crying; I didn't know what he was going to do… he just… disappeared." She dissolved into tears.

"Then what happened?"

"I started to count, but the rail came away from the wall. I tried to catch it, but the rope came off too fast. It went right out the window, but I saw only rain and water. I screamed and screamed until someone came." She crumpled back onto the sofa, sobbing softly.

"He hasn't contacted you?"

She shook her head and put her face in her hands.

"Look at me."

She looked up more from surprise at my tone than from obedience.

"What did Hedda say to you?"

"Just what I told you before. I was afraid, confused. I said he jumped. She said to me she know he will never jump. So maybe I pushed him or maybe he fell. She asked me which one happened. Did I push him or did he fall. I said he fell. She said tell that to the police." Lola lay back on the sofa, and draped a hand over her forehead. It was the studied gesture of the damsel in distress.

"Did he say where he was going?"

"No, only he will send for me."

"And you've heard nothing from him since then."

She shook her head, a tragic faraway look in her eye. "Maybe he did fall. Maybe he's dead."

"I don't think so."

She gave me a hopeful look. "You think he's alive?"

"Yes, I do."

"Why?"

"Tell me something. You weren't named in any of Edmunds' insurance policies, were you?"

"No. He left me with nothing."

"Then how do you pay for all your expensive habits?"

She gave me a look of contempt, which I returned just as hard. She lowered her eyes. "There are some ways a woman can make money if she is desperate enough."

"Who paid you to lie about Edmunds?"

"No one, I swear."

I picked up my hat and opened the door. Her voice stopped me. "Billy?" I turned. She had her pleading face on again. "You won't tell the police, will you?"

"Not for a couple of days. That's how long you have to come clean with me." I walked to the door and stopped. "By the way, do you know Randall Stroven?"

"Who?" she asked, her pleading grimace still intact. She blinked only twice, but on a dame with her skill at lying, it might be enough.

"Two days," I said, taking out a card and writing my home number on it. I threw it on the table and walked out the door, slamming it behind me.

The Boudreaux house was ablaze in lights and awash in jazz. The semicircular driveway was filled with cars. A doorman I had never seen before met me at the door and ushered me in as if I were an expected guest. The atrium was filled with people laughing and talking and dancing to a quartet of Negro jazz musicians. The saxophone player was blowing a storm out of his instrument. Most of the men were in elegant white dinner jackets, while the women wore long, clingy gowns or short flapper chemises. The place looked like an aquarium full of bright tropical fish flitting back and forth.

Hedda gave a cry of delight when she saw me and rushed to my side. She looked like the queen mermaid in a long glittery green dress. "Oh look, it's Detective Billy," she peeped and hooked an arm through mine. "I'm so pleased you came to my party. I didn't think you would." She took two glasses of Champagne from a passing waiter and gave me one. "You don't seem like the party type."

"Actually I didn't know you were having a party tonight."

"I sent you an invitation. Don't you ever open your mail?"

"About once a month."

Dominic materialized from the sea of undulating bodies and clamped an arm around my shoulders. He was flushed from dancing and tipsy from too much Champagne. A curly lock fell prettily over his forehead, and he leaned heavily on me, slurring his words slightly. "See, darling, I told you he'd come. Oh he tries to look solemn, but he's got certain joie de vivre under it all, don't you, chum?" He gave me a bear hug.

The band played the opening bars to a popular dance tune, and Hedda grabbed my arm. "My favorite song. Dance with me, Detective Billy." She took my glass and handed it to the swaying Dominic and led me to the dance floor. She slid into my arms with an almost reptilian slither and wound her arms around my neck in the same motion. It sent a chill up my spine and stiffened it. "What's the matter, Billy, you don't like to dance? I thought Latin men knew how to move with the music." She moved her hips up into mine and dropped her torso back dramatically, glued to me from the waist down.

I couldn't resist giving it back to her just a little. I ground my pelvis into her groin and then jerked her to me, tango style. I rode her around the floor a few times until she was ready to do anything in response to my slightest nudge. "How about Edmunds, did he know how to move?" I felt her body stiffen although her face carried a smooth smile.

"He was different. Not sensual like you." She wiggled into me, feeling more like a worm than a snake this time. "He was stiff and hard. But very forceful. He wouldn't dance with me, though. He wouldn't dance with anyone who was taller than he was." She giggled and loosened up in my arms.

"When did you teach him mountain climbing?"

Her shoulders twitched, and she executed a dramatic dip. "While I was training for the triathlon. He came with me a few times, and I taught him the basics." She looked at me in the eye, her face close to mine and a dreamy expression on her face. "Why?"

"I think you know why." My eyes bored into hers.

The dreaminess in her eyes was replaced by steel. "No. I don't think I do. Just what is it you want to say?" Her face was serious now, and she became heavy in my arms, no longer moving with me. I stopped, and we stood facing each other still in a dance embrace.

"You and Edmunds had it all planned, didn't you? You used Lola as a witness. You both knew she'd do whatever you told her to. And she did, but she got scared, said the wrong thing. You had to set her straight. And you did all right. You sure did set her straight. Who else was involved, Hedda? Was it Randall Stroven?"

Hedda stepped back and stared at me, her face reddening. "Are you accusing me of —"

"I know all about the suite below the stateroom, Hedda. I know he climbed down the side of the ship just like you told him to. What I want to know is where were you supposed to meet him? Where is he now?"

"How dare you—"

"Shall we ask your husband what he thinks of my theory? Maybe he—" My mouth was slammed shut by a ringing slap. Her ring bit into my flesh.

"Get out of here!" Her shout brought the attention of the rest of the party to us. I touched a hand to my stinging lip. It came away with blood on it.

Dominic stumbled to Hedda's side. "What is it, darling? Did he insult you? Shall I challenge him to pistols at dawn?" He made his hand into a pistol and pointed it at me with a silly, drunken flourish and fired.

I said loud enough for onlookers to hear, "We were just discussing how EQ Edmunds disappeared. I have a new theory. It's fascinating. Wouldn't you like to hear it?"

"Get him out of here," Hedda shouted. "Get out!"

"She can tell you all about it after I'm gone." I turned to Hedda with a bow. "Thank you for your hospitality. It was, as usual, most revealing." I took a few steps toward the door and turned back to her. "Don't forget to tell him how the rail was damaged." To Dominic I said, "Be sure to ask her about Wallace Smithers."

He still looked prettier than his wife, even with his mouth hanging dumbly open like that.

Chapter Twenty-Two
El Grotto

I figured I had stirred the pot enough for one night. It was time now to let things simmer and see what jumped out of the pot. I wasn't sure either Lola or Hedda knew where Edmunds was, but if they did, they would make a move to contact him in the next few days. I had an old friend at the phone company who would be happy to check their long distance calls for me.

I decided I had earned a little celebration. I stopped for a bite at Las Novedades and then headed out the back for La Dulceria.

The bar was smoky and noisy. I ordered rum and took it to a table of friends who were arguing about politics.

Alicia entered on the arm of a tall, oily blond twig of a man. His pallor stood out like a banana in a bowl of mangoes. Alicia hesitated before bringing him over and introducing him around. His name was Woody. I ignored the introduction, drained my glass and stood. Alicia gave me an apologetic smile and said, "Don't let us run you off."

I smiled. "Not at all. *Pero, es hora de dormir para pendejos.*" I nodded at Woody amiably and said, "Maybe you should take yours home."

Muffled laughter broke out around the table but was quickly stifled.

Her face turned white, and Woody gave me a puzzled frown. As I walked away, I heard him ask, "What'd he say?"

I stopped for a nightcap at El Grotto, a cave-like little speaky right under Seventh Avenue that only a few select people knew about. To get there, you had to go through El Goya, the nightclub portion of Circulo Cubano, The Cuban Club. At El Goya, for two dollars, you could have roast pork and yucca piled high with garlic and drink Cuban coffee until your brain was humming while you watched the best floor show in town. Gorgeous glittering costumes put peacocks to shame.

Long-legged dancers strutted out mambos, tangos, merengues, sambas, and for the Anglos in the audience, the cha-cha-cha and Charleston with a rhythm and sensuality that no blue-eyed flapper would ever come close to. The fifteen-piece band, too, was one of the best in Ybor. Congas, bongos, horns, strings, you name it. Between floor shows, the dance floor was crowded with people enjoying the band. They cooked like that all night long.

I watched from the back for a few minutes and then skirted the dining room and ducked into a door camouflaged in the same flocked paper as the wall. It wasn't hidden, but in the dim interior, you would hardly notice it if you weren't looking for it.

On the other side of the door was a tiny scarlet coffee bar which had once served liquor but was still good for a discreet tryst. I nodded at the man making coffee and headed for a door behind the bar which led to a long, dark hallway. I followed it to a series of dank stone steps and descended. A small, fragile-looking light bulb emitted a thin string of feeble light that did not penetrate the black maw below.

At the bottom of the steps I felt for the pocked wooden door. You had to know the knock or they wouldn't open the door. It was a kind of a mambo thing that a strictly Anglo guy couldn't duplicate even if you showed it to him. I rapped it out, and a tiny round hole opened like an eye in the door. A light came on over my head, illuminating me for identification.

Vincente opened the door and embraced me lavishly as I entered the underground grotto. It was cool and dark, and lit only with burning torches. The stone walls glistened with sweat. An occasional rumble overhead signaled a passing streetcar. I thought I was alone in the place with Vincente until a voice called from the deep shadow at the far end of the bar.

"Corazon," said Otto. "You're just in time to taste the wine." He sat on an end stool, his back against the wall. He poured a splash into a wine glass and slid it toward me.

I took the glass and studied its ruby color against the firelight. "The bouquet," he instructed.

I sniffed. "Smells like grapes."

"And?"

I took a deeper smell, drawing the delicate fumes into my nose. "And earth. Good dark, rich soil."

He nodded. "This wine is from the hills of the mother land, Corazon. Asturias." He poured himself a taste and took some into his mouth. His face puckered as he rolled it around on his tongue before swallowing. "Notice how it starts out on the tongue, teasing the tip with a fruity pinch."

I did. He was right.

"She rolls back smooth on the tongue, nibbles a little at the sides with a spicy bite. Right down into the palate and off like a butterfly." He took another sip and let out a long satisfied "Ahhhhh..." when he was finished.

I followed suit. Everything he said happened just as he said it would.

"What do you say, Corazon? It's a good bottle?"

"Most titillating," I said using one of his words.

"Yes," he said, pouring a round. "But not a tease. This wine, she satisfies."

We drank, and I told him about how Edmunds had made his getaway, aided by Hedda and Lola. We toasted my brilliant deductive skills and Edmunds' craftiness.

"You know Hedda," I said. "Do you think she was in love with him?"

He gave me his crooked, enigmatic smile. "In love? No. Hedda's in love only with herself. But I expect she did enjoy him. That's all she requires from her men. That, and sometimes money..."

"You think she knew about the scam?"

"Probably. It's just the kind of intrigue that would appeal to her. If anyone helped him plan it, it was Hedda, not Lola."

"That's my hunch too. I'm inclined to believe Lola didn't know about it till the last minute, just like she said. Edmunds knew how unpredictable she is. She could blow the whole thing if something happened she didn't like."

"So tell me this, Corazon. Where is he?"

"I don't know yet. I'm hoping one of the ladies will lead me to him."

"You think they know where he is?"

"Hard to say, he was very secretive. I'm not sure he'd trust either one of them with that tidbit."

"Unless he had to for some reason."

"I thought of that. He might have needed an accomplice to funnel money to him from other sources. Maybe hidden accounts or another insurance policy we haven't discovered. That man knew ways to work a buck I can't even begin to imagine."

We finished the bottle and talked of other things, everything except Alicia. I meandered home in a pleasant glow.

Halfway up the stairs to my apartment, I froze. The hair on my arms and head rose and stiffened. It took my mind a while to figure out what my body already knew. A faint scent of sweat and hair oil lingered in the stairwell. There was no sound, no movement, just an electrical charge in the air.

I realized I had been noisy coming this far up the stairs, and that my silence now would signal my wariness to whomever was in my apartment. I stumbled loudly up the rest of the stairs and thumped loudly onto the landing. Then I crept silently into the shadow behind the door and waited.

The charge in the air pulsated, and I heard a creak on the other side of the door as it opened a crack. The dark shape of a head poked out finally, and I brought both fists down with all my strength just below the base of the skull. He went down like a sack of bananas.

I leapt onto him and turned him over. It was too dark to see his face. I would have to drag him into my apartment. As I bent over to grab his shoulders, I heard a rustling behind me. A fist sank into my kidneys and sent me sprawling headfirst halfway down the stairs.

He was on me before I could get up. He grabbed a handful of my hair and beat my face against the steps. With him riding me like a bronco buster and my legs stretched up on the stairs behind me, I was in no position to gain my footing. If I didn't get him off me, my face would be mixed with my brain pretty soon.

I pushed off with my feet and pitched forward into a somersault down the stairs, carrying the hairy ape on my back with me. I rolled over him twice before we hit the landing and came up punching. I drove a hard left into his jaw and then a right deep into his stomach just below his rib cage.

I had him up against a wall and was pummeling him when the other goon staggered to his feet and came halfway down the stairs. From there, he took a flying leap with both feet pointed straight at my head. I heard a loud crack and felt the impact deep inside my skull. I remember thinking it was odd that I felt no pain, then blackness swallowed me whole.

A deep hum filled the darkness, vibrating it. It was a soothing sensation, something in the nothingness. It tickled a bit. The tickling grew into a throb, then into a deep bone pain that sang through my head. I opened my eyes and found myself lying in the backseat of a moving automobile. Lights moved past the windows above me. I tried to move, but a purple wave of pain promised to burst the veins in my head. I lay still until the car came to a stop, and someone dragged me out by my collar. I wished only to be unconscious again.

It was the voice that brought me out of it. "I told you no rough stuff," the voice said, and suddenly I was awake sitting across a desk from Santo Ciega in his study.

Everything that was not books and dark polished wood was red. The chair I sat in was a deep garnet brocade. The fabric glowed in the dim light. Santo Ciega handed me a snifter of cognac across the desk.

I put it to my nose and the fumes entered my head, soothing the screeching ache. I sipped it like medicine and felt its hot fingers bring me slowly back to life.

I realized Santo was studying me with an odd mixture of what looked like curiosity and sadness on his face. "I told them not to hurt you," he said, almost apologetically.

"I'm just glad you didn't tell them not to kill me," I sneered.

The sadness in his eyes unnerved me more than if he had told his goons to stomp my head, which felt pretty much like a cracked soft-boiled egg as it was. He motioned them from the room without taking his eyes off me.

I scanned the room with contempt, openly sizing up the man by his surroundings. Big, beautiful leather-bound books lined the shelves. Cervantes, Lorca, Shakespeare, books on history, battle strategy, medicine, politics, economics, and the occult. I smirked though it hurt my whole head to do it. "Tell me, Ciega, you ever read one word of this stuff, or is it just for display?"

"To be or not to be: that is the question: Whether 'tis nobler in the mind to suffer the slings and arrows of outrageous fortune, or to take up arms against a sea of troubles, and by opposing end them. You know who said that?"

"Hamlet."

"That's right. Just before he declared personal war on the king to avenge his father's death. A tragic war he could not win."

"You bring me here to talk literature?"

He fixed his sad brown eyes upon me again. He seemed to sag, to shrink, to age before my eyes. Instead of the robust dangerous padrone of Ybor City, there sat an old man with a heavy body to drag around. "I know you won't believe me, but I was truly sorry about what happened to your father. I never expected them to kill him. I thought they would just deport him like the others."

"It was my mother who thought you could stop them, Ciega. I knew they wouldn't have listened to you even if you had tried to stop them. To them, you're just another dago."

I was surprised when he let that one go. Instead of breathing fire, he said, "I'd like to try and make it up to you."

He paused and looked into my eyes, searching for some softness there. I gave him nothing but steel in return. "It's a little late for that."

"Better late than not at all. Look, I want some information, and I'm willing to pay top dollar for it." He smiled at his own generosity.

I kept my face a stone. "Sorry, I'm already working on a case."

He leaned over his desk toward me, voice low and a warm smile on his face. "I'll give you ten thousand dollars to tell me where Edmunds is."

I laughed in his face. "Fat chance."

"But why? This is a chance for easy money. You could buy your mother a new house…"

"My mother told me never to make a deal with the devil because you always lose."

He smiled. "A wise woman. But I am not the devil, and you will not lose." He opened a desk drawer and drew out four thick stacks of bills. He set them on the desk in front of me. "Count it if you like. It's all there. Ten thousand dollars. Just for whistling a tune."

"The only thing I'm going to whistle is over your grave, Ciega."

He drew himself up, looking more like the younger, tougher Ciega of my memory. "You know, I could just have my boys beat it out of you."

"They couldn't even beat the name out of a poor old man. They put him in a hospital trying."

He pressed a button on his desk and his boys came in. He looked at me. "One last chance to do the first sensible thing in your life."

I stared straight ahead.

"Think of your mother. Hamlet destroyed his mother; do you want to do the same?"

That did it. I lunged across the desk. "You son of a bitch. I'll kill you if you touch her." I had him by the throat and was squeezing the life out of him.

His face bulged and went from red to purple to almost blue before the goons pried me off. I spat in Santo's face as they dragged me away. A satisfying wet glob hit his left eye. He shook with rage. "You little pendejo! I'd kill you if it weren't for her." He gestured with a fist to his goons. "Get him out of here. And don't kill the bastard."

The way they went at me with fists and feet, I figured they missed that last part about not killing me. By the time I sank once more into oblivion, I didn't care.

Chapter Twenty-Three
Message in a Bottle

I awoke to the rough nudging of something hard against my chest. I opened my eyes to see a red-faced copper standing over me with this night stick. "Up you go, boy." He reached down and picked me up by the back of my collar. Pain shot through me, and I gasped. He grabbed the front of my shirt and shook me. "Come along easy or I'll give you a taste of my Lizzie." He shook the nightstick at me, and I cringed in pain. "You want to sleep in the streets like an animal in Ybor, that's your business. But you've got no right to come here and scare decent people on a morning stroll."

I looked around for my bearings and discovered I was in a lush riverfront park. Several overly well-dressed people stood a few feet away on a path, staring at me in fascinated horror. Behind them rose the silver minarets of the grand Plant Hotel. Ciega's boys had dumped me on the grounds of the most lavish resort on the west coast of Florida.

Built by railroad man Henry Plant in the 1890s when he brought the railroad to town, Tampa Bay Hotel was a luxury palace for rich men and women from the north. They came in private rail cars and were taken around in rickshaws. Thirteen exotic minarets topped with crescent moons rose over the gigantic brick building and its deep piazza overhung with horseshoe arches and elaborate wood filigree work. Just looking at it made you feel you were someplace else, say Morocco or Turkey. Two domes at either end of the sprawling structure covered opulent ballrooms opening onto terraces overlooking lush courtyards.

Few locals had ever set foot on these grounds. We never saw the mysterious millionaires from New York and Chicago, though we often wondered about them. They came unseen in curtained cars, and dined and danced in isolation from the rest of the town. Now here they were staring at me.

The copper prodded me with his stick and tried to herd me toward the waiting police paddy wagon.

"I'm a private investigator," I said, putting a hand in my pocket to retrieve my card. He must have thought I had a weapon in there because he rapped my arm hard with his stick.

The pain shot up my arm and bit my chest like a jolt of electricity. I went down on my knees. Things got dark and cloudy, and I could feel my head in the distance somewhere behind me, repeated blows raining on it, knocking out a merengue rhythm. Then a door opened, and I fell into blackness.

I woke up in a cell with Boot standing over me, shaking his head and chewing on a wet cigar stump. He handed me a cup of water. I drank half and poured the rest over my screaming head. My ears were ringing and my vision was blurry. My breathing was ragged, and I couldn't seem to take a deep breath. I struggled to get up, but something held me down. Boot put a restraining hand on my shoulder and nodded at my chest. "You had some broken ribs," he said, "and a concussion."

I saw the bandages tightly wound around my torso. "I can't breathe in this. Get it off."

"In a few days. Right now you need to go home and get in bed. But first I've got to ask you a few questions."

"Official or personal?"

"Both."

"Ciega planted me there. Yes, it was about the Edmunds case, and no, I wasn't asking for it this time. He came after me." I glared at Boot, daring him to say I told you so. He didn't. "I want to press assault charges."

He chuckled. "Glad to see they didn't beat the sense of humor out of you." He helped me into a sitting position.

"He thinks I've found Edmunds, Boot. He wants to know where he is. Why do you suppose that is?"

Boot's bushy eyebrows shot up and toward each other like a couple of caterpillars in heat. "Edmunds is alive?"

"I'm pretty sure."

"Where is he?"

"I don't know yet, but I do know how to find out." I told him about Hedda and Lola and my friend at the phone company. He agreed to take me there on one condition, that afterwards, I would go straight to bed and stay there. I gave my promise as freely as a sixteen-year-old girl gives her heart.

The operator's name was Minnie. Minuet, her mother had named her, after the dance. She was perfect Kewpie doll with apple cheeks and a tiny heart-shaped ruby-lipped mouth. Her round brown eyes were dark and vivid, and her skin was the color of roasted coffee beans. Like most people who love a good laugh, her laughter was merry and contagious.

She didn't laugh when she saw me shuffle in on Boot's arm like an old man with rheumatism. She leapt from her chair and ran to me. She and Boot got me into a chair. "Oh, Billy, poor baby," she murmured as she knelt before me, touching my lumpy head softly. "Have you been out catching bad guys again?"

"I need a favor, Minnie."

"Just say the word."

"Write these numbers down."

She got to her desk and took up a pen. I dictated Hedda's and Lola's phone numbers to her. "And get Saul Stone's home phone number and the number for Edmunds Enterprise too. I need to know every long distance call they made starting with last night and going for the next few days."

"We looking for any place in particular?"

159

"Other countries mostly. Europe, South America, the Caribbean. That sort of thing."

"I'll call you tonight and let you know what I find."

"You're an angel."

She watched with concern as Boot helped me out of the chair. "You want me to call Alicia?"

"No!"

Her eyes widened at my vehemence.

"No. I'm sorry, I just... don't need Alicia's attitude."

"I think she'd want to help."

"Please, Minnie. Don't tell her. I... I don't want her to know."

Minnie inspected me. "Who's gonna take care of you?"

"I'll be fine. Promise me."

She shook her head. "Whatever you say, Wild Bill."

I blew her a kiss and hobbled out the door.

By the time Boot helped me into bed, my head was swimming in a dark goo like cane syrup and my ears were ringing. Three Boots floated around in a lazy circle and then faded out as my eyes closed. But something nagged at me like a fresh mosquito bite. I couldn't sleep yet. What was it? What? I fought to open my eyes. "Boot?"

His head swam into view. "Hold still." I reached for his head to steady it but couldn't reach.

"I am holding still, Billy. Go to sleep now. You promised."

"Wait... find out... you gotta find out, Boot..."

"Find out what, Billy?"

What? What was it? "Why Ciega wants to find Edmunds," I heard my mouth say before sleep overtook me.

A ringing awoke me at dusk. At first I thought it was my head again, but I answered the phone anyway out of habit. It was Minnie. Neither Hedda, Lola nor Stone had made any long distance calls last night or today. Edmunds Enterprises had placed calls to New York,

160

Chicago, Atlanta, and Los Angeles, but none out the country. It was possible, I thought, that Edmunds was somewhere in the U.S. I took all the numbers down just in case. I would check them all out tomorrow.

Minnie grilled me about how I was feeling and what I had eaten, and I realized I was hungry. After we said goodbye, I turned on the lamp and got up to make some eggs. In my haze upon entering, I hadn't noticed the mess Ciega's boys had made last night while they waited for me. What the pipe bomb hadn't broken, the goons had. It looked as if a hurricane had struck. Hurricane Santo. Why did they name these storms after women? Men were far more destructive. A woman, even a criminal, would never mess up a place like this.

I fried up some potatoes and peppers and three eggs. I ate them with Cuban bread and honey and a cup of Linden flower tea. That's all I remember until I awoke with my head on the table next to half a cup of cold tea. The phone was ringing and I fought through a drowsy fog to answer it. My tongue was heavy and my voice thick around it.

Lola sounded breathless. "Billy? I must talk to you."

My mind sharpened with interest but refused to focus. She seemed fuzzy to me, not quite real. "What is it?"

"You were right about Eddie. He's not dead."

"Where is he?"

"I don't know. He won't tell me."

I heard a knocking somewhere. Was someone at my door?

"It's him. I can't talk now." The knocking again. It was her door, not mine.

"Wait."

"Come tomorrow. I'll tell you everything."

The line went dead. I had to get over there right away. Something important was happening. I struggled into my trousers and sat on the bed to put on my shoes.

When I opened my eyes, it was late morning; the sun was already ferocious in its assault. I was bathed in sweat and I hurt everywhere, but my head was clearer; my ears had stopped ringing. When I sat up, the pain in my ribs brought me fully awake, and I realized I was lying in bed with one shoe on. I had to steady myself against walls and furniture to get to the bathroom, but my balance was returning.

By the time I had bathed and shaved, I could hold one image of my face in the mirror. The floor had stopped slanting away from my feet.

I stumbled downstairs and across the street. I had four guava and cream cheese turnovers, a glass of steamed milk and two café solos. I felt the coffee go down through my spine, stiffening my backbone, clearing my head. I thought about the odd dream I had last night. Lola had called. She sounded scared. She wanted to talk to me. Come tomorrow, she had said. Or was it a dream? First Minnie called, and then I ate and fell asleep. Maybe Lola had called. Maybe I was about to get a break in this case.

By the time I boarded the streetcar and sat down, I was out of breath. The bandages constricted my chest. I couldn't breathe. Luminescent bubbles floated around my head and popped in small fizzy starbursts. I leaned back and let the breeze wash over me.

I felt the change as soon as we hit Bayshore Boulevard. The air was fresher, cooler, saltier here. It revived me. I opened my eyes as we crossed the Edmunds Island bridge and took as deep a breath as the bandages would permit.

Lola always took her time answering the door, but this was beyond her usual. I knocked again and called her name. I listened, but heard no rustling within. I tried the door. To my surprise, it wasn't locked.

"Lola?" I called, but got no answer. The place was in its usual state of disorder. I looked in each room as I walked toward the back veranda. The hair rose on the back of my neck before I was conscious of the thick stink of death. The veranda was in shambles with tables and chairs overturned, and glasses smashed.

She sat in a corner, stiff and blue-gray, her eyes glassy and staring at nothing in this world. The flesh around her neck was chafed and bruised. There was a starburst of blood on the wall above her with smear stains leading down to her head. The back of her hair was matted with dried blood. It didn't take a detective to see that someone had choked her while smashing her head against the wall. It didn't much matter which action had killed her.

It looked as if she had put up a damn good fight, though. Her hands splayed out on either side of her body. I picked up the left one and examined it closely. Small curls of flesh flecked with dried blood showed up clearly under her crimson painted fingernails. Her right hand was balled into a tight fist. I didn't want to break the rigor mortis by forcing the hand open, so I slid my pinkie under her clenched fingers and into the palm of her hand. I drew out a small wad of dark brown hair and held it up to the light. A fraction of an inch from the follicle, the hair was lighter, maybe blonde, maybe gray. I pulled a couple of the hairs out of the wad and folded them into my wallet, and then tucked the rest back into Lola's fist.

I searched the apartment, being careful to disturb nothing. There were no signs of a struggle anywhere but on the veranda, no signs of forced entry. Whoever it was, she had known him, had let him in, probably right after talking to me.

The bedroom was in no worse shape than when I had last seen it, but something was different. What was it? My brain felt thick and slow as I ran my eyes over the dressing screen draped with dresses and lingerie, the little village scene next to it on the wall, the rumpled silk sheets and comforter, the shoes and jewelry strewn about the room.

I closed my eyes to concentrate, to remember the room as it had been before. Something was different, but what? Then I had it. The jewel box. It had been the only orderly thing in her house. It was upended, and jewelry was spilled out onto the dressing table. There were plenty of expensive pieces there, diamond rings and necklaces, gold bracelets. Something was missing. Think. What was it?

Then I saw a tiny loose sapphire among the jewels. It must have fallen out of the key pin. That's what was missing, the key pin. I searched the dresser, the floor, but it was nowhere. I left the sapphire where it was. Then I remembered my fingerprints on the gun. I reached into her lingerie drawer and felt the hard steel. I wiped it down with a silk chemise and replaced it.

I froze when I heard the front door open. Whoever was there was making a racket. I ducked into the bathroom and waited. When I heard a woman scream, I ran for the veranda.

The maid screamed even louder when she saw me and picked up a coffee pot to fend me off. She heaved it at my head and ran for the front door, yelling for all she was worth. I didn't have the strength to follow.

Chapter Twenty-Four
Key Stone

Boot chewed on the soggy butt of an unlit cigar and surveyed the murder scene. "She put up a helluva fight.

"She was a fighter, all right," I answered.

"I suppose you're gonna try to tell me Ciega's involved in this."

"Come on, Boot. He grabs me first and tries to scare me into telling him where Edmunds is. That doesn't work, so the next night he tries the only other person who might know. How hard is that to put together?"

"Number one, it's way too sloppy for a professional job. Number two, she knew her assailant. She let him in, had a drink with him."

"I didn't say it was a hit."

"Then what the hell are you suggesting?"

"I want to show you something." I took him through the house, pointing out that nothing had been disturbed. In the bedroom I showed him the overturned jewelry box. "This was very neatly arranged the last time I was here."

He eyed the box. "So what?"

"There's only one thing missing."

"What's that?"

"A gold key pin to the Punch House Mez."

He stared at me a minute, letting it sink in. He knew as well as I did who held gold key pins.

"I saw it last time I was here. She said it belonged to a friend.

"Some friend."

I nodded.

"Maybe it's on the body," Boot said with a note of hope.

"I already checked."

"So you think someone knocked her off just to get the pin?"

"Most likely he just took it because it could be traced to him."

"Jesus," said Boot, "you know who holds gold key pins?"

"Both your bosses, the mayor and the chief of police. And of course, Ciega and Vincetti. Shall I go on?"

Boot glared at me.

"Don't look at me like that. I didn't kill her."

"No, but you've been here stirring things up, haven't you?"

"I've been conducting an investigation, if that's what you mean."

"I know how you work. You can't find a cat in a bush, you toss in a firecracker and blow it out."

"You want to solve this case or not?"

"Hell yes, I want to solve it. I'm a goddamn detective, ain't I? But you know as well as I do that if the finger points in certain directions, there's not one thing I can do about it except cut my own throat and then clean up the blood."

I pointed at the sapphire lying among the jewels. "You see that?"

He looked at the tangled mass. "Buncha expensive gee-gaws. So what?"

"Look closer."

He squinted at the patch of dresser where my finger was pointed. Then he saw the sapphire. His eyebrows shot up and he mashed his finger down on it and brought it up on the tip. He stared at it a long moment. "Ain't this my lucky day," he said without enthusiasm.

"Now all we've got to do is find the key with a missing stone."

"Nobody's gonna convict a man on that kind of evidence. Lots of those pins could be missing stones."

"But if we knew who it was, it might make it easier to build a case that would stand up."

"You think the chief of police is going to stand for my investigating the Key Club, Billy? Jesus, he's up there with some bimbo two nights out of three. You think he's gonna say, 'Sure, Boot. Just put a uniform on all the doors. Check their pins as they come in.' Right."

"We'll just have to do it discreetly, that all."

"And how you figure doing that?"

"I say we bring back Teddy and Tilden."

He shook his head and backed away from me. "No way. Forget it."

"You're getting lazy, Boot."

"I'm getting smart, Billy. I've outgrown some things."

"You know it's the only way."

"You call Teddy and Tilden discreet?" He shook his head but couldn't suppress a grin. "Teddy and Tilden. I almost forgot about them."

"For old times' sake?"

He chewed his cigar butt and studied me. "How is it every time you get yourself knee-deep in shit, I'm the one scraping it off my pants?"

"Seven o' clock tonight?"

"Eight," he grunted. "Northeast arcade."

SUSAN F. EDWARDS

Chapter Twenty-Five
Teddy and Tilden

I got to the northeast arcade about fifteen minutes early. A tattered bum in a once-elegant suit sat propped against the wall sleeping. Ybor had always had a few gentlemen who drank their dinners from a paper sack and slept on cobblestone beds, but since the land boom went bust, there were a lot more of them. Once-prosperous businessmen reduced to wearing tatters and frequenting soup kitchens. They usually begged just enough money to get another drink.

I gave this one a nudge with my foot and he roused looking bleary, a soggy cigar stump stuck in his face. "If it ain't my old pal Tilden," I said and flipped him a nickel.

Boot was alarmingly convincing as a bum. His wife hated it when we played Tilden and Teddy. He caught the nickel and rose unsteadily. He gave me a wobbly tip of his bowler. "Teddy, my boy," he slurred, throwing a sloppy arm around my shoulder, "I believe you've gotten some new shoes since I saw you last."

I raised my foot and stuck my toe out of the hole in the sole. "Can you believe someone was throwing these beauties away?"

We spent four hours drunkenly stumbling into the paths of prosperous-looking men, most with young women on their arms. If we couldn't get close enough to see their pins any other way, we might bump right into them or panhandle them to get a closer look.

It was fun for the first couple of hours. Every building had stairways, and Key Club holders might enter at any one of them to reach secret doors upstairs guarded by heavily armed, faceless men who saw no evil, heard no evil and spoke no evil, but looked capable of doing plenty of evil.

We were enjoying a break and counting our booty when I heard Boot say, "Oh shit," and saw him sink into a sitting position and pull his bowler over his face. I looked down the block and saw the chief of police heading toward us, a buxom petite beauty on his arm. His name was Krestakos, but everyone called him El Greco—the Greek. He even had El Greco on his campaign posters. Like Edmunds, he was short and carried himself with that almost military ramrod erectness that short men affect to appear taller and tougher. I supposed women would find him attractive in a Napoleonic sort of way. He was handsome out of uniform with his black wavy hair and noble Roman profile.

I staggered toward him, wondering if he dyed his hair.

When I was a few feet from him, singing under my breath and chuckling idiotically, I tripped over a loose sidewalk tile and sprawled into him. It was like hitting a little rock wall. He went hard and stiff and grabbed me by the hair.

"Sorry, sorry," I mumbled and gave him a cross-eyed look. He inspected my crusty suit and face. I didn't worry too much that he would recognize me. I dropped my eyes submissively and got a good look at his key pin. All four sapphires were intact.

"What are you doing here?" El Greco demanded in a hostile voice.

"My friend and I," I gestured at the cringing Boot, his hat still over his face. "We're just coming home from dinner down at the Angels of Mercy, sir. Tilden felt a little sick. Maybe you could loan us a dime so's I could take him home on the streetcar."

El Greco advanced on Boot and poked him with a toe. "You. What's the matter with you?"

Boot made some god-awful retching noises and turned his face to the wall.

"The soup was a tad ripe tonight, sir. I didn't touch the stuff, but Tilden here—" Boot was hacking and convulsing now like a cat bringing up a fur ball.

El Greco turned in disgust and started to walk away.

"Hey," I yelled, "ain't you El Greco?"

El Greco likes being famous, even with the riff-raff. He stopped and bestowed a lordly smile on me.

"I'm a big fan of yours," I told him. "I read about you in the papers all the time. You ask me, you're the one ought to be mayor." Boot made an even louder retching noise behind me.

El Greco smiled beneficently and flipped me a quarter. "Get your friend off the street. And get him a decent bowl of soup."

As he walked away, Boot muttered, "You're shameless, Heart, utterly shameless."

"Me? At least I wasn't hacking up hairballs like an alley cat."

"I'd be coughing up my cojones if he'd'a caught me."

"Hey, what's the worst that could happen? You'd be off the force. You could come into business with me."

"I'd rather take a swim with cement shoes on."

I said nothing. I was going to make him ask.

It took him a while but he finally chuffed out a sigh and said, "So?"

"So what?" Totally nonchalant.

"You know what. Did you get a look at his pin?"

"You kidding? We practically did the tango together."

Boot's face was dark, bracing for the worst. "Don't shit me on this, Billy."

I smiled. "Relax. His jewels are fully intact."

Boot let out a relieved sigh.

"Too bad. I'd love to see you arrest El Greco for murder. We all know he's committed plenty in his time."

"This is a waste of time," He said. "I'm going home."

"Hey wait. We took in a buck and a half tonight. Don't you think we owe it to the city economy to spread it around some?"

He shook his head and kept walking.

"One, Boot, at the Grotto. Vincente's been asking about you. He thinks you don't love him anymore. I told him that's not it. Your wife just won't let you out at night."

171

He stopped and turned. "What's that, psychology?"

"Come on. Just one."

"One, Heart. Then I'm off. I got a murder to investigate in case you forgot. I can't sleep in tomorrow like the private dicks."

We found Otto at his usual spot and the three of us drank a toast to Lola's spirit. "To Lola Flores," Otto said holding his glass high, "If I could command the shining of spring, could grasp it without putting it out — oh — I should wish to send it as a gift to that beautiful flower at the border of heaven."

"That's nice," I said. "Did you make that up?"

"No," he answered, "A Chinese poet named Li Tai Po did. Over a thousand years ago. Funny how it still applies."

Sometimes an oddly light spirit will visit a wake, especially after a few drinks, and people will laugh with an extra fervor. Maybe it's relief that death has come and gone and let you escape one more time. The simple joy of finding yourself still living when death has passed so close. That spirit did not visit us that night. We finished the bottle and parted soberly, the sharp edge of Lola's death not dulled by alcohol.

Who would kill such a creature? Why? What had she been about to tell me? Who was it that knocked on her door as we spoke, and why, why, why did he murder her? It was someone she knew, someone she was expecting. Did she threaten him, tell him she was going to spill the beans to me? Is that why he strangled her as I slept?

I couldn't help thinking I could have prevented her death. I owed it to her to find out who killed her and why.

My dreams were filled with Lola in her apartment, first on the veranda, then in her bedroom. In the dream, her naked body was once again silhouetted against her dressing screen. I wouldn't look — I looked around the room, at her dresser, her bed. As I stared at the wall next to her bed, suddenly it hit me.

I knew where Edmunds was.

Chapter Twenty-Six
Boot's Boot

I woke up laughing and discovered that my clothes were wet and clammy. I felt cold sweat on my chest and head. I turned on the light and saw the last of the dream vanish like a cat's tail through a doorway. The dream, what was it? A sense of urgency came over me to catch the vanishing dream.

I turned off the light and lay back down. What was the dream? What was the clue it held? Think. Lola's silhouette came back. I didn't want to look at it. Then suddenly I had the feeling I knew something big. What? The murderer? No. Edmunds. I knew where he was. I scanned the room in my mind's eye, but nothing came back. The harder I concentrated, the more foggy the image became.

I dialed the phone and Nesta answered in a sleepy voice.

"I need you to come and pick me up right now."

"Are you nuts? It's three-thirty in the morning," she said.

"That's why I need you to pick me up. The streetcars aren't running."

"Can't this wait until morning?"

"No, Nesta. It's got to be now."

There was a long pause. "Why?" she whispered.

"I think I may know where your husband is."

"Where?"

"Just come as soon as you can. I'll explain everything."

By the time I had showered and shaved, Nesta was out front honking insistently. I took the stairs in bounds, anxious to catch her before she woke up all of Ybor. Each time my foot hit a step, I could feel every punch and kick and fall I'd taken since I had met Nesta Edmunds. Somehow I felt in my bones that I was going to take plenty more before this whole thing was over.

Once in the car, I saw that she hadn't even taken the time to dress. She had just thrown a cape over her dressing gown. On the way to Edmunds Island, I told her about Lola's murder and my dream.

"We're going to her apartment in the middle of the night so you can look at her bedroom?"

"The answer is there someplace, I know it. I've just got to get a fresh look."

Nesta pulled the car up in front the Palace of Florence and looked at it doubtfully, "How are we going to get in?"

"I'm going in. You will wait in the car." I got out and closed the door before she could say anything. I wasn't surprised when she followed me. She grabbed my sleeve and whispered my name. I whirled and glared at her. "If you make one sound, I will tie you up and lock you in the bonnet of your car."

She rolled her eyes. "I'd like to see you try." But she remained silent after that, and so we went on through a door and up the service stairs. I was winded when we got to the top. My entire rib cage ached and throbbed.

Lola's apartment was posted with a Tampa Police Department handbill that read, "Crime Scene — Keep Out." I went to work on the lock with my favorite lock pick, a crochet hook purloined from my mother's sewing basket. They don't expect much crime on Edmunds Island, so it wasn't much of a lock. I had it open in thirty seconds and relocked it behind us once we were inside.

Nesta's eyes were wide as she looked around the living room. It was too dark to read her emotion. Was it fear of being caught or wonder at seeing the home of her husband's murdered lover? She followed me back to the darkened bedroom. I drew the curtains open behind the dressing screen and motioned for Nesta to stand behind it. Moonlight flooded the room, revealing Nesta's silhouette in a gauzy, dreamlike vision.

I looked away, running my gaze over the dressing table, the bed, the floor, the walls. I froze when I saw the dark square on the wall next to the window, partly obscured by the screen. I turned a light on next to the bed and examined the painted tin street scene. "Has your husband ever been to Haiti?"

Nesta came around to look at the painting. "Yes," she said. "Two years ago. I'd forgotten about it until just this minute. Yes, it all makes sense now."

"What makes sense?"

"He was always going off on business trips. Miami, Jacksonville, New York, Cuba, South America. He was secretive about his business, but he liked to brag about all the important people he met and the exotic places he went. He collected postcards from every place he visited. A couple of years ago, he said he was going to Cuba. This time he didn't bring back any postcards. I thought it was because he had been there so many times."

I turned off the light, and she went on. "A few days after he got back, I was taking his coat to the cleaners. His passport was still in the pocket. I opened it really just kind of idly. I looked at his picture and at all the visa stamps. The last stamp wasn't Cuba at all. It was Haiti."

"Did you ask him about it?"

"Yes, but he shrugged it off. He said I was mistaken, that he had told me it was Haiti all along."

"You didn't press it?"

"Edward was a habitual liar. Once he came up with a lie, he stuck to it no matter how absurd it came to be. He was meanest when he was caught in a lie. So I just let it go."

We stared at the painting in the darkness before Nesta turned away. "I'll drop you off at home to pack. I'll get the tickets. We can take the early train to Miami and ship out from there." She started to walk away, but I put a hand out to stop her. I had heard footsteps somewhere outside. An unseen hand rattled the knob on the front door. Fortunately, I had relocked it before coming back here. We held our breath and waited.

After a few moments, we heard a door open farther away and steps receding down the stairwell. They must have hired a night watchman for the building since Lola's murder. The people who live on Edmunds Island are not accustomed to murders in their midst. We waited a full ten minutes before creeping out of the apartment and down the service stairs.

Nesta was uncharacteristically silent on the drive to Ybor. I guessed she was thinking about what she might say to her husband when she finally had him cornered. I let her brood, grateful for a moment of peace.

I still didn't know who had killed Lola. I didn't much want to leave the investigation to the Tampa Police Department, even if Boot was on the case. They had shut him up before, and they could do it again if I wasn't around to stir the pot. I didn't blame him; messing in a case like this could leave his wife a widow and his kids orphans. But I couldn't stand the thought of Lola's killer drinking twelve-year-old bourbon at the yacht club while the ants ate her flesh. I wondered if I had any choice.

By ten a.m. I was packed and had fallen asleep in my armchair. When I awoke, a pug-nosed man in a short bristly haircut and a cheap rumpled suit stood over me. Behind him stood a uniformed copper at attention. The pug-nose flashed his Tampa PD detective badge and surveyed my digs. "We knocked, but I guess you didn't hear us. He spied my suitcase next to the door. "Going somewhere?"

"What'd you say your name was?"

"Schmidt."

"What are you doing here?"

"I'm asking the questions here. What's with the suitcase?"

"My mother's going to visit her sister in Miami. I'm taking her a suitcase to use. What's it to you?"

"When is the last time you saw Lola Flores alive, Mr. Heart? Or is it Mr. Corazon?"

"You on the Flores case?"

"Looks like it. Answer the question."

"Where's Boot?"

"Off the case."

"Why?"

He stuck his twisted grin down into my face. "They took him off for personal involvement with the prime suspect. Any more questions?" His face was so close to mine I could smell the cheap whisky on his breath. He examined my face with a leer. "Looks like you been in a scrap. Maybe the bird fought back while you was choking the life outta her."

"Oh, come on, even you guys wouldn't be stupid enough to try to pin that murder on me."

"Why not? We know you've been badgering her for weeks."

"I was questioning her for a case I'm on."

"Gimme a break. You—"

Just then, Nesta burst through the door. "I got the..." Her voice trailed off when she saw my guests.

"Well, well, well. This your mother, Corazon?"

"I'm his client, Nesta Edmunds," she said with enough frost to shrivel a palm tree.

"Ah, yes," he said. "You're the one who hired our boy here to harass your late husband's mistress. Where were you between ten o'clock night before last and three yesterday morning?"

Nesta drew herself up with a haughty scowl. "Am I being formally held for questioning? Because if I am, I'd like my lawyer present. Maybe you know him, Avery Sessums? He's my uncle."

Schmidt sucked his teeth and sized her up through narrowed eyes. Nobody tangled with Avery Sessums, not even the mayor. He was a former city councilman and now a state senator. *La Voz* had dubbed Sessums the only honest man in Florida politics. "Not yet, lady. But don't leave town." He turned to me. "And where were you night before last, amigo?"

"I was right here in bed. Alone."

"No witnesses, huh?"

"Boot can tell you or McCarty down in lockup, or even the jail doctor. I got beat up pretty bad the night before and dumped in Plant Park. They thought I was a vagrant and took me to the hoosegow. I had three broken ribs and a concussion. I was in no shape to strangle Lola Flores."

Schmidt took a cigar out of his jacket, bit the end off and spat it on my floor. He plugged it into his face. "Hardly an airtight alibi."

"Check it out. You'll see."

"I will, Corazon. I will." He walked toward the door, pausing just before he stepped over the threshold. "In the meantime, don't even think about leaving town, or you'll be in the hoosegow 'til judgment day."

Nesta stamped her foot when he was gone. "Damn," she said. "Damn it to hell!"

"Don't swear, angel. It doesn't work for you."

"Now what are we going to do?"

"You're going to go home like a good girl, and I'm going to find Lola's murderer."

She stamped her foot again like a spoiled child. "I don't give a fig who killed her."

"You're such a warm and caring person."

She ignored my sarcasm. "Murder is a matter for the police, Mr. Heart. May I remind you that you are in my employ, and I want you to find Edward."

"I'm their prime suspect now and I can't do anything until I find out who the murderer really is, don't you see that? Besides, I do care who killed her."

"Sounds like a personal problem to me, Mr. Heart. This is business."

"She was a human being, Nesta. And she loved your husband. Probably more than you did. What he did to her was just as cruel as what he did to you. Probably crueler."

Her face turned a bitter gray. "You don't know what he did to me," she spat. "Did you know he gave me syphilis, Mr. Heart? Courtesy, probably of Miss Flores or someone like her. I nearly died in a shack of a hospital in Key West. I couldn't go to a decent hospital close to home, could I? Then everyone would know. My family couldn't have that. In a town like this, your reputation is all you have."

"At least you're still alive."

"Am I?" Her mouth was set in hard lines. "I can live with the shame. God knows, I've had enough practice since I met him. Did you know that he once boasted he would marry the Queen of Gasparilla? He liked to remind me that he made that vow long before I was crowned. He didn't marry *me*. He bagged Tampa's sacrificial virgin. And everyone knew it except for me." Tears filled her eyes, and she turned away from me.

"Look," I said, softened by her shame, "that's all over now. You've got to look toward the future. You're young; you can start over."

"Can I?" She spat the words out like something rotten she had just bitten into. "Even if someone would have me after Edward wiped his feet on me, I couldn't—" A sob broke her voice. She shook her head, fighting for control. "Never mind," she said in a strangled voice. "You're right—it's over and done."

"What is it, Nesta? What has made you so bitter?"

She looked at me a long moment. The starch had come back into her now and the only sign of a struggle was the flaring of her nostrils. "The syphilis," she whispered. "I—I'll never have children." The horrible sadness in her eyes was made more terrible by the trembling smile on her lips.

"I'm so sorry. I didn't know."

She waved me off and turned away. "I didn't mean what I said about Miss Flores. No one deserves to die like that."

"You know whoever murdered her is connected with your husband's disappearance. Lola knew where Edmunds was. And someone was trying to choke it out of her."

"Either that or someone was trying to keep her from telling you."

"I've thought about that too," I said. "Tell me, how well do you know Hedda and Dominic Boudreaux?"

"Not nearly as well as Edward knew them. Dom was Edward's little lap dog. He was always dragging the two of them on trips with us. He'd send Dom out on some job, and then Edward and Hedda would disappear. I hated traveling with them." She looked at me. "Do you think they murdered Lola?"

"Not really," I said, stunned at what she had just revealed. Given his obvious philandering, we both knew exactly what Hedda and Edmunds had probably been up to when they disappeared together. I wondered why Nesta had waited until now to tell me about the two of them. But after all the humiliation she had already endured tonight, I wasn't going to give her a hard time about withholding information. Instead, I said, "I think Hedda helped your husband with his disappearance. And she's tried to shut Lola up once before."

"What does that mean?"

"I don't know. But she knows more than she's telling."

After Nesta left, I dialed Boot's desk at the precinct. He answered on the first ring. "Boot Simms."

"Boot, what the hell's going on down there? Who's this bulldog, Schmidt?"

"You know I can't talk here. Especially to you."

"You off the case for good?"

"What do you think?" When I didn't answer, he said, "Call me tonight. We'll talk." Then the line went dead.

My head was beginning to scream again, and my body felt as if it had been run over by a Packard. I lay down and tried to sleep, but I couldn't get the questions out of my head. I kept going over my last conversation with Lola. She had said I was right, Edmunds was alive. She needed to talk to me. Then there was a knock at the door and she said, "He's here." She had sounded scared but not surprised. She had been expecting him, whoever he was. She must not have been too frightened because she evidently let him in.

"That doesn't fit with the Ciega angle, does it," said Otto when he stopped by to bring me a *Chronicle* and a bottle of malta that afternoon. "If one of his boys was trying to get something out of her, he wouldn't call before he came."

"Not necessarily. Maybe she was trying to cut a deal with Vincetti. Edmunds didn't leave her any money. Maybe she was going to sell him out to the highest bidder."

"So why would Vincetti kill her?"

I sighed. "You're right. It just doesn't fit. No matter how hard I try, it just doesn't fit."

"You said Edmunds didn't leave her anything. What's she living on?"

"She wouldn't say. I'm hoping Boot'll have a fix on her finances when I call him tonight."

I scanned the paper after Otto left. It was the usual stuff. Schools were teaching high school girls, future wives they called them, to serve meals on sixty cents a day. A lucky monkey had survived two shipwrecks. And Randall Stroven had been named by the Chamber of Commerce as Civic Leader of the Year. There was a photo of Chamber President Terrance Quattlebaum handing Stroven a plaque over a staged handshake. It was all so damned cozy. I threw the paper down and stood up. I'd had about all the rest I could stand.

I found Ciega at his table in El Dorado, having his afternoon coffee. Boot was right. When all else failed, I couldn't resist tossing a firecracker in the bushes to see what I could flush out. He drew on his giant cigar and eyed me as I approached his table. "I see my boys followed directions this time."

"Too bad you didn't give them the same instructions about Lola Flores."

"What are you talking about?"

"I'm talking about the woman Vincetti iced two nights ago trying to find out where Edmunds is."

Ciega gave me an amused smile. "Vincetti, hah! Vincetti's a businessman. He never made a hit in his life."

"That explains why it was so sloppy."

He didn't seem so amused now. "Get outta here, kid. I don't want to hurt you again."

"Oh my, you look surprised. He did tell you, didn't he?"

"Beat it," he said, eyeing his goons who rolled their shoulders and cracked their knuckles, loosening up like boxers.

I took a couple of steps toward the door and then turned back to Ciega. "Don't be too hard on Vincetti. I'm sure he meant to tell you."

I still had some time to kill before I could call Boot, and I was hungry. Mama had a skillet full of tomato and basil simmering on the stove when I arrived. She took one look at my beat-up face and asked, "Do I even want to know?"

I told her about my run-in with Ciega while I set the table. I had forgotten a comment he had made at the end of our interview. It suddenly came back to me there in the kitchen. "He said if it wasn't for you, he would kill me. What do you suppose he meant by that?"

She was pouring a hot potful of steaming linguini into a colander. The steam burned her hand and she dropped the pot with a shout of pain. I picked up the pot in silence as she snapped a stalk of aloe from a plant in the window. She rubbed it on her hand, avoiding my look.

"Mama, how well do you and Santo Ciega know each other?"

She dropped her head. "He was my sweetheart when I met your father. He swore vengeance on the man who stole my heart. And he took it."

"Why did I never know this?"

She smiled sadly and touched my hair. "I have spent most of my life trying to forget the existence of the Yellow Rat. When I think of him, when I speak to him, my heart is filled with hate. I do not want a hateful heart. So I push him out of my memory."

I told her about Lola over dinner. I described how she had met Edmunds when she was a taxi dancer in Havana, how she had gone with him to Miami, there to find out he was married. How when Edmunds' wife died, he had brought Lola to Tampa and had married the Queen of Gasparilla. Still Lola stayed with him and traveled with him. "She must have loved him very much to put up with all that."

"Not necessarily," said my mother, sounding uncharacteristically cynical. "Maybe she liked the independence of being kept by a married man, and a busy one at that."

I looked at her with surprise.

"Don't make Lola into something she was not. It does not honor her memory." She raised her chin in an almost defiant gesture. "Not all women want a man around all the time, Billy. But most of them still have to depend on one."

After we finished our tea, my mother donned a shawl and beckoned me out for a walk. We made the promenade down Seventh Avenue, stopping to talk with friends and exchange embraces, Mama showing me off like a newborn babe. She even tried to buy me one of those cone-shaped lollipops I used to love from the piruli man. We settled on helados instead, a coconut for her, mango for me. Although I lived in Ybor, I no longer felt of Ybor very often. This was like coming home.

We stopped in front of St. Mary's Cathedral. Mama drew her shawl up over her head and went in. I followed. We lit candles for Lola and prayed for her spirit. Finally, I felt at peace.

Back at her house, Mama seemed to know I would spend the night. She kissed me and went to bed, leaving the door to my old room open, the dim comforting light next to the bed on. For a moment I was ten years old again, safe in blissful ignorance. As I drifted off to sleep, I remembered Boot. Damn. His wife would skin me alive if I called this late. Ah, well, he'd keep. Everything would keep until tomorrow. My sleep was surprisingly deep and untroubled.

Chapter Twenty-Seven
A Deal with the Devil

The door to my apartment stood open when I arrived the next morning. I sidled up to it and peeked in. There amid the charred wreckage and ransacked clutter from previous visitors stood Rocky Vincetti, surveying the mess. I was surprised to see a sad expression rather than an angry one when he turned to me.

"You come to finish the job, Vincetti? Maybe throw some acid on the walls, release a plague of locusts? How about riddling the place with a machine gun? You haven't tried that yet."

"Look. I admit I had you thrown off The Mez, Corazon. That was business. In my business I can't afford to have people see some punk push me around in my own place, you know what I mean?"

"Yeah? And what about the pineapple, was that business too?"

"I keep telling you I didn't do that. Look, asshole, haven't you figured out yet there's another player in this? Someone who has never wanted you on this case?"

"You're the ones who wanted me off."

"We didn't even know you was on the case until you came around snorting and pawing the ground like a toro charging a red cape." He scowled at me. "Someone had you tailed. Someone tossed a pipe bomb in your window. Someone iced the girl. But I'm telling you, Corazon, it wasn't us."

"Long as we're being so candid here, why were you on the same ship as Edmunds? What did you say to him when you and your brothers dragged him into a cabin on the deck?"

His jaw muscles tightened and his nostrils flared as if he were fighting the impulse to sock me. Then his eyes softened in resignation and he slumped into a chair. His skill at the gesture reminded me of Lola. I didn't trust him as far as I could toss a cow.

"Edmunds owed Ciega money," he said with a sigh. "It's kind of complicated. Some gambling debts and loans. And something about an insurance policy for half a million dollars."

I laughed. So Edmunds had nailed Ciega with the same scam. I wondered how many other suckers were out there holding worthless insurance policies on Edmunds' life. It certainly gave them all a motive for murder, either before or after they found out they'd been trimmed.

"So you were trying to collect on the ship?"

"We'd been watching him for a while. We knew he was taking a wad of cash to Europe. My brothers and I were due for a trip anyway. My mother really was sick. She died last week. Aldo and Frankie were there." A fat tear grew in his eye and spilled down his face. He made no attempt to wipe it away. Whether he was acting or not, it was a shameless gesture. It made me want to cry, but I kept my face a rock and said nothing.

"We waited until he was alone on deck and grabbed him. Demanded our money. He said he didn't have it on him, but he would bring it to us that night."

"And you Girl Scouts just believed him."

"Hell no. But we were on a boat in the middle of the ocean. Where was he gonna go? We figured if he didn't show that night, we'd just muscle in the next day and take what was ours."

I didn't bother to suppress a chuckle. "I hope that story's true because it sure makes you look like a witless bastard."

He bit down on his cigar savagely. "Yeah, he had a real talent for making people look stupid. So far he's done all right with you too."

"That what you came here for, Vincetti, to have a contest on who's stupider? I could have saved you the trouble and conceded. You win, *no lo contendre*."

"Yeah, well I was drinking martinis with the mayor while you was dressed like a drunk bum and bumping into El Greco. Which one seems stupider to you?"

186

"Why are you here?" I growled.

"Looks to me like you're looking for something. I thought maybe I could help you find it."

"Your generosity is truly heartwarming."

He affected a grave, avuncular smile. "You got us all wrong. Especially Ciega. He tried to help your father. The Committee wouldn't listen to him. This is his way of making it up to you."

"What a guy."

"People change, Corazon. They lose people that mean everything to them. They know what it's like, and it makes everything different."

I wanted to hit him so badly, my knuckles ached. "What's the deal?"

"He wants me to open The Mez to you, no questions asked. You don't even have to tell us what you're looking for. All I ask is that you keep a low profile."

"And you ask nothing in return."

He shrugged magnanimously. "We're just trying to repay an old debt."

"Forget it, Vincetti. I'm not your bird dog."

He crossed his arms over his heart. "You wound me."

"I'd like to wound you worse."

You're a bigger fool than I thought, Corazon." He flicked his cigar ash out the broken window and looked out over Seventh Avenue. "The Anglos run everything in this town. They always have. We're just their pawns."

"You're giving them too much credit."

"You don't think they call the shots?"

"You know what happens when you put fifty rats in a barrel, Vincetti?"

He gave me a skeptical scowl. "What's this, a riddle?"

"The big rats eat the little ones."

"So what?"

"The Anglos aren't chess players moving us around like pieces on a board. They're just the big rats."

He looked at me and shook his head. "How do you sleep nights with thoughts like those in your head?"

Chapter Twenty-Eight
Midnight Underground

I stopped at Otto's on the way to my office. "What's the news, my friend?" I asked and picked up a *Chronicle*.

His lips went tight. "Billy, you need to get out of here right now."

"Why?"

"Coppers got a murder warrant out for you. They were just through here on their way from your office, wanted to know if I'd seen you today. I told 'em you bought a paper and mentioned an appointment in south Tampa."

"Dios mio."

He threw me a set of keys. "Go to my place now. We'll talk when I get home."

"They've got no evidence against me."

"Word has it they've got an eyewitness who says you were there the night of her murder."

"Who?"

"I don't know but you don't stand a chance if they get you in their jail. Go."

I looked around the place to see who might be watching. It was deserted at this time of day. Everyone was tucked away in an office, busily adding up columns of numbers or typing up lists, or whatever it is they do all day in those offices. "Thanks, Otto. I owe you."

"Go," he urged, motioning me away.

I took the exit at a purposeful clip, checking the impulse to break into a run.

The door to Otto's place was nestled into a back corner in an interior Ybor courtyard. The apartment itself was set into a larger building and had no windows at all. No light penetrated Otto's snug cave. He had no need of lamps, but friends had bought him some so they could see when they visited him. These gifts he politely refused, insisting that in his house, one must enter his world, a world in which seeing with the eyes was not a factor.

Coming from the harsh heat and brightness of the midday Florida sun into Otto's cool, dark cave was like returning to the womb. You experienced Otto's place by touch, sound, smell, and most importantly, by taste. Otto was a fabulous cook. No one ever saw his place except in brief snatches of light from a match lit for a cigar or pipe. That newcomers took overlong in lighting their many smokes did not escape Otto, I'm certain.

However, those of us who spent a lot of time there didn't need to see the place. We had a deeper acquaintance with it. We knew the placement, texture, and shape of every piece of furniture, the scent of good wine and well-aged cheese, the yeasty smell of bread and roasted garlic.

I had spent many evenings in this blackness and navigated the place with a sure foot, feeling the air circulated by overhead fans in currents and eddies around doorways and furniture. I sat in my favorite chair, a huge, slouchy overstuffed thing, covered with an old silk damask throw.

I reached my left hand straight out at nine o'clock and felt the reassuring smooth cool touch of soapstone. This was my favorite sculpture, and Otto kept it next to my favorite chair. That's the kind of host he was. It had a substantial heft and weight. I pulled it into my lap and ran my hands over its smooth lines, which swept up to a point. Some people had described it as a fancy teardrop shape, but to me it was a frozen flame. I can't tell you what it was about that object, why I found its weight, its shape, its surface comforting, but I did.

Otto had other sculptures. He owned a dazzling collection of nudes from human-size marble classic Greek figures to the graceful elongated forms of a new artist named Erté. His collection of Asian precious stone carvings included Chinese jades so intricately carved

190

that you could spend an evening getting to know just one in the darkness while the conversation went on around you.

There were African tribal masks, clay vessels, mahogany carvings, and many more objects to delight the fingers. Although seduction was not Otto's aim in collecting sculpture, I have witnessed more than one woman swooning in his arms while he guided her hands over texture, along contours and into crevices.

I got up and walked unfalteringly through the blackness to the bar and poured myself a brandy. I took my drink and one of Otto's handmade Sobranos back to my chair. I allowed myself a few moments of peace before turning my thoughts to the fix I was in.

I dialed my mother's number and sat back to wait out the rings. She never hurried to answer the phone, considering it more a nuisance than a tool. If she was busy, she might not answer it at all. She picked up on the sixth ring, a land speed record for my mother.

News travels fast in Tampa, especially if you're plugged in. I wasn't surprised she already knew about the warrant. Her friend Mrs. Rodriguez had a son on the force. Her voice was husky and thick with tears.

"You must not let them catch you," she whispered. "I have some money—"

"I don't need money right now, I—"

"You must take it. Go to Italy, to my sisters. I will come later."

"I can't leave, Mama."

"You must..." her voice broke, and she sobbed softly, fighting to maintain control. But the tears tore out of her. "They killed my husband. They must not kill my son."

Her sobs brought a deep ache to my chest, rang my bones, "Mama, Mama...I'm not going to let them kill me. And I'm not going to let them run me out of town. This is my place, my home. Not Italy."

"That's what your father said. And where is he now? Under the dirt of his home! Where are we now? Is this our home? Are these our people who kill us and take our sons?"

"I'm going to find out who did this, Mama. They are not going to catch me."

She let out a ragged sigh. "Sometimes knowledge is danger, not power."

"No. I will never believe that."

She said nothing. "I want you to go stay with Aunt Rosa," I told her.

"You will not leave your home to stay alive, but you tell me to go stay with my sister?"

"But the police—"

"I will go to the police tomorrow with my lawyer. I will protest this warrant.

"No, please, Mama. Let me handle this."

Her voice hardened. "Don't you say that to me. You want to fight a war, don't tell me to go hide in the house."

"Can't you see you'll just make trouble for yourself?"

"You want me to behave myself, eh?"

"Yes, I do. Very much."

"When you get on the ship for Italy, then I will behave."

"You know I can't do that."

There was a long pause at the other end of the line. I could hear her take a deep breath. "I know." Her voice trembled when she said she would light a candle for me. I promised to call her again soon.

Next I called Nesta. The cops had already been by to shake her down, but her uncle had been there, and they had backed right down.

"Uncle's not happy about this whole thing. He told me if I don't give up the search, he'll let them hang me out to dry next time."

"Will he?"

"Never. It would be too hard on the family name."

I gave that some thought before I told her to pack a bag and get some cash together, and to be ready to bolt at a moment's notice.

I pushed the phone away and felt the hands of Otto's clock. Five o'clock. Boot wouldn't be home for at least another hour. My stomach growled about the time I became aware of the smell of ripe mango. I followed my nose to the kitchen, where I found not only a perfect mango but a thick wedge of asiago cheese, some fresh crusty bread, and a fat chorizo sausage. The hot mustard was in its usual place, as was a half-full bottle of red wine. There was always a bottle of wine in progress at Otto's. We called it the perpetual fountain of Dionysus. Otto had a fine stone statue of him.

I had just finishing setting out the repast when Otto entered quietly and locked the door behind him. I smelled fresh mussels in his bag. We drank and nibbled while Otto, as if by magic, produced mussels in marinara sauce over fresh linguini within about twenty minutes. Like the perpetual fountain, there was the eternal pot of marinara in Otto's kitchen. Tomatoes, peppers and herbs continually brewing and marrying in the best Spanish virgin olive oil.

Over dinner we batted the facts around. He told me the police had gone over my place pretty good and asked all the neighbors about me. I told him about Vincetti's offer.

"That's great," he said. "The most wanted man in Tampa hanging around The Mez with the mayor and the chief of police, and at least half the Committee. Can I come watch?"

"Sometimes you've gotta make a deal with the devil."

"No," he said. "There's always another choice."

"There might be one," I replied as I dialed up Boot.

"Holy Mary, Mother of God," he said when he answered. "You're in deep, buddy. I was you, I'd get out of town while you still can. The *Chronicle*'s had a reporter on this story all day."

"You know me better than that."

"Yeah. I guess I just hoped you'd grown some brains since your youth."

"Let's not fight, Boot. I need all the friends I can get."

"They got a witness puts you at the dame's at one a.m."

"Who?"

"They pulled me off the case before I was able to find out."

"I need to know, Boot."

"I'm working on it." The tone of his voice told me not to push. "Call me tomorrow night. I'll see what I can have by then… You lay low until then, you hear me?"

I gave him my assurances that I would stay out of sight and said goodbye. "There went my choice," I told Otto as I replaced that earpiece.

When I emerged from Otto's the next morning into the blazing sun, I felt like a mole caught above ground, blinded in a whole new way. The sun's rays pierced my eyes painfully and all the sights rushing at me made me dizzy. I had to sit down and close my eyes until it passed and my eyes adjusted before setting out again.

I was waiting for Vincetti outside his private door to Punch House when he arrived. He didn't recognize me because I was dressed in the uniform of all old Cuban men in Ybor, a rumpled guayabera shirt and straw hat with a wide brim that hid my face in deep shadow. Vincetti slowed and put a hand inside his suit, feeling no doubt for the .38 he kept in a holster next to his heart.

I raised the brim of the hat long enough to give him a look and then flipped it back down. A grin slithered across his face. "Every time I think I've seen the last of you, you pop up like a loaded bolita ball," he said, bringing a key out of his vest pocket and fitting it into the lock. "What's with the caballero act?"

"For a guy who thinks he's on the inside, you don't know much."

"I keep up on what counts, Corazon." We had arrived at his office. He motioned me into a chair and sat down behind his desk. "You keep thinking you count."

"There's a warrant out for my arrest for the murder of Lola Flores."

A smile pulled his cruel thin lips so tight they disappeared. He looked like a hissing ferret. "For a Boy Scout, you sure get in a lotta trouble."

"Seems to be a family trait."

Yeah, you screw up and then you come to us to fix it. Like I told you before, the Anglos—"

"Save it, Vincetti. I know all about your impotence. All I need is some information, and I can't hang around The Mez and get it myself now."

His features snapped into a predatory alertness. "Sure, companero," he said smoothly, "just tell me what you need to know."

"Not so fast, *compadre*." I spat out the last word with as much contempt as I could muster. "I know why you were so eager to let me stake the place out. You think whoever I'm looking for can lead you to Edmunds."

He clamped his features down in his best poker face, but I didn't need confirmation.

"But it's not that simple," I told him. "I already know where Edmunds is."

His eyes narrowed, but he said nothing.

"This man I'm looking for doesn't know. I'm pretty sure that's why he killed Lola. He thought she knew and was trying to get it out of her."

"So why do you want to find him?"

"Try to keep up, Vincetti. There's a warrant out for my arrest for the murder of Lola Flores. I can't run down Edmunds until I give them her killer, now can I?"

"Funny how you were looking for him before that warrant came down ain't it?"

I stared him down. "Look I know this won't mean much to you. But I don't like to see a man get away with murder. Maybe I've just seen too much of that in this town."

He took a cigar out of his desk, bit the tip off and hocked it across the room. "I'm still waiting for you to tell me what you're looking for."

"First I need your word, for whatever that's worth."

He lit his stogie and blew a thick cloud of smoke at me. "On what?"

"You give me the name of this person, and you make no move on him whatsoever." He nodded. "You do that, and I'll tell you where Edmunds is when I'm done with him."

"How do I know you know where Edmunds is?"

"I guess you're just going to have to trust me on that."

He eyed me suspiciously. "Why should I?"

"You blew this job once and kept your head on your neck. You think Ciega's going to be so generous if you blow it again?"

A twitch tugged at the corner of his left eye.

"I'm a pro at this stuff, Vincetti. Let me handle it alone, and I'll see to it you come out smelling like a gardenia."

"How do I know you'll hold up your end of the bargain?"

"You're saving my neck by giving me this guy's name. I don't like feeling indebted. Especially to you. Besides, I want you to get Edmunds. He's a no-good scumbag who deserves everything that's coming to him. I can't give it to him, but you can."

I could see the thoughts bubbling in his tiny brain. "Okay," he said at last. "We'll lay off the guy for forty-eight hours after we give you his name. I give you my word. Then you gotta give me Edmunds."

"How do I know your word is any good?"

"I only went back on my word once, and that was to save a man's life." He gave me his most sincere look. "Besides, what choice do you got?"

I told him about the key pin with one sapphire missing and watched his face. If it worried him, he hid it well. I told him to call El Goya and leave a message for Olgamar when he had something for me.

Back at Otto's, I paced. Boot wouldn't be home for several hours and I couldn't afford to be out on the streets any more than necessary. I didn't like being out of the action with a noose out there waiting for me. I had to do something. I dialed up the Boudreaux house and was surprised to hear Dominic answer the phone. I identified myself, and there was a long pause on his end of the line.

"Sorry if I spoiled your party the other night."

"Hedda is spitting mad. What did you say to her?"

"She didn't tell you?"

"No. All she does is curse you when I bring it up."

"Has your wife taken any vacations without you this past year?"

"Oh gawd yes. She's gone more than she's home."

"Where has she gone?"

"Well, we went to France together in the fall. She went from there to Africa, but I had to come back to work. She's gone to New York a couple of times to shop and see theatre. And to Puerto Rico, I believe."

"Are you sure it was Puerto Rico?"

"I think so, why?"

"It's very important that I know whether it was Puerto Rico for sure. Is her passport in the house?

He was silent for a long moment. When he spoke, his voice held a note of suspicion. "Why do you want to know?"

"I can't tell you that. Your wife asked me not to. That's why she was so angry with me at the party. I threatened to tell you."

"Tell me what, old man?"

"Listen, Dominic. Whatever else I may be, I'm a man of discretion. It goes with the business. You'll have to get it out of her yourself."

He said nothing.

"If you were in her place, I wouldn't snitch you out either."

Another long pause and then, "Hold on."

I sat in the blackness for what seemed like hours. At last he returned. "I've got it." I could hear him rifling through the pages. "Here it is, January…hmmm… Guess I was wrong, it was Haiti. Port au Prince. I could have sworn she said Puerto Rico."

"Thanks for checking anyway."

"What is this about? Is it Eddie? Do you think he was in Puerto Rico?

"Maybe."

"And you thought Hedda went there to see him."

"I didn't say that."

"I'm not stupid, Heart. Why else would you ask if she went to Puerto Rico?"

"Was your wife having an affair with Edmunds?"

"They had a flirtation. Hedda flirts with everyone. So did Eddie. It was harmless enough. I hope you're not suggesting she had a hand in his disappearance."

"I'm not suggesting anything."

"No wonder she had a fit. I can't say I blame her," he said coldly.

"I have to explore all the angles. I'm sorry if I've offended you and your wife."

He put on his best lawyer voice and said, "You've done your exploring. I don't want to hear another word from you about this. And please don't bother my wife with it. We were both quite fond of you. I would hate to have you hauled into court for criminal harassment."

"That would be the least of my problems."

"Don't count on it."

"Lola Flores is dead, Dominic. Murdered in her home." I hated to give it away without being able to see his face, but it didn't matter much. I didn't figure he knew anything. "There's a warrant out for my arrest. They think I did it."

He sputtered but didn't really say anything. I thanked him for his time, and I could swear he sounded almost regretful when we said goodbye.

Next, I called Olgamar, the hostess at El Goya. Like I said, word travels fast in Ybor. She had already heard I was underground and was eager to help. I gave her the number of the pay phone in the City Hall lobby next to Otto's stand. I told her to call it if someone left a message for me at El Goya. She agreed instantly and asked if there was anything else she could do.

"Look in on my mother. Make sure she's okay."

"I already have. Alicia is staying with her until this thing blows over. Don't worry, people are looking out for her... and, well you know, Billy, a lot of people are pulling for you. This thing won't go down without a fight."

"Thanks, Olga. I'm hoping it won't come to that."

"Be careful," she said before hanging up. I slumped back in the chair. My thoughts ran dizzily over my predicament. I wondered if they planned to make me just disappear like they had my father. Or if they would take me in dead and say I was killed resisting arrest.

Either way, they would hang Lola's murder on me and close the file. Justice done, Tampa style. No loose ends, no messy, expensive trials with those unpredictable juries. Clean, quick, and at tremendous savings to the taxpayers. This must have been how my father felt all those years ago when he saw his name on the Committee's list of undesirable agitators in the Chronicle. Full of anger and impotence.

I had to stop these thoughts. If I let them get to my mind, they had me. I closed the door on bitterness and helplessness. I felt the clock face. Five-fifteen. Boot probably wouldn't be home yet, but I couldn't wait any longer.

"Libby," I said when his wife answered.

"Hi, Mom," she said conversationally.

"Have you got someone there?"

"Mmmhmm," she said. "Listen, can you call me back in about an hour? I've got company right now."

"Sure, is everything okay?"

"No problem. Bye bye," she sang before hanging up. I had never known what a good actor she was. I wondered if Boot knew.

I stretched out on the sofa, a magnificent leather monster with the clean earthy scent of cow hide. My head swam pleasantly with deep comfort despite my wondering who was grilling Libby. She didn't seem concerned, so I let it go for the moment and gave myself to the sofa.

I woke when Otto entered. "What time is it?" I asked.

"A little after seven," he answered as he headed for the kitchen with bags that wafted the briny smell of fresh shrimp.

I leapt on the phone and dialed. Boot answered on the first ring. "What took you so long?" he demanded.

"I'm sorry, Boot. I fell asleep." It seemed I was always apologizing to Boot. Someday maybe I'd get the chance to forgive him for something. "What have you got?"

"Guy's a snoop. Says he was tailing you for a client."

"Who?"

"Won't say. He's claiming client privilege, and nobody's pushing too hard on the point. Says he saw you enter the Flores apartment building at midnight and come out about an hour later."

"What's his name?"

"Jack Cunningham. You remember him?"

"Ex-cop, right?"

"Yeah, a little after your time on the force. Got bounced for icing one too many guys in the line of duty."

"Swell."

He gave me Cunningham's home and office addresses.

"Thanks, Boot. You're a true pal."

"Listen, I..." There was a long awkward pause. "Schmidt was here when you called. He was grilling Libby about you."

"That's what I figured."

"She didn't give him nothing, but..."

"Look, partner. I understand. You've done more than your part. I won't call again until this whole thing's behind us."

He thanked me, and we broke the connection without any goodbyes.

I dialed up Nesta and told her to drive past the corner of Ninth Avenue and Avenida de Cuba Street three times before stopping to pick me up at nine o'clock. "Make sure you aren't followed."

"What do I do if someone's following me?"

"Go to the Colonnade on Bayshore and have a root beer. Then go back home and wait for me to call."

By the time I was finished with my phone calls, Otto was setting shrimp al ajillo on the table and vermicelli topped with mounds of fresh grated parmesan. He uncorked a bottle of Italian white and poured us both a generous snootful. I brought him up to date over dinner and told him my plan.

"What if it's a trap to draw you out?"

"Boot wouldn't do that to me."

"He wouldn't have to know. They just plant the information on him and let it find its way to you."

"They don't think that far ahead."

"I hope you're right."

"Believe me, I know them. They're not that smart."

"Never underestimate your opponent, Billy. Even if he's stupid."

SUSAN F. EDWARDS

Chapter Twenty-Nine
Witness for the Persecution

I had second thoughts about involving Nesta as I watched the corner of Ninth and Avenida de Cuba from a second-floor cantina down the street. Just by giving me a ride, she was breaking the law. A few people milled at the corner, on their way home or out for an evening stroll. A *chavatero* stood on the corner, sharpening a knife for an old woman. An occasional car rolled by.

I saw Nesta's Packard come from the south up the Avenida and turn west on Ninth. A few moments later, a taupe Jaguar executed the same move. All I could see was two men with hats in the front seat. A police cruiser came creeping up Ninth, headed in the opposite direction.

Nesta came up Avenida again a few minutes later but continued past Ninth this time and hung a left on the next street up. Some kids in a Model A puttered behind her but didn't follow her turn. No jaguar this time. I headed down, scoping from street level now the faces and cars on both streets. She came up Ninth this time, looking pretty clean and pulled over. I hopped in and gave her directions, keeping an eye out the back window. No one was behind us.

"I can't believe they didn't put a man on you," I said.

"Who says they didn't? They just don't give them cars that can keep up with a Packard."

"You ditched a tail?"

"Let's put it this way. There's a copper still wandering the alleys of Hyde Park looking for me."

"Maybe I should deputize you."

"Deputize me?"

"It's just a something Hedda said. She wanted to be my assistant."

"How quaint."

"What's quaint about it?"

"The idea of my being your assistant, like I'm some gum-snapping, nail-painting receptionist in a seedy office."

"I didn't say that."

"You didn't have to. I hired you, Billy. That makes you my assistant."

All the worries I had about involving her in a crime suddenly vanished. I was the one who would take the fall here. She had not the slightest fear of getting caught. Her uncle would simply take her home and send the hired help to jail for her sins, just like every other rich Anglo in this town.

We parked a couple of blocks from the building that held Cunningham's office. It was a run-down two-story brick cube at the north end of downtown, a shabby neighborhood close to the jail. A lot of bail bondsmen and pool halls and all-night hash joints. Cunningham's building was completely dark.

We walked around the alley in back. A thick wooden door was set into the back of the building. Its keyhole was painted shut, which probably meant it had an interior bolt. I gave it a pull just to make sure. It didn't budge. I stepped back and looked the building over.

The windows on the first floor were guarded with wrought iron panels set in concrete frames. The second story had casement windows that opened with a crank on the inside. The latches on this kind of window were often sprung and it was easy enough to pry them open from the outside.

I started to climb onto the first story window ledge and from there onto the top of the door ledge.

"What are you doing?" Nesta demanded.

"Taking the path of least resistance."

"Can't you pick the lock on the door?"

"It's bolted from the inside."

"What about the front door?"

"Right. I'm going to stand on the front porch, picking the lock with the police station two blocks away."

"What about me?"

"Go wait in the car." I had gained the tip of the door frame and was working the window above, wiggling the frame back and forth. I felt the latch give. The window opened easily.

"I will not. When you get in, I want you to open the door for me."

"Forget it, lady. Your trained monkey has slipped the leash. It's my neck not yours in the noose." I grasped the window sill above me and pulled myself up and through the window.

I found myself in a small office. The letterhead on the stationary said Hallmark Real Estate. As I was unlocking the office door, I heard a noise at the window behind me. I saw Nesta's reddened face as she clutched the windowsill, "Don't just stand there, help me," she grunted.

I ran to the window and pulled her up. When she was inside, she spluttered and grumbled and brushed off her ruined dress. Her silk stockings sagged from large holes ripped in them by the rough brick. She gave me a murderous glare. "I know it's your neck in the noose. Why do you think I'm here?"

A noise in the alley shut us both up. I carefully cranked the window shut and peeked out. A couple of old drunks were weaving down the alley in search of a cozy doorway. They spied the red high heels Nesta had left behind and went for them.

Nesta looked over my shoulder in time to see one man take up a shoe and dance it around the alley like a fine lady, running his grimy grizzled cheek against it. She gave a disgusted groan and turned toward the outer door. I followed her out.

Cunningham's office was the last one on the left. It had an old loose lock on it. I used my crochet hook, better than any lock pick ever engineered.

Cunningham's office was one room with a flat top desk, one four-drawer metal filing cabinet, and two folding chairs, not much to show for a lifetime of work. I headed for the desk and told Nesta to start on the files.

"What am I looking for?"

"I don't know exactly. Files on anyone related to this case or to Haiti, anything dated the past couple of weeks."

The top right desk drawer held a cheap loaded .32 automatic and a few pencils, envelopes, paper clips. The drawer below it contained a flask and two grimy glasses. I opened it and sniffed. Homemade rot-gut. The guy had no class. Crumpled bills and overdue notices spilled out of the top left drawer. In the last drawer I found two lengths of pipe, some smoke bombs, and one stick of dynamite.

So Vincetti had told the truth for once. Unless it was he who had hired this thug, but that didn't seem likely. Vincetti had enough meat on his payroll. Why hire an outside man to bomb my apartment, and an Anglo at that?

"This is sickening," Nesta muttered over the files.

"What is it?"

She showed me a lurid black-and-white photo of a man and woman entering a cheap motel.

"Looks like he mostly handles divorce work."

She popped the pictures back into a file and continued scanning. I looked over her shoulder and spied it immediately. "There—Corazon."

She pulled it out and opened it. On top of the stack of papers lay a photo of me leaving Lola's apartment building. It was a dark picture, but my identity was clearly discernable. The date of Lola's death was written in pen across the bottom. I resisted the urge to crumple it. I just put it in my pocket for future reference. The papers were handwritten logs of my movements over the last two weeks.

"None of his other files are this detailed," said Nesta.

"Yeah, well I hope they're more accurate than this. Half of this stuff is baloney. Looks like every time I ditched him, he just made stuff up. Here it is. He's got me at Lola's at midnight, when I was home nursing broken ribs and passed out on morphine."

The file had no client name anywhere. I pocketed the logs and returned the file to its place. Then I went through all four drawers and came up with nothing else. Nesta was going through a ledger we had found in the bottom drawer. "Whoever it is is paying him well," she said. "Two-fifty a week it looks like. That's four times what I'm paying you to take this stuff."

"You can't tell who the checks are from?"

"Nope. No names at all."

"There must be check stubs somewhere, billing records."

"All the other bills are in the folders along with check stubs and receipts. Cunningham's been careful to keep his client on your case secret."

Just the same, we went through everything again and came up empty-handed.

The sky was just beginning to lighten as we slipped out the front door and walked off down the street. In an hour, these streets would be crawling with coppers coming off and going on duty, and with the sleepy prisoners, mostly bums who had done their time in the Graybar Hotel. Right now the streets were totally deserted, so there was no one to witness an old Cuban gentleman in guayabera and straw hat and a rumpled shoeless woman with torn hose slip into a Packard and drive away.

Nesta balked when I directed her next to Cunningham's house. "I'm tired. I'm hungry. Can't we do this another time?"

"Easy for you to say."

"You know, this martyr act is getting kind of worn out. I know you're in trouble. I know it happened while you were working for me, and I'm trying to help. But this isn't my fault. You can't blame every white person in Tampa for what happened to your father."

She knew she had gone too far as soon as the words were out of her mouth. She covered her lips with both hands and stared at me. "I'm sorry. I didn't mean that the way it sounded."

"How do you know about my father?"

207

"My uncle did some checking and found out who you were. He remembers what happened. He was a city councilman then and he fought to open an investigation. The mayor and the other councilmen were all against him. He knew that two of those men had been there at the...the abduction." There were tears in her eyes and she looked at me with genuine feeling. "I'm sorry about what happened. I wish I could make it right."

I looked out the window to hide my own tears. "Let's get some breakfast before we hit Cunningham's place."

By seven-thirty we were sitting in Nesta's car about a block from Cunningham's house, washing down Cuban cheese toast with hot black coffee in silence.

"I guess I've been pretty hard on you," I said at last.

"No worse than I've been on you."

"My father never trusted Anglos. He always said they'd smile and offer you a drink, then stick a knife in your belly while you drank it."

"My father always said everyone in Ybor was a red who wanted to take over Tampa and destroy the American way of life. He said we had to keep them in line or they'd bring down the whole country."

We looked at each other a long moment. I saw an awkward young woman struggling to understand the lies she had grown up with. Everything she had once believed in, had once wanted, had been torn from her. She was a woman who had lost her innocence.

I don't know what she saw when she looked at me, but her eyes were sad and gentle. We came together without effort, neither willing nor fighting it. The kiss held not so much passion as comfort, acceptance, love. When it was over, we looked at each other with twin expressions of surprise, eyes wide, mouths open.

She collected herself and sat up, straightening her clothes and hair. "Well. Don't you think you'd better..." She motioned in the direction of Cunningham's house.

I nodded with an embarrassed grin. "Oh. Uh, yeah..." I ducked out of her car and closed the door quietly behind me. Its soft click for some reason make me feel like weeping.

Cunningham's place was an unpainted Florida pine bungalow with a deep front porch. At the top of the house was the usual belvedere, a small sleeping porch lined with windows on all four sides to make the most of precious summer breezes. It was a surprise after the gloom and austerity of his office. I slipped into the carport and spied the tan Chevy. I got in on the passenger side and slumped down low in the seat.

I didn't have a long wait before Cunningham ambled out of his house with a newspaper tucked under his arm. He was in the car with the door closed before he saw me. By that time I had the blade of my stiletto at his throat. He froze.

I told him to start the car and drive, keeping the tip of the knife firmly against his carotid artery. "One false move, and you'll be gushing like a fire hose," I told him, waggling the knife to emphasize my point.

Beads of sweat gathered above his upper lip, and red patches mottled his bloated face. He had that peculiar smell of animal tissue pickled in formaldehyde that characterizes certain men who drink too much.

"I ought to waste you right here," I growled, giving him a jab with the blade. "There'd be one less liar in the world. Who put you up to it?"

"You think I'm scared of a punk like you?" He gave me a disdainful once-over. "I could eat three of you for breakfast,"

"Yeah, and I could make enough blood sausage outta your neck to feed a family of four for a month." I wiggled the blade savagely, drawing some surface blood.

"You ain't gonna do nothing to me, punk. You're in enough trouble as it is." He shoved his newspaper at me. I opened it and saw the *Chronicle*'s screaming headline, "Private investigator sought in brutal murder." There, printed large and lurid, was Cunningham's photo of me leaving Lola's apartment building.

The article quoted sources close to the investigation as saying they had evidence that I had harassed the victim repeatedly before her death, and that she had hired private investigator Jack Cunningham to discover who was employing me and why. Cunningham had followed me to the victim's home on the night of the murder and had snapped a photo of me coming out.

The writer went on to say that Miss Flores' maid had discovered me in the apartment the next morning. The reporter conjectured that I had returned to the scene of the crime to retrieve incriminating evidence. The story detailed the grisly murder scene and the struggle it suggested. Hair matching the color of mine had been found in one of the victim's hands, and flesh had been found under her fingernails.

Anonymous sources were again quoted as saying contusions and lacerations on my face were observed by police when they questioned me after the murder. Anyone with information about my whereabouts was encouraged to call the newspaper or the police.

"How's it gonna look if you kill the eyewitness?" Cunningham asked.

"I'm a dead man anyway. At least I'd have the satisfaction of slitting your throat before I die."

"And I'm as good as dead if I squeal, so what's the difference to me?"

"Why did you bomb my apartment?"

"That was the job. Follow you and report on your movements. Twenty bucks a day, plus expenses. It was a hundred extra clams for planting the pineapple. Nothing personal. Just business."

"Was that supposed to scare me off the Edmunds case?"

"I don't ask them kinds of questions. Especially for that kind of pay."

"How much did he pay you to finger me?"

"Enough."

"Enough to commit perjury? That's a federal offense. You know what they do to cops in jail?"

"I got a picture, Heart. It's there in black and white."

"You could have taken that any one of the times I interviewed Miss Flores."

He pulled the car over to the side of the road.

"I didn't tell you to stop."

"I'm not gonna tell you nothing, and we both know you're not gonna kill me." He turned the motor off and looked at me. "You're stupid, but you're not that stupid. You didn't nip the bird—you figure you can still prove that. But if you kill me, you really are a dead man."

"I probably am anyway."

"Yeah, but if you kill me, no one will ever believe you were innocent of the girl's murder. And that's worse than dying for you, isn't it?"

I put the knife away and stared at him. A jolt went through me and my fist shot out, landing with a satisfying crack against his jaw and slamming his head into the window.

He wiped the blood off his mouth and felt his jaw and teeth. He gave me a funny half-smile.

"Now you have something else to put in your testimony. You can tell them I attacked the star witness. That ought to clinch the case."

"I ain't gonna tell 'em anything about it."

"Why not?"

"You think I like these guys? You think I want to lie on the witness stand? They got me by the short hairs too. But I'm not gonna give 'em anything they don't ask for." His face softened and he smiled. "It ain't much, but it's the only rebellion I can afford."

"What do they have on you?"

He snorted and started the car. "Like I'm gonna tell you." He asked me where he could drop me like we were old friends who had just been out for coffee. I told him my car was in his neighborhood.

"Did you kill the girl for him?"

He gave me an indignant look. "I ain't no hit man."

"Maybe you didn't mean to kill her. Maybe you were just supposed to scare her like you did me. Or to retrieve a certain item."

"Like what?"

"You tell me."

"Forget it. I was never in her place."

"You said they had you by the short hairs, Cunningham. What else could they have on you that would make you perjure yourself in a murder case?"

He pulled over to the side of the road. "Get out."

I opened the door. "Looks like I hit a nerve."

"You don't know nothing. These guys don't need nothing on you to squash you like a bug. You ought to know that by now." He looked me in the eye. "I know who you are, Corazon. It's just a matter of time before they figure it out. If I was you, I'd get out of town. Fast."

I got out, and he spat gravel taking off.

Nesta was right where I had left her, fast asleep behind the wheel. She woke when I opened the door. She smiled sleepily. "What'd you find out?"

"Exactly ten times nothing," I muttered.

We rode in silence back to Ybor. I had her stop on a little back street. I looked at her, but she avoided my eyes. "Nesta, what happened this morning. Between you and me…"

She waved me off. "It's okay. You don't have to…" Her voice trailed off and she bit her lip.

"We both know it could never work out," I said softly.

She nodded, still not looking at me. "I know. But still..." She turned sad eyes on me, her lip trembling. "It was a very nice kiss."

I smiled and nodded. "It was better than nice." I squeezed her arm, kissed her cheek and got out.

I dialed up El Goya as soon as I got to Otto's place, but Olgamar hadn't gotten a call for me yet. I slugged down a glass of water and dragged myself back to the guest room. My face had no sooner touched the satin case of the goose down pillow than I fell asleep. I slept straight through to the morning.

The smell of Cuban coffee woke me. I followed my nose to the kitchen where Otto poured me a cup. "You saw the *Chronicle*?" he asked.

"Yeah," I said, and told him the story of my meeting with Cunningham.

"You think the snoop killed her?"

"Naw. For one thing he doesn't have dyed brown hair." I related finding brown hair with light roots in Lola's hand.

"There's got to be a way to find out who his boss is."

"Maybe Vincetti will come through."

"What makes you so sure he'll tell you the truth?"

"He needs a bird dog. If he's got any sense, he'll tell me the name and follow me to the quarry."

Otto finished his breakfast and left for work. It was almost five a.m. I lit a match and looked at the photo of myself exiting Lola's building. There was something wrong with this picture. What was it? I flicked the match out before it burned my fingers.

The answer came to me in the darkness.

SUSAN F. EDWARDS

Chapter Thirty
The Missing Sapphire

I lit another match. The picture was too dark around the edges. Lola's building always had an electric lamp on at night next to the entrance. It should have lighted the left side of the picture, but that part lay in such deep shadow I could barely make out its outline in the dark. However, my face was quite light. Where did the light come from? Surely I would have seen, in fact been blinded by a flash if Cunningham had used one. He would have had to use one to illuminate my face like that.

I extinguished the match and lit another. I turned the picture over and saw that it had been developed by the Burgert Brothers photography shop downtown.

I called Nesta and told her to take a streetcar downtown to the Tampa Theatre for the one o'clock matinee of *Flesh and the Devil* with Greta Garbo. She groaned about how much easier it was just to drive, but I nixed that. If the cops on her tail were as lazy and sloppy as I hoped, they would be watching her car. If she slipped out the back door and left on foot, they wouldn't even know she was gone.

I showered but didn't shave. I had a nice disguise going that I wanted to keep. I dusted my hair and beard with flour from Otto's kitchen, put on one of his suits and clamped a gray fedora on my head. It took me a while to find my shoes in the blackness. I don't have Otto's habit of carefully placing objects where I can find them later.

I staggered down the street, blinded by the harsh sunlight and looking every bit a wobbly old gentleman high on nerve tonic. I took the streetcar, keeping a sharp eye out beneath sleepy-looking lids. I got out at Tyler and Franklin and slipped over to Florida Avenue. I entered the back door to the office building into which the theatre was set and quietly took the service stairs ten flights up to the top of the building. I walked out onto the roof and looked down over all of Franklin Street. From here it would be easy to spot anyone following Nesta. If she had a shadow, I would simply slip out the back door of the office building and make tracks.

I was soaked with sweat and nearly swooning from the heat by the time she showed. I scanned the streets for a full five minutes before following her down and buying my ticket. I slipped into the cool dark lobby lit with little flickering bulbs that looked like flames. It was an opulent place and the only building in town with refrigerated air.

The unreal feeling of cold air on a hot day was compounded by the phantasmagoric décor. The place was supposed to resemble a Moorish pleasure garden with statues, ferns and even peacocks beneath a dark blue evening sky that twinkled with ten thousand stars. Clouds even drifted over the sky occasionally, thanks to the marvel of what they called the Brenkert Cloud Machine. I knew I was supposed to be impressed, but all I could think was thank God it wasn't my job to change ten thousand light bulbs to keep the stars twinkling over the heads of over-privileged Anglos. In Ybor, we watched our movies on sheets under the real stars.

I found Nesta near the back where I had told her to sit. The auditorium was even more splendid and garish than the lobby. The newsreel was over, and the magnificent organ rose through a trap door on stage while the organist played the theme song to *Flesh and the Devil.*

I sat behind Nesta and slipped the photograph between the seats to her. She agreed to take it to the Burgert Brothers studio and find out who had paid for the developing. I also asked her to find out if there was anything strange about the way it was developed.

She left first. I gave her a ten-minute lead and then slipped out the back door. I arrived at Otto's around two-thirty and made myself a roast pork sandwich and heated some fried plantains Otto had left out for me.

When I finished my lunch, I called Nesta. The maid answered and said Mrs. Edmunds was not home yet. I paced. All this waiting and having to let other people do all my leg work was getting to me. I called Otto.

"No word yet," he told me. "I'll call the minute I hear from her."

I needed to move; I felt caged. I dropped to the floor and did pushups until the muscles in my arms burned and trembled. I collapsed in a cold sweat. Maybe I should pay Vincetti a visit. I flipped onto my back and started doing sit-ups, counting. By the time I got to a hundred, my muscles refused me. I lay there panting. I poured myself a double bourbon and took a cold bath.

When I had done everything I could think of, I called Nesta's number again. This time she answered, breathless, on the fourth ring. She had just gotten in.

"It took some doing," she said, "but I found out some very interesting things."

"Who paid for it?"

"They wanted to know who I was, of course, and why I was asking all these questions. I said I was the D.A.'s assistant and that the photo had been entered as evidence in a murder case. I told them we needed to check its authenticity. Quick thinking, huh?"

"You're a genius. What'd you find out?"

"It worked. They answered all my questions. I think I have a talent for this."

"Nesta. What did he tell you?"

She sniffed and said coolly, "For one thing that photo wasn't taken after dark. The man who brought the film in asked them to print it like that, all dark like night but with the face visible. They can do that right in the darkroom. He told me how—"

"Who, Nesta? Who was it?"

"The man who brought in the film was stout, maybe fifty-five, mostly bald but with a little graying reddish hair and mustache, and a flat nose. They said he looked Irish."

217

"Cunningham."

"Mmm hmm. He signed the name Mallory, but guess whose account he charged it to?"

"Stroven?"

"Nope," she said in a self-satisfied voice.

My thoughts ran over the possibilities. "Saul Stone probably has an account with Burgert Brothers. They've shot every building and crane on Edmunds Island."

She was silent for a moment. "Forget Saul. It's not him," she said tersely.

I had almost forgotten my early suspicions that the two had once had more than a business relationship. Who else would have an account with a photographer's studio? Of course. Insurance companies often had photos taken of insured properties and items. That was it. "Victory Life," I said.

"Yep," she said happily. "I knew old Mullethead had something to do with this. I never liked him."

"What's his relationship to Stroven?"

"He's Stroven's puppet. Everyone knows Terrence Quattlebaum does whatever Stroven tells him to."

"We'll have to wait until tonight and go to Mullet's house. Maybe when he sees what we've got on him, he'll give us Stroven." I told her where to pick me up at seven and hung up. The phone rang again almost immediately. I picked up the earpiece but did not speak.

"Bingo," I heard Otto say at the other end of the line. I suppose I should have just flicked Vincetti off like a cockroach on my sleeve. I didn't need his information now. But I had some time to kill, and I badly needed some action. Besides, I wanted to see his face when I beat him to the punch.

I donned a pair of Otto's dress trousers, a white shirt and black dinner jacket and slicked my hair flat with his hair pomade. I figured

MAN OVERBOARD

I would look enough like a waiter to get me through the kitchen. I pulled a fedora down over my eyes for the trip.

SUSAN F. EDWARDS

Chapter Thirty-One
The Black Hole

Ten minutes later, I was standing next to Vincetti on The Mez of Punch House.

"I hate it when you do that," he muttered and steered me quickly toward his office in the back.

Unlike the rat hole he worked in downstairs behind the kitchen, this was undoubtedly the office he used for meeting important men and for trysts with women who were not quick enough to elude him. Red brocade drapes and divan and a massive carved mahogany desk. He looked even more ferret-like behind it, dwarfed by its size, his face and teeth rendered even more pointy by its curved carvings. "So," he said with a smug smile. "You want to know who's missing a sapphire form his key pin, eh?"

"No thanks. I'm not interested anymore."

Surprise and disappointment flashed across his face, but he quickly tucked them behind a poker face. "Why not?"

"For one thing, I already know who it is. For another, he's no longer a part of the picture."

"Are you saying he didn't ice the cupcake?"

"I'm saying he doesn't know where Edmunds is."

"You're bluffing. You don't even know who it is, do you?"

"Terrance Quattlebaum," I said. "Also known as Mullethead."

His face reddened, and a fat wormy vein throbbed at his narrow temple. He leapt from his chair, knocking it over. "Oh yeah, wise guy?" He punched a button on his desk, and his two simian bodyguards entered. "Take him to the hole."

They grabbed me on each side and dragged me from the chair. "I thought you only went back on your word to save someone's life."

"I do," he sneered. "Mine."

"You'll never find Edmunds without me."

221

He gave me an evil grin. "But we have you, Corazon. In case we need you. That's why I'm not turning you over to Tampa's finest. Yet." He nodded at his boys, and off we went.

In a small room off the kitchen, one ape kicked aside a rug and threw back a wooden bolt in the floor. He opened a trap door and his partner shoved me in.

The hole turned out to be just that, a black cellar with no windows, not one needle of light. It was like being at Otto's again for the first time, only without his gentle presence or any of the comforts of his home.

I felt for the ceiling. It was about a foot above my head and supported by thick, splintery wood beams. The trap door was locked up tight and did not budge a fraction of an inch when I pushed on it. The place smelled damp and musty, and I could faintly hear the clang of pots and pans above. I would have to learn the lay of the land the same way I had Otto's.

First I followed the wall around the perimeter, shuffling my feet out front. The room was long and narrow, roughly thirty by sixty feet. Large, heavy cases of bottles lined the walls and were stacked in the center of the room. I got one open and pulled out a square bottle I figured to be gin. I opened it and sniffed the piney scent of good stuff.

I went through a few other boxes until I located a bottle of Jamaican rum. I took a long pull at it and carried it with me while I examined the room for any means of egress besides the trap door, feeling every inch of ceiling and wall. It was tedious work made unnerving for the occasional skittering sound of rodent claws.

Something light and spidery landed on my hand and sent a heebie-jeebie up my spine. I flung it off, shuddering from the sensation. Scorpions love darkness, as do giant cockroaches and certain kinds of poisonous spiders. My flesh crawled at the thought as I forced my hand back to the wall. I began thumping the wall every few inches to warn away any creatures nearby. I took another swig of rum to quiet my shaky limbs.

At the far narrow end, I found a metal grate at the bottom of the wall. It was large and heavy. I felt around its frame and located four corner bolts with large wing nuts frozen in place. I could hear the faint sounds of water flowing somewhere beyond the grate.

Nesta was probably circling the block for the tenth time by now, wondering what had happened to me. I only hoped she had the sense not to try to tackle Mullethead alone. I felt around the room for something that might help me loosen the wing nuts.

I stuck my hand into one box and felt something hairy move away. I sprang back into another stack of crates, knocking them over. I heard bottles breaking and smelled the sweetish metallic aroma of liquor. I was sprawled out against the crates and something hard poked into my back. I felt for it. A crowbar used for opening crates lay wedged between two slats.

Even with the crowbar, it seemed to take hours to scrape, hack, whack the wing nuts until they finally moved. At last I got the grate open and crawled into a concrete pipe about four feet in diameter, about the size of Edmunds' porthole, I thought with a shudder. The bottom contained about two inches of damp, stinky sludge. The water sounds got closer as I advanced. At last the pipe opened out to a larger chamber with about a foot of water in it. I stood and saw that the blackness softened to a gray off to the right.

As I neared the lighter patch, I heard a muffled streetcar bell, and then I saw bars of blackness above me slicing up a dark blue sky. I could barely reach the grate with the tips of my fingers.

I dreaded the thought of dragging a case back through the pipe to stand on, but I didn't let myself dwell on it. I slogged back through the water, steeling myself for another crawl through the slime.

By the time I got back with the crate, the sun was starting to rise. It sent rosy rays down through the grate that looked like the gates of heaven to me in that moment. The grate was heavy, but it wasn't bolted down. I got it off and hoisted myself upward to freedom. I found myself in a cobblestone alley a block away from Punch House. I was covered with a dark, evil-smelling sludge.

Chapter Thirty-Two
The Road to Freedom

Otto sniffed the air loudly when I arrived. "Dios mio, you smell as if you've been crawling in the sewer."

"You always spoil my surprises," I grumbled as I headed for the bathroom.

After a shower and a glass of port, my humor improved, and I told Otto about the double-cross. He wasn't surprised, but he did refrain from saying I told you so.

I dialed up Nesta. As I feared, she had gone to Quattlebaum's house alone. His wife had told her that he had left yesterday morning for Chicago on business.

"Did you find out what time his train was?"

"Way ahead of you. She said that the train left at seven-fifteen. I called the station, and they said they didn't have at train to Chicago then. I asked if they had anything going out at seven-fifteen." She paused for dramatic effect.

"And?"

"Just one, Tampa to Miami. I'm betting he shipped out to Haiti from there."

"When does the next train for Miami leave?"

"One o'clock this afternoon, I booked two tickets, in case you decided to show up."

"You're an angel," I said, meaning it.

"Admit it, I'm good at this."

"A regular Mata Hari. Meet me at the station at noon. And make sure you're not followed."

"I'll be careful, but I'm not too worried about it. Uncle called the police commissioner and threatened a lawsuit with lots of publicity if they didn't stop harassing a helpless widow who has already been through perfect hell." When she finished congratulating herself, we rang off.

"Ai," I said to Otto after hanging up, "Schmidt's stupid, but even he's going to think far enough ahead to have a man the train station."

"Leave everything to me," Otto said and patted my grizzled jaw. I didn't have to see him to hear that crooked Otto smile in the dark. First he called a friend with a car. Then he shaved me smooth as a baby's butt with his straight razor, leaving only a pencil-thin mustache. Then he oiled his hands lightly and ran them through my hair. He combed it back into a smooth shell and trimmed a bit around the ears and neck. Then he gave me his favorite tropical traveling suit, a fawn-colored linen with a buttery panama hat. The final touch was a pair of his spare glasses with black disk lenses and a rattan cane from Trinidad.

By the time he finished with me, it was almost eleven. Outside the door he folded a small bag into my hand and embraced me before pushing me toward a waiting Ford coupe and nodded to the driver.

"I don't know how to thank you, Otto."

"Just don't come back before they lay that warrant to rest."

It wasn't hard to move like a blind man with the black disks obscuring my vision. I stumbled toward the car and got in. As we pulled away, I looked into the bag. It held some bread and cheese, four fifty-dollar bills, and Otto's passport.

Fortunately, this was the busiest time of day at the train station. I spotted the coppers right away despite their plain clothes attempts to blend in with the crowd. Their spines were too rigid, their loitering too alert. They also had selected the two ugliest mugs in the force.

I stood near the door and saw Nesta arrive and go to the ticket counter. I didn't dare watch her much, but her walk was as cool as a coconut. She bought the tickets and scanned the room. Her glance slid over me without the slightest flicker of recognition and continued on around the room.

226

Nesta came toward me to the door and looked out. I stumbled toward her from the side with my cane tapping in front of me and smashed into her. She dropped her bags with a startled, "Oh!"

"Sorry," I mumbled, as we both knelt down to retrieve her things. In the confusion, I slipped one of the tickets out of her bag and into my pocket. She started to protest, but I lowered the glasses an instant and gave her a wink. "Sit as far away from me as possible on the train. We'll talk in Miami."

"Right," she said, standing up with her bags.

"Are you sure you're all right?" I asked patting her arm blindly.

"Oh yes, I'm fine. Don't worry about me," she replied a little too loudly, too theatrically. And then she abruptly walked away.

As I tapped my way toward a row of seats, my nose drew me toward a light floral scent. I sat down next to it. I reclined quietly for a few moments and then sniffed the air. "Is that orange blossom you're wearing?"

"Yes," came the girlish voice of a young woman.

"Very nice," I said, settling back. "Some people feel sorry for a blind man, but I tell them, this blind man knows the beauty of a flower in ways they don't even imagine. The softness of the petals, the different scents." I knew I was somehow becoming Otto, imitating his grand charm and putting this young woman at ease in the way only he could do.

"I never thought about it that way," she said.

"For example, orange blossom is sweet, light. Delicate. The perfect scent for a young lady like yourself. Tea rose would be too musty, too old for you. Gardenia too flirtatious. No, you have selected the right scent for you. Modest. Not overwhelming. Thank you for improving my olfactory landscape."

She giggled. "Are you going to Miami?" she asked.

I nodded.

"Me too," she said. "Let's sit together."

"I would like that," I replied and executed a languid stretch, turning so I could peer over the glasses to see first one copper, who was now by the entrance and then the other, who was standing by the door that led to the trains. Both scanned the crowd, but neither gave me second glance.

This was almost too easy. It was starting to make me nervous. At last the boarding call was given, and we rose to join the crowd at the doors. This would be the test. I pushed my glasses far up on my nose and gave myself over to Orange Blossom's arm. I could feel the copper's eye upon me as we passed. My neck prickled with his gaze and didn't let up until we were on the train. I realized suddenly I had been holding my breath and let it out in a loud sigh.

"Are you all right?" she asked as we found places to sit.

"Oh yes," I said, sinking into the seat. "I guess I'm just tired." I hadn't slept for forty-eight hours, so this was no lie. I felt fatigue dragging at my bones. I thanked her and closed my eyes and promptly fell asleep.

I felt a tapping on my shoulder. I was afraid if I opened my eyes, I would see Detective Schmidt standing over me with a set of steel bracelets. "Mister," came the soft voice of my companion. "I'm going to the dining car. Would you like me to bring something back for you?"

"What time is it?"

"Six o'clock. We'll be there in another hour."

"Ah, thank you. A cup of coffee would be nice. Black with sugar."

When she returned, I was finishing the bread and cheese Otto had packed for me. I drank the stale coffee gratefully and tried to entertain Orange Blossom for the rest of the ride although my mind was already on the next leg of my journey.

Two hours later Nesta and I sat on a bench in the ship terminal under slowly turning ceiling fans that churned the hot, damp air like melted butter, thickening rather than cooling it. I was jumpy waiting to get through the next obstacle between me and freedom.

While we waited in line, I began to sweat profusely. The more I mopped, the worse it seemed to get. Guilty men sweated — I knew it, and so did customs officers. My breath came in shallow short gasps. I tried to get control, inhaling deeply, slowly. Then we were face to face with the customs officer. I was morbidly self-conscious of my breathing and grateful I didn't have to look him in the eye as I held out my passport upon his command.

Nesta explained that I was blind, and she was my traveling attendant. More out of curiosity than duty, he insisted I take my glasses off. I rolled my eyeballs up as far as I could so that only the bottom crescents of iris lolled into view, and removed my glasses. He gave a snort of disgust and told me to put my glasses back on.

He pressed my passport into my hand and said, "Go." Nesta guided me out the door and onto the ship.

It was a stormy night, much like the one on which Edmunds had disappeared. I gazed out a porthole at the roiling water and tried to imagine climbing out in this weather with nothing but a rope between me and the angry water.

Nesta came up behind me and looked out over my shoulder. "Sometimes," she said, "I almost wish she had cut the rope."

We arrived at Havana under clear morning skies; the hot Cuban sun made the damp ship decks steamy. We didn't want to deal with customs agents any more than necessary, so we stayed on board until the ship left port a few hours later. We drank fruit juice with rum and took a stroll on deck before siesta time. I could feel my jaws unclenching, my muscles loosening, my gait slowing to island time. A feeling I could not at first identify came over me. And then I remembered it. Relaxation.

All I had to do was get through Haitian customs and I would be safe. They would have to extradite me to get at me then. If they ever even found me. Fortunately, the Tampa police are not known for their detective work, only for their brutality.

When we arrived at the airstrip at Port au Prince, I was unnerved to see the place was crawling with American naval ships. Two armed American MPs worked their way down the line of new arrivals in customs, asking countries of citizenship. When Nesta told them we were Americans, they directed us to a different line.

Chapter Thirty-Three
Native Son

The line moved fast, and when we got to the front, a Haitian customs officer gave our passports a cursory glance and asked the usual questions. Then he stamped our visas and waved us through without even inspecting our bags.

I wanted to kiss the earth as we stepped out of the building onto foreign soil. Instead, I took off the glasses and drank in the sight of Haiti, thirsty to see again.

A small wiry Negro man who could have been anywhere from twenty to fifty sprang forward and seized our bags with a broad smile. "Taxi," he said, dragging our bags with us still attached toward a beat-up old Model A Ford stuck together with wire and rags and festooned with root dolls and other talismans. He said that for ten cents, he would take us to the finest hotel on the island.

As we bounced off down the muddy, rutted road, our driver, whose name was François, pointed out things of interest, old banana and sugar cane plantations, cinnamon and nutmeg trees. A line of military jeeps appeared on the road headed toward us in the opposite direction. They honked insistently until Francois pulled of the road and stopped. He plastered a grin on his face and waved at the soldiers, most of whom ignored him, although a few waved back.

"Why are there so many American soldiers here?" I asked.

He gave me a surprised look. "Been here since 1915. July 28."

"But why?"

"Someone killed our president. Your president sent in the Marines, just to keep the peace, he said. That was thirteen years ago. They still keeping the peace, I guess."

"That's nice of them," said Nesta absently.

Francois slanted his eyes at her under half-closed lids. "So nice," he said unconvincingly.

"Do you have a new president?" I asked.

He snorted. "You might call him that."

I was intrigued with his sarcastic tone. "What do you call him?"

"We have many names for him," he replied and pulled into a circular driveway and under a porte cochere overhung with brilliant crimson bougainvillea. It was indeed a lovely hotel, a sprawling tropical French Colonial building with a deep veranda filled with flowers and ferns.

Before we said our goodbyes to Francois, I gave him a quarter and showed him the photo of Edmunds. "You know this man?"

He looked at the photograph carefully and shook his head. "Maybe I could find him for you. What is his name?"

"Wallace Smithers. We're also looking for another man who might have arrived yesterday or even this morning. A little taller than me and about twice as heavy. Dark hair, maybe fifty-five years old. Terrance Quattlebaum. You see anyone like that?"

"I see many fat American men, Monsieur. I do not remember the name, but I will find out some things for you." He gave us a dazzling smile that showed teeth as straight and white as Miss America's.

It was late afternoon by the time I got to my room after making arrangements to meet Nesta for dinner in an hour. My room faced west and opened onto a courtyard with exotic trees and flowers. A hidden spring burbled somewhere within in the garden.

I had a shave and a cool bath and enjoyed the vermillion rays of the evening sun. The soap had a sweet cinnamon scent and tingled on my skin. Refreshed and revived, I was ready to close this case.

Nesta was already in the dining room when I arrived, looking fresh and radiant and well-pressed. She smiled as I sat down. The waiter brought us tall, cool glasses of water, perfumed with fresh fruit, and broad shallow china bowls of a chilled creamy chowder.

I ordered the island's best rum. It was the first alcoholic drink I had ordered legally in my life. The soup was rich and delicious and held the surprise of a dollop of mango chutney nestled at the bottom of the bowl. Next came raw conch marinated in a spicy lime juice, fried tannia cakes and lobster in a golden ginger sauce.

When we could eat no more, we leaned back, Nesta with a French cigarette and café au lait and me with strong black island coffee and a Dominican cigar. A conga band played outside as I outlined our search strategy. We would hit all the hotels first. We were almost sure to come up with someone who had seen Edmunds or Mullethead. If not, we would start on bars and restaurants.

Nesta had been uncharacteristically silent through dinner. She smoked and stared out into the velvet evening. "It's strange," she said finally, still searching the night. "I've thought — dreamed — about this day. What I would say to the man who ruined my life." She finished her coffee and took a deep pull on the cigarette. She seemed to have forgotten my presence.

"And what will you say to him?"

"I honestly don't know."

The waiter brought a folded piece of paper to us on a pewter dish. I unfolded it and read the spidery handwriting: "Francois has found your man." I passed the note to Nesta and looked toward the front gate. There was Francois on the other side, attended by a hotel security man, his brilliant white grin taking a bite out of the night. Maybe he would save me some shoe leather after all.

The air was warm and heavy with the perfume of tropical flowers. Francois had a small boy of about four with him, whom he introduced as his son, Cristophe. The boy looked at us solemnly through eyes as gentle and heavily fringed as a fawn's. Nesta took him into her lap for the ride, cooing and petting him and giving him treats and trinkets from her handbag, trying to coax a smile from him.

Francois told her how smart his son was. On Francois' command, Cristophe counted to ten in pretty baby French, and giggled. Nesta was enchanted. "It's too sad," Francois lamented.

"What do you mean?" asked Nesta, taking the bait like a hungry fish.

"I would like to send him to the Catholic school this year so he can learn to write."

"But why can't you send Cristophe to school?"

"It costs too much. We have eight children, Madame. It would take food from their mouths to send one little one to school. It's too bad. He is such a smart boy."

As if on cue, Cristophe gave us a dazzling smile and said, "Smart boy," nodding his head vigorously.

Francois pulled his ancient car into an overgrown weedy driveway and stopped in front of a once-magnificent two-story building. Its deep veranda was empty and vine-choked. A single feeble light bulb flickered over the door. Nesta stared at the place.

"Welcome to the Hotel Haiti. Your man owns this place. But he goes by a different name here. Jean Jacques LeClerc. He says he will make us all millionaires one day." He chuckled at the thought.

"So you knew him all along," I said.

"I wasn't sure when you said the name, so I came by today to have a look and see if he was the man in your picture. He looks different now, but it is Monsieur LeClerc. I am sure." Francois looked at Nesta. "He is your family?"

Nesta nodded.

"I am sorry for you."

Nesta smiled and rummaged in her bag. She pulled out a twenty-dollar bill and pressed it into Francois' hand. "Send Cristophe to school." Francois nodded solemnly and kissed her hand.

The dusty lobby was dim and deserted when we entered. A distant scream pierced the thick air, followed by a single shot. We ran toward the back in the direction of the sounds.

Chapter Thirty-Four
Brains and Brawn

The rear veranda was empty except for thirty or so rattan tables with chairs and a bar lined with dusty bottles. A twisting wooden walkway covered with a sagging thatched roof disappeared into the dense jungley growth.

A high-pitched, insane cackle broke through from the darkness and seemed to echo around us.

I saw Nesta shudder and felt a cold finger run down my spine. We crept down the walkway toward the noise. The muffled sound of a man's voice, deep and angry, came to us, but we could not make out the words.

The walkway took a hard right turn, and suddenly the jungle fell away. The jeweled night sky leapt into full view over sparkling silver sand running down to the sea. The smell, the sound, the feel of the air abruptly changed when we came out of the overgrowth. The warm salty breeze was a soft caress. The walkway ran on stilts about fifty feet out of the jungle and ended in an elevated octagonal porch with a palm-thatched roof and lit with torches.

In the darkness, we advanced until we could see and hear better. A young woman, her skin the burnished blue-black of the night sky, stood off to one side watching two men. One was compact and smaller than the other with long wavy hair and a full beard.

The other I recognized instantly as Quattlebaum. His tiny, shovel-shaped head atop that barrel body was unmistakable from any distance. He waved a gun wildly and fired another shot over the smaller man's head. "You don't think I'll shoot you," he bellowed, a drunken edge to his voice.

We inched closer to see the man with the long matted hair sink onto his hands and knees and crawl around, barking and panting like a mad dog. "Arf! Arf! Shoot me."

Nesta's eyes widened. "It's Edward," she whispered.

"Mullethead! That's what everyone calls you behind your back!" Edmunds dissolved into laughter. "Because you've got a big ugly fish face," he crowed.

We were close enough by now to see Mullethead's red bloated face pouring sweat. "You lied to me. You're a liar!"

"And you're a murderer," screamed Edmunds, his shaggy hair obscuring his face.

"I did it for you, Eddie. She was going to expose you to everyone. I saved your life."

"You strangled the love of my life, you fat moron."

"He told me to shut her up. He said she was going to blow everything we worked so hard for."

"I hate you! You're pathetic."

"You said we were a team, you and me and Randy. The Three Musketeers, remember? She was going to ruin it all. I had to shut her up."

"Get out, you murderer!"

"I've got nowhere to go, Eddie. I lost everything. You've got to help me." Mullethead sank to his knees and clutched Edmunds' legs. Edmunds kicked him in the face, screaming like a panther.

Mullet fell back, and Edmunds leapt onto his stomach, punching and gouging at his face until Mullet finally lay still on his back, weeping as Edmunds spat words into his face. "I hate you, you bloated overfed sissy. You make me sick."

Quattlebaum gave Edmunds an odd smile and brought the pistol up. Nesta buried her head in my chest as the shot cracked. An inhuman howl rose up, and Nesta turned before I could stop her. When she saw the bloody sight, she dropped to her knees and gave up her dinner.

Edmunds sat back against a post, spattered with bloody clots, his eyes rolled back in his head, moaning.

Terrance Quattlebaum lay dead at Edmunds' feet, blood oozing from a wound in his temple. I ran toward the porch with Nesta behind me. I found a dirty rag and pan of murky water on a table. I used the rag to cover Quattlebaum's head. I threw the water from the pan into Edmunds' face.

Nesta stood over him, her eyes dull with repugnance as she saw the dark deep pits of his sunken eye sockets, his matted hair.

He looked at her with deep self-pity. "Nesta, I'm sick. You've got to get me to a doctor."

She knelt down and examined the livid blisters and crusty scabs that covered his face and hands. His lip quivered pitifully.

"You're my wife. You've got to help me."

She looked at me. "We've got to get him to a hospital," she said.

Just then, I heard a familiar voice behind me say, "Nobody's going anywhere just yet." There stood Rocky Vincetti and his two brothers. A smile slithered across Rocky's face as he looked at Edmunds. "I gotta tell you, Eddie, you don't look so good."

Edmunds smiled idiotically, his head beginning to loll back on a rubbery neck. He looked at Rocky's gun and muttered, "Everybody wants to shoot me tonight. Tch, tch, tch." And then he passed out.

"We've got to get him to a hospital," Nesta repeated.

"I want my money," Rocky said.

"Does he look like he's got a lot of money on him?" Nesta asked with irritation.

"He doesn't pay up, he's a dead man."

"He's a dead man anyway, you idiot. Can't you see that? He's in the third stage of syphilis."

Rocky's face twitched in irritation. He wasn't used to being spoken to like that, especially by a woman.

"I can't let him die like this," Nesta moaned.

Rocky put his pistol to Edmunds' temple. "Yeah? How about like this?"

Nesta brushed the gun away as if it were a toy and Rocky a naughty boy. "I'll see to it you get your money. Just help us get him to a hospital."

Rocky sucked his teeth and shook his head. "You ought to be begging me to shoot him after what he did to you."

She looked at him with tears in her eyes. "He's a liar and a thief without a shred of conscience," she said. "But I once loved him, and I can't let him die in this filth." The tears spilled down her cheeks.

Rocky sucked his teeth some more and looked at her long and hard. Then he eyed his brothers and jerked his head toward Edmunds. Aldo hooked his arms under Edmunds' armpits and hoisted him up. Frankie took his feet. "For you," Rocky said to Nesta, "not for him."

"Thank you," she replied and followed them down the wooden walkway.

Chapter Thirty-Five
Chez Caribe

The next few days saw an odd kind of vigil over the deathbed of EQ Edmunds. Rocky sent his brothers home but refused to leave until he saw Edmunds dead. He sat in a corner of Edmunds' hospital room with his arms folded and waited.

Nesta handled the hospital staff with the sure hand of someone accustomed to giving orders. She managed to keep Edmunds reasonably comfortable as he drifted around, lost in his own mind.

At times, he was perfectly lucid, even brilliant and witty. I caught glimpses of the man who had made millions and charmed men and women alike. At other times he hallucinated, becoming terrified or vicious like some wild animal, cornered and fighting desperately for its life.

Francois found a legitimate Haitian judge who consented to take Nesta's and Edmunds' statements without telling the American authorities of my presence in Haiti. His court reporter, a British woman of about fifty, took Edmunds' testimony down in shorthand and transcribed it into a document for him to sign. It took three days and lots of patience to get all the answers.

Edmunds explained how he and Terrance Quattlebaum and Randall Stroven had arranged fifteen different insurance policies on his life for a total pay-off of over three million dollars, all mortgaged to the maximum at banks all over the country and funneled to Haiti through various ghost corporations. Edmunds had paid off his partners handsomely and then used some funds to buy the hotel and other property. He had hidden the rest in cash after paying off his blackmailer.

It turned out that Hedda had not been in on the escape but had put two and two together and wormed Edmunds' whereabouts out of Mullet. She had visited Edmunds and offered to keep mum for a cool million.

"Where did you hide the rest of the money?" I asked.

Edmunds gave me a sly look. "You'll never find it."

"Your wife needs it to pay your hospital bills."

"My wife?" He seemed confused. His eyes began to glaze. "My wife is dead."

"Your second wife, Nesta."

"Nesta… Ahhh, my little ticket to Tampa high society. That wife." He chuckled. "A fool. They're all fools." He sat up in bed shaking his fist. "You think you're better than me. I'll show you who the best man is. Here's your precious queen, all soiled and syphilitic." He crowed like a rooster, then dissolved into tears. "She always thought she was better than me."

"She is better than you," Vincetti told him. "She's the only reason you're still alive."

Edmunds died two weeks later on a Monday. By then, Nesta, with the help of the skeletal hotel staff and Francois and Cristophe, had found over two hundred thousand dollars squirreled away in odd places around the hotel, in books, pockets, radios. She gave them ten percent of everything they found. It was a tidy sum in Haiti, and Francois bought his family a house in Port au Prince. They would be moving from a corrugated tin shack in a nearby village with no plumbing or electricity.

Nesta had funneled Edmunds' notarized statement through her uncle to the DA's office in Tampa. The warrant for my arrest was dropped two days later, on the day of Edmunds' funeral.

Vincetti was there along with a sprinkling of townspeople, mostly hotel employees and their families. The ceremony at graveside was brief, conducted by Francois' cousin who was a Baptist minister. He sang "Swing Low, Sweet Chariot," in French, and the few tears that fell were for the singer's sweet and mournful voice, not for the deceased.

Nesta stared at the casket long after it was lowered into the ground, and at last took a shovelful of dirt and dropped it on top of the casket, then another and another. Her eyes had a glazed, hysterical look to them, and she began to perspire. Her hair came loose from her bun and stuck to her face. But still she shoveled.

Francois gave me a concerned look. I stepped forward and put a hand on her arm. "Nesta. I think you can trust them to finish up here."

She looked at me through dazed eyes as if trying to place me. "What?" She looked at the grave and the pile of dirt next to it. "Oh. Yes...yes." She dropped the shovel and turned to me. Her shoulders were trembling and her legs wobbly. I put an arm around her and led her away. She never shed a tear.

That night we had dinner on the back veranda of the Hotel Haiti. A wonderful callaloo stew. Nesta had recovered herself after a nap and a dip in the ocean. She barely resembled the over-groomed, tight-lipped woman who had invaded my office on Gasparilla Day. She had been swimming every day and her muscles rippled under glowing sun-burnished skin. She seemed suddenly more vivid, more alive. Or maybe it was just the rum and torchlight and the bamboo flute music that drifted in on the ocean breeze.

"I suppose you'll be going back soon," she said.

I nodded. "Tomorrow."

"I'll never be able to repay you for all you've done."

"All in a day's work, ma'am."

She smiled and sat back in her chair, turning her face to catch the breeze. "The air is so exquisite here. It's like a soft caress."

I watched her stretch out comfortably. "You're not going back, are you?"

She smiled and took a sip of her drink. "You're in the right business, Billy."

"I know."

"That's what I've always envied about you. You're always so sure what to do, how to think. You do what you think is right, regardless of what anyone else thinks."

"I haven't always."

"All I've ever done is what's expected of me. Marry, keep a gracious home, be a good daughter, a good wife, a respectable matron of the community. But I'm free of all that now. I lost everything in Tampa, my honor, my place in the community."

"People forget in time."

"No, I don't want to go back. I want to stay here and fix this place. I've already hired Francois to oversee the restoration. He's quite a carpenter, you know. I'm changing the name, too. Something French and exotic like Chez Caribe. With high French service, of course. Rich Americans will eat it up."

"What about your promising career as a detective?"

"I'll make myself chief of hotel security," she said. "Unless, of course, you know anyone who wants the job."

Our eyes met across the table. "We said before it couldn't work."

"We're not in Tampa anymore. The rules are different here."

I didn't know what to say. She looked so beautiful then, so real, so like everything I had ever wanted in a woman. She reached out a hand and I took it.

"I know you have to go back," she said. "And to tell you the truth, I'm kind of glad. I need some time alone, but..." She looked into my eyes and shook her head.

I squeezed her hand, still not knowing what to say.

"I won't say I'll wait for you. I plan to follow my own inclinations for a change. But maybe someday..." She rose from her chair and came around the table and sat in my lap. Her body was fragrant and smooth. "For tonight," she whispered, "let's forget it all. Who we are, where we come from, what's ahead. Tonight is just tonight. Nothing else exists."

Her lips were soft and sweet, like a ripe fig, something to be lingered over, tasted and savored. There was no rush. We had all night.

Dawn found us more hungry for each other instead of less, more urgent in the rhythms we had found together. We had to finally count to three and leap apart to break the magnetic pull between our bodies, laughing, on the verge of tears, and wobbly on our legs as if returning from a sea voyage.

Francois drove me to the docks. Nesta sat in the front seat, looking like a modern Madonna with Cristophe nestled in her lap. We drank each other in sadly with our eyes. We had said our goodbyes all night. All that was left when we parted was a look, a smile, the last sweet drop at the bottom of the cup.

SUSAN F. EDWARDS

Chapter Thirty-Six
Case Closed

I came back to Tampa to close out the file on the EQ Edmunds case. Based on Edmunds' testimony, Randall Stroven was indicted on fraud and racketeering charges. He has, of course, hired a posse of Tampa's most influential lawyers to defend him, and he has been the judge's golf partner for twenty-five years.

Somehow, I doubt Stroven will ever go to prison. But circulation went way up on his competitor's newspaper, the *Tampa Herald* since they have been reporting all the salacious details of the trial, unlike Stroven's own paper, the *Chronicle*, which has ignored the story entirely in favor of covering Amy Semple MacPherson's latest abduction.

Stroven was declared ineligible to run for City Council while the investigation is pending. I like to think that no one will ever respond to his calls for lynch mobs again.

Hedda was found innocent of extortion charges, but the I.R.S. did make her pay taxes on her booty. Her husband has stood with her through it all, though Dominic spends most of his time with the handsome muscular gardener in his cottage out back. It's an arrangement they live with to keep up appearances. No one knows except a few trusted close friends.

Otto keeps in touch with Hedda. She visits him often in his dark grotto, staying sometimes for days before setting sail for Africa or South America.

The Feds have been cracking down on gambling lately. They have declared Tampa one of the battlefields in their war on vice. One senator even said that Tampa is more wicked than gay Paree. The local fathers, of course, sacrificed Ciega to the altar of federal virtue. He was arrested on something like seventeen different charges of gambling, tax evasion, and racketeering. I only hope he lives long enough to sing the names of Tampa's richest men before he meets with one of those unfortunate accidents so common among Negro and Latin men in the city jail.

Ybor is changing. Cigar factories are closing. People seem to prefer cigarettes these days to fine handmade cigars. Tired of low wages and poor working conditions, cigar workers are drifting away to take jobs in other parts of the city. They want to be Americans now.

No one talks about anarchy or socialism or workers' rights anymore. Instead they discuss easy payment plans to buy refrigerators and automobiles and one of those little bungalows in west Tampa. This is the quest now—acquisition is the new measure of a person's worth. An era is coming to an end in Ybor. I am not sure how or why, but this place is disappearing, being erased from the face of Tampa.

Women are changing too. Alicia sold her store and went off to New York to work for legalized birth control. She writes my mother long letters about women's rights. She is giving her life to this cause like my father gave his to workers' rights. She always sends fond regards to me, as if I were her younger brother.

I think of Nesta often, making a new life, reinventing herself. Maybe someday I'll do the same.

About the Author

Susan F. Edwards is an award-winning writer, editor and journalist in Tampa, Florida.

Made in the USA
Monee, IL
18 November 2023